K.M. HARRELL

NYIRA
AND THE
INVISIBLE
BOY

THE GRAVEYARD CLUB, BOOK 1

Cover design and book design by (damonza.com)

ISBN: 978-0-9997144-1-6 (hardcover)

ISBN-13: 978-0-692-99468-9 (paperback)

ISBN: 978-0-9997144-0-9 (ebook)

First Edition January 2018

gatekeeper press
Where Authors are Family

Hey, mom. I…ah, wrote a book. Miss you.

This story is a work of fiction, and is not meant as an
accurate representation of Taíno or African culture.

Nyira

Near the Congo River, 1760

THE MIKONI CREPT across the Yguni plateau while her village was asleep. Their medicine man shrouded them in the mist. But Nyira's father, Ahmed, could smell the mist men in his sleep. He awoke.

"Get up, child," he whispered to her.

Nyira loved how her father appeared in her dreams, as a butterfly or a raindrop, or as the wind. It was his way of not startling her from her sleep. Such an act could damage a child's spirit and fuel nightmares. This time he was himself: tall and lean, wearing his blue cotton sleeping robes.

"You must hide, child," he said, without smiling. "Wake now!"

A shadow rose behind him.

"Papa…?" When she sat up, she heard people running and screaming. She rushed to the door of her hut and saw some of the village structures were ablaze. She ran to the well at the center of the village and almost couldn't get through. All her people were pushing and fighting past the square, trying to escape the fire and the Mikoni. Her only thought was to get to her father. When she finally broke through,

Gnangi, the chief's massive wife, reached out and caught her by the arm.

"You're going the wrong way, child."

"Let me go! I have to find papa!"

"No, Nyira. We must leave." She snatched the seven-year-old up and tucked her onto her hip. Nyira was enveloped by Gnangi's coconut oil aroma as she disappeared into the folds of her Kente robe.

"Please Gnangi! Papa woke me from my dream, and there was a shadow behind him." She kicked and squirmed.

"If you don't behave, I will pull a reed," said Gnangi. "You must escape, Nyira, the slavers are slaught—" Gnangi's grip slackened, and Nyira slid from her grasp. When she fell over, Nyira saw a red spear with yellow lines painted on it protruding from Gnangi's back. She also saw the warrior who threw it; he stood beside a burning lodge about twenty feet away: an almost seven-foot heavily-muscled ebony man painted with yellow, white and bright green, upon his chest shoulders and thighs. When they locked eyes, he said:

"Come here, girl."

Nyira turned and fled down the path to the jungle. She felt the warrior's footsteps as he pursued her. "Don't make me chase you, girl," he snarled. "I will be angry if you make me chase you!" The heat of him was on her back, and just as he lunged to grab her, she darted into the darkness of the bush. He wouldn't follow her there. No one went into the jungle at night. Not even warriors. They hunted there during the day, and the women of her village collected the banana and coconuts and other fruit from its many trees, but they always left before sundown. Only Nyira, the medicine man's strange daughter, who had no mother to teach her better, ventured into the hot teeming blackness.

She stopped about thirty yards into the foliage. The warrior had stopped as well, right at the edge of the darkness.

"The jungle is not safe for a child," he said. "Come out, girl." He sounded almost pleading. Nyira wasn't listening, and the blur of her tears made the village's burning huts appear distorted. Where was Papa? Why couldn't she hear his mind? She stood still and closed her eyes.

Papa? Where are you?

An image appeared to her—though it wasn't very substantial. It was as if her father had turned into a kind of smoke, like she was dreaming. This was no dream. He wore the cream-colored garments he preferred when traveling in the spirit realm.

Nyira, my daughter, he said. *Don't hide in the jungle too long. I don't want you to get wild. I know you could hide forever if you chose to. Don't, my princess. There is a place you must go. You'll know when it's time to let them take you. I love you…*

When she came out of her trance, the warrior held her in his embrace. His smell was sweaty with a thick musk she knew was fear.

"You didn't go far enough, girl. Now you will pay—" Something bumped him. It was huge but smooth, and there was more than one.

He looked around him; his eyes got wider. Nyira watched the warrior's face in the darkness—she had moon vision. That's what her papa called it, so she only needed a minute amount of light to make out his expression. He had beautiful eyes, not the green of a sorcerer, a light hazel. Like Gnangi or some of the other women of her village. The big thing bumped him again. The warrior's musk got stronger, and the sweat of his brow fell onto her face like large raindrops.

"Let me go!" she told him, kicking and wriggling.

"No… you… you are mine. I will—" The thing hit them harder, and knocked him off his feet. She broke away then. But he stood, breathing fast as he reached for her.

"What…? What was—" The thing smacked him again. It knocked him flat. "I—stop! Stop it!" He jumped up, took out a knife, and slashed at the darkness. His sweat glistened in the moonlight. The thing let out a low booming growl. The warrior backed away, trembling. He then turned his head toward the opening at the edge of the jungle, and Nyira could see he thought there was a chance.

"Don't run," said Nyira. He wasn't listening. "You won't—" He bolted for the clearing. He barely made five steps and was ripped back into the blackness. They tossed him around, like a straw ju-ju doll. "Help me!" he screamed. ""Stop it! He—" Nyira turned her head away. She heard him make a gurgling sound from his throat, then nothing.

She turned and moved further into the jungle, but the thing bumped her now. She smelled the warrior's fear on it. There was a rumbling moan, so deep it vibrated the ground, and then a huff. She reached out and touched it. A heavy, muscled form rolled itself around her.

Aboo, she admonished. *You were bad.*

Brothers see run, grumbled Aboo. *Should not run. It not moving. Can have it?*

Nyira fought back tears thinking about Gnangi lying face down, with a spear in her back.

Yes, she said. *Take him.*

After her encounter with the Mikoni warrior, Nyira stayed up in the mahogany trees. The monkeys tried to bring her fruit, but she couldn't eat as she gazed at the remains of her village—so they cried with her and did all they could to ease her grief.

The Mikoni herded most of her people into boats for transport up the river. The next day, some of the warriors searched the jungle, like they were looking for her, or for the other warrior. One of them, a big tall man wearing a long black and gold *pagne* that was secured by a gold skull brooch at his shoulder, leaned down at the edge of the clearing and picked up a knife that was on the ground. He looked up as if he could hear something. Nyira wasn't moving, so it wasn't her he could hear. His mind reached out, asking a question:

Where is my son?

Nyira wanted to ask: *where is my papa?* But kept the thought to herself.

After the Mikoni had left and her village was deserted, she went back to search the men's lodge. She never made it that far. The hyenas got to the village first. She'd seen what they did to a water buffalo that died along the banks of the river. She only got as far as Gnangi's body. Nyira let out a scream that scattered the hyenas and then ran back into the jungle, howling in sorrow. She did that for the rest of the day. The other creatures of the bush must have wondered what type of animal howled while the sun was up.

She spent the next few weeks mourning and sleeping on the backs of hippos near the bank of the Congo River. At one point, the bonobos coaxed her into a game of catch the monkey-fruit, but she never mustered the enthusiasm they were hoping for. The Mikoni returned to her village—a few times during that period. She never showed herself, and had no plans to give herself up, not yet. The big man in the *pagne* was always with them.

One morning, as she roamed the forest, a banana dropped from the tree above. She looked up and saw a young gorilla dangling from the vine in the tree above her.

"I am called Gord," he said. "Are you not too small to be away from your mother?"

"I am called Nyira. And I have no mother." She picked up the fruit and tossed it back to him.

"Thank you. My mother is sad, since the loss of my sister."

"I am sad, too. I lost my papa. Why are you away from your band?"

"I must find my courage. Father says I must learn to be brave—or I will not win a breeding group. But I have an idea that will make mother happy." He dropped to the ground. "Come. Climb onto my back. We will go and meet mother." Nyira was apprehensive, but still intrigued, so she hopped onto the ape's back, and he climbed back into the tree and sprang quickly from branch to branch until they reached his home. It was deeper into the jungle, but still not far from her village.

Gord's mother, Nje, sat sullenly near a copse of mahogany trees in the clearing. His older brothers, Dyil, Biko, and Djat, were performing feats of strength to lift her spirits.

Dyil, the eldest, picked up a small boulder.

"Look mother! See how far I can throw this!" He heaved the rock a good distance across the field. Nje hardly noticed the display. She smiled when she saw her youngest drop from a tree with something on his back.

"Look, mother!" cried Gord. "I bring something to cheer you." He stopped in front of the sad-eyed old female and Nyira climbed off his back.

"That is a human!" roared Dyil, charging up as if he might trample Nyira. "You cannot bring a human here!" Nje approached Nyira very slowly, as though afraid to frighten her.

"Ooh… such a tiny. Where did you find her?"

"She was alone in the forest."

"Oh, you are such a thing. Such a tiny, tiny." She reached her arms out. There were tears in her eyes. "I would like to hold the tiny—"

"Nje!" A massive male charged out of the bush. He was so tall he cast a shadow over Nje and little Nyira. "What are you doing, woman?"

"Mogi. Don't be so loud. You will frighten her."

"Why is there a human here?" growled the big male.

"My youngest has found a tiny for me to hold." Mogi turned his gaze upon Gord, and the youngster almost fled.

"I—ugh—mother was so sad," stammered Gord, not able to meet his father's eyes. "She was lost in the forest."

"I have seen this creature," said Mogi. "It is she who converses with the night force, Aboo. She has a village. They will be searching for her. Humans are dangerous."

"Her village was destroyed by her own kind," said Gord. "Her father was killed."

"As I said. These creatures are dangerous."

"I want to hold her, Mogi," whined Nje, she was crying. "She is so small and has no one. Can I not hold the tiny one?" Mogi looked upon Nyira as she sat quietly on the grass in the clearing.

"I don't think this will be good for us, Nje. We have done well to keep clear of them."

Nje clenched her arms to her chest and rocked back and forth, as she made a groaning sound in her throat.

"Do not make the mothering sound at me! I didn't take your child! I—all right! But keep it out of my nest!" He snatched a medium sized gum tree up by the roots and hurled it past Dyil's stone.

For the next couple weeks, Nje toted and groomed Nyira like a small child. She realized that this couldn't possibly go on forever, but enjoyed the attention, and needed it almost as much as Nje. The older males kept their distance. Nje threw coconut shells and sticks if they got too close.

"Stay away from my tiny tiny! You will scare her!"

One evening Mogi made a decision.

"We must leave this valley. The humans are searching for the tiny tiny. They will attack if we stay here. Tomorrow I will go find a place deeper in the forest. You must all remain concealed until I return." The younger apes took to the trees. But Nje had some tasks to complete before the journey.

"If you put me down, I can help," said Nyira.

"Are you strong enough?" She handed the girl one coconut.

"I could maybe carry two." Nje looked suspicious of this claim.

Gord and his brothers left the clearing for a monkey-fruit tree at the edge of the valley. At night, while Nje was asleep, Nyira and Gord leaped and cavorted through the trees. To make sure she could keep up, Gord had Nyira ride on his back.

"I didn't get to play with my sister," Gord said. "You are a good replacement."

"I didn't have a sister," replied Nyira. "But I played with the girls in my village. When their mothers allowed it. That changed when I got older." Gord led her to secret berry bushes that even his brothers and father were not aware of. They made sure to get back to the band before Nje awoke the next morning.

On the following day, when the young males left the clearing, Nje put Nyira down and went about her final tasks before the journey. Suddenly a leopard rushed out of the high grass and pounced on Nyira. When it closed its jaws on one of her little arms, it received a jolt of pain. Nyira broke free and ran for the trees.

"Run, Nje!" she cried. The leopard recovered and was quickly on her tail.

Unfortunately, Nje showed no regard for her own safety. She ran straight at the leopard.

"Not my tiny tiny!" she screamed, flinging sticks and coconut shells. The flimsy debris bounced off the cat; and it paused briefly, as it focused on a much larger prey. That was the moment Nje seemed to realize the danger she was in, and turned, trying to get away. The leopard jumped on her back. She flung it off and kept running. The leopard was quicker than the old ape though, and cut her off. Cornered, the gorilla displayed her considerable fangs and swatted at the cat. The cat swatted back, tearing out her right eye and a good part of her jaw. Nje took off again, only in the wrong direction—away from the trees. The cat jumped her again, sunk its teeth into the back of her head, and dragged her off her feet. By the time Gord and his brothers responded to the sound of their mother's cries, she was dead.

Nyira hid in the bush and sobbed. Her first instinct was to run away, fearing herself pulled back into despair. She fought against it for the sake of Gord. She climbed into the trees with Gord and the rest of his brothers and watched, as the leopard dragged the body of Nje under a nearby sycamore, and fed.

"Don't look," Nyira told Gord.

She took her own advice and kept her eyes closed. She periodically stole a peek at Dyil. Nyira sensed he was hurting, but he would never allow his brothers to see him cry.

"We must fight!" cried Gord. "Why are we sitting while that monster feeds on our mother?"

"Shut up!" said Hjat. He smacked his younger brother across his nose. "You know nothing. You speak when you're asked." Gord touched his nose and looked at his paw. There was a bit of blood, but he wasn't finished.

"Papa wouldn't want us to be cowards! We shoul—" Hjat struck him so hard this time he knocked him from the tree. He reached out and caught a branch as he fell. Gord didn't say anything more after that. The other brothers wouldn't protect him from Hjat.

"I must leave," he told Nyira, as they slept in the trees that night.

"Why? Your papa will be back soon." She envied Gord that fact. At least he had a father who could return.

"I couldn't face him. Mother must be avenged."

"Can I go with you?"

"It may be dangerous. Stay here, my brothers will protect you."

"I—I could help you…"

The leopard wasn't difficult to track. After it had had its fill of Nje, it picked up the carcass and carried it out of the clearing.

"Maybe she has cubs nearby," said Nyira.

"That would slow her down," replied Gord. "It could be an advantage."

They moved within the thick canopies of the trees and managed to keep pace with the cat, but Nyira needed to inform Gord of something.

"She senses us."

"No. How?" said Gord. "We've been very quiet."

"I don't know. But she does," said Nyira. "I can tell how she drops Nje and pretends to take a bite. She's listening."

"Then this will be harder. I was hoping for surprise."

"We could wait," said Nyira. "Your papa could—"

"I can't," replied Gord. "That beast carries my mother in its jaws. I have to get her back!"

"But if she feeds her to the cubs…" She couldn't say it. "Oh, Gord! I'm sorry." Gord stayed quiet for a long time. They both remained in the trees.

"We can just go back," Nyira finally said. "Your brothers won't know."

"Yes, they will. They'll know by now," said Gord. "To them I'm nothing, so I can at least die with honor. Father will respect that."

Nyira threw her arms around him. "No! I don't want you to die, Gord!" She began to sob.

"That's why I didn't want you come, so you wouldn't have to see."

"I came to help so you wouldn't die. Please, let's wait and try to think of something."

"But I don't want to lose her."

"We won't. I can hear what she's thinking. She won't get away."

Gord climbed to a lower limb and never took his eyes off the leopard.

The leopard reached her lair where her cubs awaited the arrival of their meal.

The lair was located in the western valley, off a tributary of the Congo River. Nyira liked that there was a rear approach to the cave. The river flowed past it as well. So the leopard wouldn't have to look for water.

"She goes into the cave," cried Gord. "We have her trapped!"

"But… she might be waiting for us to come through the mouth of the cave."

"I don't care if she is waiting." He jumped to the ground and lumbered toward the cave opening. Nyira had no time to react.

"Gord! Wait—"

"Come out, monster!" roared Gord, beating his chest and flinging dirt at the entrance. "Come out and face me!"

Nyira realized that if she was going to help, she needed to leave the trees as well. As she got closer, she saw the leopard crouched at the mouth of the cave. Nyira could sense she was unnerved by the young gorilla's brazen challenge, and wanted to make sure there weren't others with him, who might attack her from the rear. Nyira had an idea. She ran around the side of the cave and came over the top, and hid in the brush. Once there, she mimicked the sounds of Gord's three other brothers. The sounds were so realistic, Gord apparently thought his brothers had actually joined him. This was not what Nyira intended, because Gord got much bolder.

"My brothers! Join me!" cried Gord. "Dyil, Hjat, and Biko! Let's avenge our mother!" He snatched up a large stick from the bank of the river and charged the leopard.

"Gord, don't!" cried Nyira. But it was too late. Gord ran up and smacked the confused feline across the face with his club. She swatted him away and tried to run, thinking that others would be upon her. Instead of taking the victory and letting her go, Gord grabbed her tail. This was not a good idea. The leopard spun around and caught him across the face with a vicious swipe. Gord staggered—blinded by the blood in his eyes. But he kept calling to his brothers and swinging the club. He hit the beast a solid blow on the top of her head. He pushed the blood out of his eyes and backed her up to the river, while Nyira increased her echoes and threw rocks and dirt, too—making it seem like the brothers were attacking from the left side of the cave, out of the bush. Gord took the opportunity of her confusion to beat the cat toward the river. Nyira wasn't sure what he intended. Gord didn't swim, or at least not that well. That didn't stop him from pushing the leopard into the water while flailing away at her with his stick. Leopards are usually adept swimmers. Although in this instance, Gord had the advantage. He was upright, and the waist-high water helped blunt the swipes the leopard took at him. Gord was able to land a number of significant blows. Nyira just hoped he didn't lose his weapon in the water. Otherwise, he was dead. The last blow to the leopard's skull was so vicious it broke Gord's club, and the creature didn't come up again.

When Gord emerged from the water, he collapsed onto the bank, and Nyira saw the bloody gashes on his chest and torso.

"Gord, lie down!" she said when he tried to get up. She quickly gathered moss to pack his wounds. "Let me help you." But Gord wasn't happy.

"I failed. I couldn't get her," he said, breathless, as he watched the leopard float further out of his reach. "I wanted to take her body back to my papa. I failed, Nyira. It was all for nothing!" He began to cry.

"Don't Gord. Please rest. I'll find something to put on your wounds, and we can get back to your brothers."

"Why should I go back? They won't believe me. And I don't have anything to show for my efforts."

"Yes they will. Every animal in the bush saw what you did, and your papa and brothers will hear of it."

Nyira was able to get him to relax then. She left Gord on the bank and went into the jungle to find herbs to put on his wounds. She shouldn't have left him.

When Nyira was returning, she heard the sound of Gord in distress, so she moved quietly and concealed herself in the bush. When she climbed the trees overlooking the bank near the leopard's cave, she saw Gord tied down by a net and a group of men standing over him, as he struggled to free himself. One of them was the big man from the Mikoni.

Nyira didn't know what she should do. She was afraid of the Mikoni, but couldn't just leave her friend in their clutches.

"Let him go!" she demanded. "What do you want?"

The big man turned and faced the direction her voice was coming from.

"Good day, my little sorceress," said the man. He was actually smiling. This irritated Nyira very much for some reason.

"Let him go! He's hurt!"

"Yes, I see," said the man. "But he was magnificent against the leopard. I've never seen a gorilla use a weapon."

"He was brave!" yelled Nyira, as if that fact alone should be enough. "Let him go!"

"You speak animal very well, by the way. I've been watching you with them. Your gorilla will command a high price at my village market."

"You can't take him! I won't let you!"

"You don't have a choice. My warriors will kill him rather than let him go. His large head alone will make a great prize."

"No! Please…" she said and began to cry a little. "He was… brave."

"Yes, I saw. That will make him worth the price."

Nyira didn't speak for a while, as she considered what might happen to her friend.

The big man turned to his men.

"Let's go," he commanded. "Pick him up."

"No wait!" cried Nyira. "I… I'll give you something else."

"What would that be?"

"Take him home, and I… will come with you. And you promise not to hunt him or his brothers?"

The big man seemed to think about that for a moment.

"That's a good offer, child. How do I know you'll honor it?"

"If I don't, you'll know where to find him."

The big man smiled.

"It is agreed."

She stayed in the bush and followed as the warriors carried Gord back to his band, in the jungle near her burned out village.

CHAPTER 2

SAINT DOMINGUE (HAITI)

TEN-YEAR-OLD ENRIQUILLO NOTED that the French soldiers were too encumbered to pursue him. It often puzzled him how the white men expected to be successful in the thick jungle, dressed as they were—every inch of them covered in the tight garments they wore. Add to that the long fire spear they carried propped upon their shoulders. But the most curious was the thing they wore upon their heads. It sat black and squat like a fat petulant crow and seemed to increase their misery in the dense heat of the bush. Also, when *Hurucane* showed up, he would take them with him as he raged through the island.

Enriquillo was perched high above, within the branches of a cedar tree, as the troop marched up the trail into the jungle. He had to restrain himself from scampering down the trunk and snatching one of the head things. If for no other reason than to say: This item is worthless! Can't you see that?

Enriquillo used one finger to stroke Taki, his hawk, on the crown of her head. She was situated near his knee on a branch. She didn't like it when he did that, and if anyone else tried it they would lose part of a finger, but she seemed to understand that calm was required at this moment. Although she did flutter up to a branch above him, and then eyed him suspiciously. He had grown bored with this hide and seek game. But Enriquillo had brought this upon himself.

He had snuck onto the Bissett plantation and stolen a prize Arabian colt. It wasn't a fair trade for his friend, Arak, and Higuamota wasn't happy when he led the animal into the village cave.

"You can't keep it, Enriquillo," she told him.

"I have to have something, mother," he replied, as the horse whinnied and pawed the cave floor.

"This won't bring him back."

"I can sacrifice it. Arak will…" He knew the argument was flawed before he finished.

"You must return this creature, Enriquillo. The white men covet them. They will be searching for it. Besides, it didn't cause Arak's death, so it shouldn't have to suffer for it."

Enriquillo looked at the horse's face. It twitched its ears and dipped its head as if to say: *You know your mother speaks truth.* Dejected, he dropped the *bejuco* tied around the animal's neck. At that moment, a bat dove from the cave rafters and spooked the colt; it bolted toward the far corner of the cave and disappeared into one of the dark chambers. Enriquillo didn't feel like pursuing it.

"If you don't go and get it, you will have to replace it," his mother told him.

"How will I do that, mother? I don't have another one."

"In the way we always do it, my son, with fish."

"The boat will have to be repaired," replied Enriquillo. "It still has the hole in it. That won't be easy without Arak."

She went and embraced him. Enriquillo was almost as tall as his mother. Higuamota stroked his forlorn face, and then kissed the flattened forehead that was common among the Taíno people.

"You will do it, Enriquillo," she said. "You must." She turned and headed toward the front porch of her *caney*, the customary house of the tribe's *cacique*, which she was. Enriquillo decided to go and retrieve the colt instead. He couldn't yet look at the hole the white man's fire spear had made, that stopped funny, playful Arak from moving.

Enriquillo had waited until nightfall to lead the colt back along the eastern edge of the town. The Bissett plantation was a sprawling property about two miles from the beach. That's how the white man had spied the two Taíno boys playing in the surf, bringing their boat in from a late evening fishing expedition. Enriquillo was usually very careful. He normally went on these treks alone, because while he was young, he was the only member of the tribe who had invisibility. But there was to be a gathering of the remaining Taíno tribes—decimated and driven into hiding with the arrival of Columbus and the Castilians over three hundred years ago. They were coming out of the mountains to Higuamota's village cave—so more fish would be needed. Arak had offered to accompany his friend, and help manage the larger catch.

They had been frolicking in the waves. Arak had become a stronger swimmer that summer and was racing the boat as Enriquillo paddled through the calm blue water. When they got through the surf, Enriquillo was blinking in and out of invisibility, teasing Arak as they commenced to tug the boat onto the shore. When Arak got into the vessel to retrieve the large haul of fish, Enriquillo heard a small explosion and saw the hole in the boat after his friend fell and didn't get up. The white man had not seen Enriquillo. He had still been invisible when the man pointed his weapon at Arak. He hadn't even bothered to come and look at Arak after he'd fallen, but simply turned and strode away, as if all he'd felled was a bird. Enriquillo could only sit and cry as the man walked back through the acres of sugarcane that faced the beach at the edge of the property.

The colt did not make a sound as they made their way through the canebrake. Once they were through, Enriquillo found himself in the middle of a massive field of sweet potatoes. The crop seemed to stretch for miles and was a testament to the white man's wealth. Enriquillo thought that perhaps on his way back, he would pick a few as a surprise for his mother—and then decided that he wouldn't. Higuamota would ask how he'd managed to pick them when the tribe's crop was in a valley to the west of the mother cave.

The moon and clouds were not cooperating as they had on his initial foray to take the colt. The clouds now receded and the moon caught the white of the horse's coat and set him ablaze like a walking, four-legged star. Enriquillo panicked a bit when he noticed the effect. He reached down and grabbed a handful of the dark, moist soil and tried to rub some upon the colt, to diminish its glow. The animal wouldn't stand still for it, as if it knew the dirt would take away its luster.

Enriquillo finally gave up when the colt reared up in protest. He managed to calm it down and simply walked it quietly through the rows of potatoes. When he got to the edge of the field, they were in the yard behind the stables. The colt could obviously smell the other horses, as it pawed the ground and pranced a bit. *You can let me go, now. I'm home. I'm home*! it seemed to say. But Enriquillo still had to put the horse back where he had taken him from. He put his hand on the beast's muzzle, and stroked it a bit, hoping to make it settle down.

The trouble started when they got through the front door of the stable. Enriquillo had not considered what the horses already in the stables would do when the colt returned. They began a loud, exuberant ruckus: whinnying and neighing, some of them even pawed the floor of the stables and reared up in excitement, and the colt responded to the energy of its stablemates. Enriquillo realized he should've just let the animal go when they were in the stable yard. It was too late for that now. He was then struck on the head from behind.

When Enriquillo awoke, he was laying on his side in a stall filled with the grass the white men called "hay." The strong smell of the horses made him cough, and he had a difficult time sitting up because his hands were bound behind his back. When he finally accomplished it, he saw that another boy was in the stall with him. It was one of the dark people the white men had brought to his land. The boy was thin and had a large scar on his face below his left eye. It was a fresh scar. Enriquillo wasn't surprised. The Taíno knew the white men were kinder to their animals. The dark boy backed away when he saw Enriquillo was awake.

"Hello," said Enriquillo. He smiled at the boy who was about his age, but a little taller, and dressed in rags. "What's your name?"

The boy retreated all the way to the gate at the front of the stall.

"Massah! Massah! He wake!" cried the dark boy.

"Massah, Massah, He wake?" replied Enriquillo. "That is a… well, I am Enriquillo."

Enriquillo stood up and went toward the boy. The boy climbed onto the stall gate, and continued his cry: "Massah! Massah! He wake!"

"Yes. I heard you the first time," replied Enriquillo. "Don't be afraid. I'm of the good people."

"No! You stop!" said the boy, kicking out at him and practically falling off the gate. "Stay from me! You evil!"

Enriquillo stopped and looked at the boy. He was shocked.

"That's not true. I am…"

"Massah! Stay from me demon! Massah say you eat eyes!" He continued to try and kick out at Enriquillo.

"I am not… Who is this 'Massah' you speak of?"

The boy sat precariously on the gate, barely managing to keep his balance. He seemed to consider Enriquillo's question.

"Massah… is… Massah. Him… own this," he said, regarding the building. "Him… own all. Own… me…"

"I have never met this 'Massah'," said Enriquillo. "So how could he say that I… and how can someone own you? You're a person… like me. We can't be owned."

The boy just stared at him, as if he didn't comprehend what he was saying.

"I've heard that the cannibalistic Caribs take people and

keep them," continued Enriquillo. "But that's only until they eat them. Why don't you just run away?"

The boy sat there for a moment, with his mouth open, as if he had something to say, but couldn't say it. Finally, he slid from the gate and landed on the floor of the stall, and sobbed.

"I can't run away," he said, with heaves of breath. "Where would I go? They have taken me too far from my home!"

Enriquillo sat down beside the boy.

"I'm sorry. I hadn't considered that," said Enriquillo. "I don't know what I'd do if I were too far from my mother and my people."

"I didn't even have a chance to say goodbye," replied the dark boy. "My mother and father, they... Are you a sorcerer?"

"I don't think so," replied Enriquillo. "What is that?"

"It is one who has magical powers. If not, then how are you understanding my language, and speaking it? We're not allowed to speak our language here. But you seem to know it."

"I... I don't know. I can do some things. But only Agueybana has magic."

"Who is Agueybana?"

"He is *behike* in our tribe. He heals wounds and walks in our dreams."

"That's like a medicine man," said the dark boy.

"Yes. That sounds like Agueybana," replied Enriquillo. "Medicine man. He would like that name. And what's your name?"

"Pierre," replied the boy. "That is the name the white men gave me when they brought me here."

"What is the name your mother and father gave you?"

"Abiodun," the boy replied. "I was born during festival. People were happy. But I'm not now, and never will be again."

"I believe you will be, Abiodun. You will be happy again."

"How will that be possible? I'm far from those I love."

"You could start by being free. That would be a good beginning."

"I can't just run away. Where would I go?"

"My people have hidden in the caves below the mountains for hundreds of years. I could help you."

"But I'd be alone."

"Yes. But you'd also be the first. And if you're first, you will be *cacique* when others who escape come."

"What is *cacique*?"

"He is the leader of the tribe."

"Like a chief," replied Abiodun. "I'm too young to be chief."

"Are you too young to be free?"

"No. I was free before."

"Then just go and be free, until you're old enough to be chief."

Enriquillo began to work his shackled hands under his bottom and past his legs until they were in front of him.

"Are you strong, too?" asked Abiodun. "Can you break those chains?"

"No," replied Enriquillo. "But I did learn a trick from Agueybana. He calls it: Small. I use it when I need to hide in a place I'm too big for. I'll see if it will work on these." He closed his eyes and held his shackled wrists out before him.

Abiodun saw the shape of Enriquillo's hands change, and the shackles just slid off.

"Amazing!" cried the dark boy. "You are truly a medicine man."

Enriquillo stood up and began to climb over the stall gate.

"Wait!" said Abiodun. "We'll have to find another way out. The master's big dog will be waiting in the stable yard. We could get out through the hayloft."

Enriquillo smiled.

"No. We won't need to. I'll lead the dog away. Just head for the cane fields behind the stables." He climbed over the gate and turned invisible.

Abiodun let out a gasp.

"You are a sorcerer!"

"Just wait a few moments," replied Enriquillo. "I will give a bird whistle when the dog is gone."

Abiodun waited. After a short while, he heard the booming bark of the master's giant bull mastiff; the dog quickly went silent. He wanted to run out and see what Enriquillo had done to quiet the beast but restrained himself. He then heard a familiar chirping, a sound that often floated out over the cane fields as he was bent hacking in the unyielding sun. He was afraid but started moving toward the stable door. The yard was empty when he got outside. Though the moon was still bright and cast an eerie shadow off the stables and onto the front yard—he could see the residence of Etienne Devereaux, the overseer. The house was small and white with a pillared front veranda—a tiny imitation of the master's palatial quarters. It was less than thirty-five yards from the stable yard. Abiodun had a notion that cruel Etienne could see him through the front window of his house. He was suddenly gripped by fear and forgot everything Enriquillo had said to him. Where was he? wondered Abiodun. What if he had gone back into the mountains? How could he have trusted his fate to a horse thief? What was he to do now? He realized that all he needed to do was go to the overseer's house, and say that the horse thief had escaped. They would blame him, of course. He was supposed to keep watch over him. Etienne was quick with the whip. But perhaps they would do something other than the whip. White men were creative in their cruelties. He didn't wish to die in some of the ways others like him had been killed: feet chopped off and bleeding out, or strung from a tree and gutted like a boar. Perhaps it would be better if he presented himself to master Bissett. Though there was no guarantee that the master would save him from Etienne. Since it was obvious that the overseer carried out his barbarity with the master's blessing. He was lost, irrevocably lost… but then he heard another sound.

"What are you waiting for?" asked a voice from the left side of the stable. "Come this way. Let's go."

"You must go back, Enriquillo," said Agueybana. They were sitting by a fire not far from the mother cave, as he applied healing herbs to the dark boy's facial wounds. "This dark one says there was a hound. You must take the dark one's scent away from the path near our cave."

So there Enriquillo sat, watching from above. He had taken some of Abiodun's rags and placed pieces of them in fifty different places around the town. The hounds had gotten very confused. The only legitimate lead the soldiers had was that they knew Enriquillo was Indian and was likely hiding in the mountains. With that knowledge, they began a search of the surrounding mountain valleys. The trail was cold before they started. He just wished Arak was there hiding up in the tree with him. He always knew the right face or the right sound to make him laugh.

He hoped to make a friend of Abiodun but knew the white men wouldn't give up their property so easily.

CHAPTER 3

THE MIKONI VILLAGE was a long way up the river. It took the warriors guiding the barges two days to navigate with her and the rest of the captives. As they approached the dock, there were a number of boats moving in and out of the area, each of them filled with people and supplies, and what Nyira took to be other slaves, as they were chained together like those in her transport.

The village had no huts. Most of its structures appeared to be made of a type of green clay. But the roofs were thatched with flat reeds that made them look more substantial than regular palm. As she was taken from the barge, Nyira could make out the roof of a much larger building. It reminded her of the men's lodge in her village. The roof was very strange; it appeared to be made of shiny material that she had never seen. It caught the sunlight and gave a slight glint. While she could see the large structure, what caught her immediate attention was the market they herded the slaves through. Nyira had only left her village a few times with her father, so this area was like none she had ever experienced. To her, a market was where farmers came to bring their fruits and vegetables, and the fishermen brought what they caught in the river. The Mikoni market had fruits and vegetables, too—although beside them stood strange men dressed in animal skins, and on the tables before them were displayed human heads. Some were shrunken, others appeared to have been recently removed from someone's body. Nyira was appalled. Apparently, the men were trying to show what they could do. There were also people who were volunteering to be set on fire. A group of nearly naked men were standing behind a gentleman wearing a beautiful red, yellow and green *pagne*. This man was haggling with the customers. Once a deal was made, the customer was handed a lighted torch and pointed toward one of the nearly naked men, who allowed a substance to be poured over his head and torso.

Further along was a giant crocodile wearing a diamond the size of a small guava, in a setting at the top of its head. It sat at the mouth of a large ditch next to the market. Nyira didn't initially understand the purpose of this display, but a number of raggedly dressed young men were marched to the ditch. The men with them had spears and machetes. Once they were in place another man dressed in a beautiful Kente garment, stepped up and called for patrons to come and bet on one of the young men being able to retrieve the diamond. The lucky winner would receive the stone. As she moved past, Nyira made eye contact with the giant crocodile.

I am Reyta, it answered when she asked its name.

Why are you not in the river, Reyta?

I'm not allowed in the river. I am a slave.

I'm sorry, Reyta. I'm a slave, too, replied Nyira.

I have also not been fed in a week. I'm so—

A man came near with a long pointed pole and jabbed Reyta right behind her eye.

"Get ready you monster!" he bellowed.

They hurt me. So I must do as they command, or I will be killed.

Nyira wondered if markets in other villages were as cruel as the Mikoni's. She couldn't imagine people going there to buy food.

Along with the evil displays, the Mikoni market also had other live animals, like elephants and leopards and gorillas. She tried to slow down to see if anyone she knew was there, but the shackles on her ankles kept her in step with those in front of her.

"Don't slow down, child," said a woman's voice behind her. Nyira tried to turn around and have a look at the person. "Don't look back. If we fall, someone will be whipped. That's what happened yesterday."

"Since yesterday? How far is your village?" asked Nyira.

"Don't talk so loud. A long way. We've been traveling for a week."

"Oh, my! Is your family still…?" She stopped when she realized that what happened to her family probably happened to this person's as well. "What is your name?" she asked instead.

"I'm Benzia," replied the woman. "I'm from Dotha."

"I'm Nyira, from Mael. My papa is… was the medicine man of my village. His name was Ahmed."

"I have heard of Ahmed, the medicine man from Mael. He was known for healing through your dreams."

"Yes. He was. And he…" Nyira paused, as a wave of sadness swept over her. She wasn't yet accustomed to discussing her father's demise with humans. Animals were much easier. They didn't ask questions, nor wondered where you came from. Gord and his desire for revenge was the most human reference she'd had in months. She swallowed her unhappiness, and the woman didn't ask her about her papa. Nyira was grateful for that.

The slaves were marched through the middle of the village, past the square where the well and the baker's oven were located. Nyira thought that perhaps someone would raise an alarm at seeing all these people chained together. But the Mikoni villagers, in their colorful, well-weaved robes and solid clay houses looked past them.

"Don't they see us?" asked Nyira.

"No," replied Benzia. "We're not people to them."

"I must try to like them," replied Nyira. "Papa said to start by liking everyone, and you'll always find some good."

"Your father was a wise man, child. But they don't care if you like them. You're their property." Nyira had no response to that.

They were led to the lodge at the center of the village. The closer Nyira drew to the structure, the more wondrous it became. It sat on a flat green promontory surrounded by a steadily moving backwater off the Lualau River. It didn't really look like a lodge. Not in the sense that it was constructed of wood. It appeared to be made of... gold. And there were various other gold creatures arrayed on the grounds around it, in postures of attack—some of them molded into the wall of the structure. The building was much larger than any dwelling in her village and looked to be a village itself. It was as tall as a mahogany tree and wider than five giant baobabs. There was a high barrier constructed around it, and a number of large, fierce-looking warriors guarded various points along the wall, each of them painted with the yellow, white and bright green of the warrior she encountered the night her village was attacked. Their spears were long with sharp four-sided spearheads. Nyira wanted to cry as she remembered what this weapon did to Gnangi.

When they came into the huge front courtyard, there was a tall stern-looking young woman standing at the side of a cobbled walkway, waiting for them. She was as tall as Gnangi, about six feet, and dressed in the most beautiful kente garment Nyira had ever beheld. The fabric seemed alive the colors were so vibrant, and the weave was very fine. It fit the woman so well it seemed to have been woven directly upon her. But it was the woman's eyes Nyira found the most captivating. One of them was a turquoise color, while the other resembled that of a panther. It was a deep golden yellow with the iris like that of the giant feline. Nyira couldn't help but stare. She also noted that when she wasn't scowling, the woman's features were quite beautiful.

"Divide out the women and children!" the woman barked to the warriors. "And what are you looking at, girl?" She had noticed Nyira.

"You have a pretty panther eye," said Nyira innocently, and smiled up at the woman.

They were just beginning to unshackle the slaves, but the woman came up and snatched Nyira out of the group by her leg irons, and turned her upside down, like a fish she'd just caught in the river.

"What did you call me?" snarled the woman. "Martolé, fetch me the cane!"

A boy of about eleven, who was naked from the waist up, but wore a clean, bright *pagne* from the waist down, brought her a large bamboo stick.

The woman tossed Nyira to the ground and started hitting her with it.

No one had ever struck Nyira, so she was shocked by the pain, and felt a charge of heat erupt behind her eyes.

"Ow! Stop please!" cried Nyira. "You're hurting me! Why are you hurting me?"

"Because I can!" screamed the woman. "And I don't like slaves who look me in the eyes!"

She got in a few good whacks, but when Nyira made eye contact with her, the woman stumbled and dropped to her knees, holding her head.

"My head!" cried the woman. "My head! It's going to explode!"

Nyira had never been so angry, so she was frightened by the results of it. It was like a fire raged inside her skull, and she screamed from the pain. Even her tears burned.

That's when the big man with the skull brooch burst from the front door of the lodge and ran down the steps toward her.

"Let her go, girl!"

The panther woman howled in agony as she writhed around on the ground. Nyira didn't know what to do; her anger wouldn't let go—it was like a hand of fire gripped her skull.

Desperate, the big man snatched one of the warrior's long-bladed spears and dragged an old woman from amongst the slaves.

"Take your eyes off my wife, sorceress! Or I will kill this old crone!"

Nyira realized that this old woman was Benzia. Something in the old woman's bloodshot yellow eyes, a twinkle of friendliness, allowed her to take hold of her anger and push it down. She turned her face away from the panther woman and ran to Benzia.

When the panther woman was released from her agony, she got up slowly, took a machete from one of the warriors nearby, and raised it to strike Nyira.

The big man, whose name was Chief Abdullah, took the weapon from her.

"I command you to stay away from her, Vandella."

Vandella stood for a while, glaring down at the child as if her body couldn't move on its own. Her fine kente garment was now as filthy as the slaves.

"Go make yourself look like a chief's wife," Abdullah directed. Vandella was able to move then but was still glaring. So he stood in the path of her vision.

"And don't look upon her! Looking has nearly killed you. Now go!"

Nyira was still crying. She had sat on the ground and had drawn her knees to her chest as she rocked and sobbed. Benzia sheltered her in an embrace.

"He must see you as very valuable, Nyira," said Benzia. "Otherwise, he would've let her kill you."

"I don't know how I did that. I didn't mean to, but when she hurt me, my head started burning."

"Well, I promise never to hurt you, little one. You obviously inherited some power from your father."

"Papa never hurt anyone. Now I've made that Vandella woman angry."

"She's more than angry, Nyira. You have a lot to learn about being a slave."

"What have I to learn?"

"For one, you should never look the slaver in the eye. I learned this when a boy was tossed into the river, for the crocodiles. His crime: he had given one of the warriors the evil eye. That's how they make examples. So I'm afraid for you, Nyira. That panther woman has been made to look weak."

"What else?" asked Nyira.

"What do you mean?"

"You said there were a few things. That was only one."

"The next is: you should never speak. Not ever. Because no matter what you say, you will get a beating…"

By the time they were allowed to sleep that night—in a pile at the center of the courtyard—Nyira knew her mistake: she shouldn't have given herself up.

CHAPTER 4

UNCLE JACEUX HAD staked out a small cave in the western mountains, which he decided to give Abiodun for his home. But first, he had taken Enriquillo and Abiodun to his lower camp and had his *behike* walk through the dark boy's dreams.

"We must be sure that he is not one who would reveal our hiding places to the white men," he said.

"I have spoken with him, uncle," said Enriquillo. "He is sad to be away from his home, but happy to be free. He would never return to slavery of his own free will."

"We still must be vigilant, nephew. The dark ones are treated badly by the French planters, and some of them have weak spirits that will respond to fake kindness and give anything to their masters."

"I understand, uncle."

"Now take the dark one to his cave, and if he proves to be true, then in time you may take him to your mother cave."

"Thank you, uncle. Are we to fish tonight?"

"Yes. I will show you a secret cove that your father used exclusively."

When Enriquillo visited Abiodun, he brought cassava

bread, fruit from Jaceux's lower orchards in the jungle, and fish he had caught. Abiodun was delighted by the company, but Enriquillo couldn't convince him to leave his hiding place. Abiodun was afraid of being re-captured. In his mind, the overseer had eyes everywhere. He was certain that were he to set foot outside the cave, Etienne would descend from the cliffs above, bent on his destruction.

"White men don't live in the mountains," said Enriquillo. "They never leave the town or their plantations."

Abiodun grew quiet when Enriquillo spoke of white men.

"He is searching everywhere," whispered Abiodun. "I hear him at night, shuffling along the cliffs." He sat at the little fire in his cave, with his hands folded in his lap; he looked down at them as if to ponder the relentlessness of Etienne.

Enriquillo, who had been hiding all his life, still had trouble comprehending his friend's fear.

"We are high above the valley. He would need wings to get up here. White men don't have wings!"

"Some of them do," replied Abiodun. "I've heard stories. Others who ran away were captured within a few days. They don't—"

"Where did you hear such stories?" asked Enriquillo, looking around inside the enclosure. "There's no one here but you."

"I've heard them," replied Abiodun, stubbornly. "All slaves know of them."

"But you're not a slave anymore. You're free! I don't understand." He was so frustrated he couldn't speak. He sat on the ground near the entrance of the cave and leaned his head against the rock. It was like trying to convince water it was wet.

"What good is being free, if you can't 'be' free?"

Abiodun looked at his friend.

"Thank you for what you've done for me, Enriquillo. I didn't realize being free was so hard. I don't think I'll ever really be free, until I can go home, to my family."

Enriquillo gazed about the cave at the strange keepsakes Abiodun took with them during their escape. One item was a long-handled tool with two curved blades at the end.

"It is used to open the soil for seeds to be planted," he said when asked why he wanted it. It leaned against the cave wall in the far corner. He also had the remains of the ragged garment he'd worn, suspended from a protrusion in the wall. The flimsy item performed a mocking dance when a breeze made its way into the enclosure.

Enriquillo became angry.

"The overseer doesn't need to find you," he said, as he stood up to leave. "You never escaped. You've just imprisoned yourself in here."

The sun had started to go down, and the shadows crept into the cave.

"If you never go outside, what chance do you have to return home?" He stepped out onto the trail and walked to the ridge overlooking the valley above the town. Enriquillo cried. He missed Arak, who died because he wanted to be outside with him, and here was Abiodun, afraid to be. What could he do?

"All right," he heard Abiodun say. He turned and saw him standing in the mouth of the cave.

At first, Enriquillo was excited. While Abiodun looked like he was staring over the edge of the cliff—he didn't want to scare him back into the cave. The sun had gone down, and the sky was cloudy, covering the moon, so he decided to try something different.

"What kind of games did you play in your village, when the sun went down?" he asked. The question seemed to make Abiodun forget his fear.

"Chase the Leopard," he replied and smiled. A good sign.

"That sounds like fun," said Enriquillo. He went to stand beside his friend. "How is it played?"

Abiodun gazed at the cliffs above and at the rocks and boulders strewn about the ridge. "We would need to be in the jungle," replied Abiodun.

"That's not very far away," said Enriquillo, smiling. "I'll race you there."

Abiodun got quiet, and Enriquillo was afraid he'd asked too much. Then his bright teeth showed as he smiled. "I'll give you a head start," he said. "I've always been the fastest in my village."

Enriquillo soon discovered it was no idle boast. Even with a significant lead, Abiodun blew past him like a hot wind, just as they got to the edge of the jungle. He then explained the rules of Chase the Leopard.

"You can't use your invisibility, Enriquillo. That would be cheating," said Abiodun. "Leopards are quiet and strike from almost anywhere, but they're not invisible. They just appear to be sometime. So I, as the hunter, must search and find you, before you can attack. We are hunting each other."

The game was intense and fun. Enriquillo never had a chance, because Abiodun was an adept tracker—even at night. Enriquillo was only momentarily tempted to use his invisibility to gain an advantage, but he was having too much fun for it to matter.

CHAPTER 5

THE NEXT DAY, the women and children were moved into a large tent at the eastern corner of the courtyard, behind the lodge. They were fed a meal of hard bread and a watered down soup with barely any meat. Nyira didn't like the taste of it. She preferred fruit from the jungle.

"At least they're feeding us," said Benzia.

Vandella apparently wasn't ready to let go of her revenge just yet. Toward the end of the day, Nyira saw her at the eastern end of the wall, furiously stabbing the barrier with a spear. She wouldn't look directly at her, but Nyira knew it was a message to her. And she started delivering it the following day.

The tent was stiflingly hot, and the breeze and mosquitos wafting in off the backwater, didn't help. The following morning, warriors showed up and took women from the tent. The first one was a tired, cheerful mother, who had held onto her child through the long trek across the jungle and up the river to the village. Her name was Abena. She was very fastidious about keeping her child clean and making the baby as comfortable as possible. The baby's name was Efuru. Abena was happy when the other slaves paid attention to Efuru because she'd gotten a lot of love from everyone in her village.

But when Abena came back later that morning, she was badly injured. Her clothes were in shreds, and her back was bleeding. She had left her child with Nyira.

"Give me my baby!" screamed Abena, who needed help walking now. "That panther woman said you're responsible for this! You sent an evil spell that told her to do it!"

"That's not true," replied Nyira, hurt by the accusation. "I never—"

"But you are a sorceress," declared Abena. "We heard the chief name you. After what you did to his wife."

"She hurt me. I—"

"So you don't deny it!" She snatched her child away a little too roughly, causing her to cry. Abena was a short, plump young woman with ritual scarring on her face and arms. Her eyes were large and expressive. They reflected her anger as she glared at Nyira and cradled a bawling Efuru to her shoulder. The rest of the women who returned were in the same condition and had the same accusation. But that was not the end of it.

Vandella was apparently not content to punish just a few. Anyone that Nyira said a kind word to, or spoke to at all, was viciously beaten. And one woman, named Bosede, never returned. The only slave spared, besides Nyira, was Benzia. Nyira wasn't sure if this was calculated, but it added weight to the women's indictment of her: That as a sorceress, she could ensure that no harm came to her beloved old crone.

When a second slave did not return from the beatings, Nyira decided it was time to make amends with Vandella. So she asked one of the warriors stationed outside the tent to request an audience with the panther woman. Benzia was opposed to the idea.

"Nyira, what are you doing? You can't go into her lair. You'll be trapped."

"I have to tell her I'm sorry for hurting her."

"That's insane, child. And it won't stop her from hurting us."

"I have to try, Benzia. Or she may kill all of you."

"That's only because she wants to kill you. She can kill a thousand of us, and it won't matter. Please, Nyira. I fear for you."

"I'm sorry, Benzia. What choice do we have?"

Benzia was a stooped old woman. Her skin was black as soot and her eyes yellow and bloodshot. She had told Nyira that at one time, she was held captive in the diamond mines of Ndogi when she was a young girl, and the gases produced by the deep caverns had caused her eyes to look the way they did. At this point, she was worn-looking, in a faded *pagne* that had been washed too many times but not recently. Her head was covered by a ragged scarf through which her gray braided hair was visible and on top of that was a piece of discarded fisherman's net, tied in a knot behind her head. She was referred to as the witch by the other slaves, and Nyira knew she relished the description because people were wary of her. But Benzia was no witch. She reached out and pulled Nyira into a tender embrace.

"I don't know what will become of us if we lose you, child. I believe they haven't been as cruel to us because they fear you."

"I don't want to be feared," said Nyira. "I'm just like the rest of you."

"You're not like the rest of us, Nyira. You're not like any child I've ever known."

A tear rolled down the old woman's withered cheek. Nyira reached up and touched it. She wasn't used to seeing grownups cry, but found the old woman's tears felt just like her own.

The warrior returned with instructions to bring Nyira to the lodge. She followed him out of the tent and across the courtyard to the front steps of the gold building.

She had trouble keeping up with the tall warrior. The steps appeared to be made for a giant. Nyira had to go on her hands and knees a few times to get up them. The warrior didn't help, but he waited patiently for her to catch up. The front door was twice as tall as the warrior, and made of the same red metal as the roof. Just above it, within the gold exterior of the structure, a massive lion was taking a bite from the top of the door. The warrior grabbed the high brass loop and pushed the door opened for Nyira, and then quickly jumped away, as if afraid to go inside. As she stared into the dark foyer, Nyira was also apprehensive, conscious that Vandella may have set traps for her. But she could sense someone or something was there waiting for her, and it didn't feel evil.

"Hello," said a child's voice.

Nyira stepped inside.

As she walked into the foyer, Nyira heard what sounded like bird-song, and flinched when a colorful little hummingbird buzzed past her head. When she looked up, she discovered the most beautiful sight: A garden suspended from the high ceiling. It was bursting with bright flowers and small trees, and there were also openings notched in the ceiling that let in sunlight. The garden was teeming with every type and color of bird: from grey parrots, peafowls, toucans, kingfishers and many, many more.

"Do you like birds?" asked the voice.

"Oh!" said Nyira. She had been so absorbed by the hanging garden she'd forgotten the person in front of her. This was another unusual sight: a boy covered from head to foot in gold. He was bald, quite a bit taller than her and wearing nothing but a small loincloth. "Yes," replied Nyira. "I do like birds." As she moved further inside, she was startled by a sudden boom.

"Don't be afraid," said the boy. "That's just the door closing. It makes an awful sound, but you get used to it."

"What's your name?" asked Nyira.

"No."

"No? No what?" asked Nyira.

"That's my name. I am called No."

"Pleased to meet you, No. I am called Nyira."

He came up and grasped her hand.

"I am to take you to my mistress," he said. It was such a casual gesture that she didn't even consider resisting, and allowed herself to be taken.

As they made their way through the long entryway, Nyira gazed down at No's hand.

The gold didn't appear to rub off or to flake.

"How did you get covered in gold?" she asked

"What is 'gold?'" replied No, looking at her. Nyira noted that his eyes were the color of morning sky.

"It's what's on your skin. How did they do it without burning you?"

"This is not… whatever you called it. This is the color of my skin. It has always been the color of my skin."

They soon came upon a series of very large paintings. Each of them depicted men who were obviously related to chief Abdullah. One was almost his twin, while others had similar eyes, noses, and various other features. They all were tall and just as big, wearing beautiful *pagne* or kente garments. There were ten of the paintings, and all had one thing in common: a golden person kneeling beside the men. There were different types of strange objects on the wall facing the paintings. It was covered from the floor up to about twenty feet with gold bones. The bones went unbroken for about ten yards, and then they got to the doorway out of the foyer. Nyira was speechless. Mounted twenty feet above the doorway, was the head of a hairy elephant. She had never known elephants to be hairy, but this one's head was larger than many huts in her village, and the tusks that curled down around the doorway were longer than some palm trees, and just as thick.

They left the foyer and entered a large room at the center of the lodge. The room contained a giant staircase that seemed to go all the way to the ceiling. The banister running along the length of it was composed entirely of gold bones, but it was the thing at the beginning of the banister that stopped Nyira in her tracks: another gold boy. He appeared to be made into the banister.

"Oh my goodness," cried Nyira. "What is… who is this?"

"That is Yes," replied No.

"He looks just like… is it a statue of you?"

"No. It's my twin. Do you have a twin?" asked No, as if to perhaps change the subject.

"What happened to him?"

"He's dead," replied No. "They put him at the front of the stairs. So that I—"

An awful roar erupted from the top of the stairs. Nyira shrieked and hid behind No. When she gazed up, there stood chief Abdullah, dressed in a purple and gold kente robe, and beside him, a massive male lion.

"What is the meaning of this, No?" demanded Abdullah. "What is this slave doing here?"

No dived to the floor in front of the stairs and looked to be either a rug for the chief or a meal for the lion.

"I've been commanded to bring her to mistress, my chief." He said all this to the stones in the floor.

"Whose idea was this? She shouldn't be here."

"I asked to come," replied Nyira. "I want to say I'm sorry."

"Have you lost your senses, girl? I've been trying to keep her away from you. You're worth more to me alive. I wi—"

"Stay out of this!" This was Vandella, who had come up a hallway just to the left of the stairs. She was standing in the doorway, hands on her hips and eyes locked onto Nyira. She was clean now, and her hair was done up in an elaborate tiered creation rising up from her scalp. Abdullah was quick for a man of his bulk; he raced down the stairs and towered over Vandella like a shadow over the sun.

"What did you say to me?" boomed Abdullah.

The lion didn't even bother to follow. Instead, he lay himself down at the top of the landing, as if to enjoy the show.

Vandella's expression quickly changed from one of hatred to one of fear.

"I—I'm sorry, my chief," she said. "I forgot myself. Please forgive me. The slave has asked for an audience so that she might apologize for her attack upon me."

Nyira had been so caught up in the grandeur of the lodge that she had not noticed the other occupants. There were other gold servants. Many of them adults, and non-servants as well. She got a better look at the boy who'd brought Vandella the cane she'd used to beat her a week before. He came up an adjacent hall, among a group of other children. He was wearing a long yellow and blue *pagne*, and it was held at the shoulder by a jeweled brooch, shaped like a crocodile. When Nyira gave him a smile, he smiled back. He looked very much like his father then. But one of the children—a pretty pouting girl of about nine, with thick braids infused with bits of gold—said:

"We shouldn't smile at slaves, Prince Martolé."

The boy turned to the girl and then grabbed one of her braids and jerked her head around.

"I will smile at whomever I like!" snarled Martolé . "You don't tell me who I can smile at!"

The girl started to cry, and when Martolé released her braid, she ran back up the hallway. Nyira immediately didn't like him. But Martolé continued to smile at her as if he'd done nothing unusual.

"I don't like this, Vandella," said Abdullah. "I've told you this slave is very valuable. The Dutchmen pay ten times as much for a sorceress. They like to present them to their king."

"Yes. I know, my chief," replied Vandella. "I promise that I won't lay a hand on the child."

"I will hold you to that." He turned, but before he went back up the stairs, looked at Nyira.

"Don't hurt my wife, child," he said. "If you do, you'll be sorry." He went up before she had a chance to reply.

When Nyira looked at Vandella, she quickly turned her face away.

"Don't look at me, slave! Get up, No!"

The gold child sprang to his feet.

"Yes, mistress."

"Take the girl to the parlor. I'll be there in a moment."

No happily took Nyira's hand again and escorted her up the hallway past Martolé and the other children with him.

The parlor was smaller than the central room but still very large. There were ebony and gold statues situated in various corners around the room and a large colorful patterned rug in the center of the floor. The walls in the room were decorated with tribal designs that seemed to depict the various conquests of chief Abdullah's ancestors. A massive diamond and ebony throne stood before a large window facing the doorway. A gold boy was stationed next to the throne. His head down, hands out before him, palms up. The floor underneath the colorful rug was composed of quartz stone from the mountains. Nyira had to do a double take, because she'd somehow missed another gold boy, floating on his back above the floor, and also a masked man sitting beneath him, as he rotated like meat on a spit. Nyira noted that the boy was crying. His tears plunked like big raindrops onto the quartz floor. The masked man was very casual in the tasks he performed over the floating boy as if he was bored. He too wore nothing but a loincloth and was as black and wrinkled as Benzia. He was also very slim. Arrayed on the floor beside him were a series of small decorated wooden bowls. Some of them glowed with tiny flames. The old man dipped his fingers into one of the bowls and then sprinkled the substance over the rotating boy. The child let out a shriek of agony.

"Stop! You're hurting him!" cried Nyira.

"Shhhh," replied No. From his clenched hand, she felt him trembling.

The old man glanced over at them then. His mask was carved with the image of some hideous fanged creature.

Ahhh, No. There you are. The old man's voice was a deep vibration that emanated from the walls and ceilings. No dropped Nyira's hand and ran for the door. The old man casually dipped his fingers into another bowl and blew its contents toward him. Nyira heard No squeal as he raced through the central room.

The old man clapped his hands, and the floating boy exploded in a cloud of gold dust. He then stared at Nyira.

Come sit with me, child, the voice said.

Nyira noticed something strange about the old man's voice. She didn't really hear it. She felt it and saw it. And she didn't like its color. Her papa had warned her that certain dangers had strange colors, particularly voices.

"I am to see the mistress," replied Nyira. "Not to sit with you."

Are you afraid? asked the voice. *Don't be. I just want to taste a bit of your powers, child.*

"I don't have powers."

Oh yes you do, said the voice. *You use them so easily you don't even realize it. No one can resist my request to sit with me. Yet you wade through me like I was water. It is I who should be afraid. But you've made a mistake. Look closer.*

The light in the room changed, and Nyira found herself in the middle of a different landscape: a dry Sahara. The land was flat and windy. Thick brown grass and brush covered the area. Then she saw the lioness. Just to the right of her, in her peripheral vision. She suddenly remembered this area, because her papa had once brought her to this region. She also knew why the beast was there: It was going to kill her because somehow she had changed into a gazelle. And then the lioness was upon her.

CHAPTER 6

AGUEYBANA DIDN'T OCCUPY a cedar hut, like other nobles in the tribe. The *behike* had instead chosen a cave in the far corner of the village enclosure. It was more of a crevice, really. But entering it was no easy task. You had to crawl through a small tunnel in the rock, and once inside, it was totally black.

"Why would I need a torch in my own home," replied Agueybana, when asked. "When all that wasn't there when I came, I brought."

Enriquillo stood outside the opening for a long time before he had the courage to crawl through the tunnel. When he emerged into the room, Agueybana was lighting a small coral pipe. The flame momentarily illuminated the old man's ancient features. Enriquillo was relieved when the light went out because he didn't want the *behike* to see he was crying. For a long time, he was content to sit in the dark and endure the bitter aroma of the old man's pipe tobacco. Agueybana seemed to enjoy his pipe and the silence, too. But finally said:

"You wanted it more than he did, Enriquillo."

"You're wrong, old man!" cried Enriquillo. He got up to crawl back through the tunnel.

"Your anger is poisoning you," replied Agueybana. "It has mixed up your mind."

"I'm not mixed up!" Enriquillo screamed in the darkness. "You weren't there!"

"Then say what happened."

They had been playing along the trail that led from the mountains down into the bush. Enriquillo had finally gotten the hang of Chase the Leopard and had even won a few times. Not many, but enough to make it competitive. Abiodun continued to gain courage outside his cave. He'd also grown more comfortable coming out during the daylight. Though Enriquillo knew he couldn't push him too far. But after two weeks of racing through the jungle, climbing up into the upper branches of the pine trees, and chasing Taki along the cliffs near his hideaway, Abiodun was a different person.

"I can't play today, my friend," Enriquillo told him that morning. "I must go down to the cove and catch some fish for the tribe."

Abiodun got a strange look.

"I was the best fisherman in my family," he declared. "I could help you bring back more."

Enriquillo wasn't comfortable with this suggestion.

"Thank you, Abiodun. But I don't need any help. I've always done most of the fishing for my village—since I was eight."

"But with the two of us, we could catch hundreds more fish."

"I… well, we just shouldn't though," replied Enriquillo.

They were standing outside the cave after Enriquillo had brought fruit for his friend. The day was bright with a few flimsy clouds floating over the eastern mountain range. There was also a slight breeze, and Abiodun was feeling invigorated by the salty air coming in off the ocean.

"You don't have to worry about me. I want to live. I know I can't hide in my cave forever."

"It's good that your fear is gone, Abiodun. But we should wait for another day. When there's not a task to be performed."

"I can't believe this! I'm finally ready to live my life. To 'be' free—like you said. Am I only to be free when you need a playmate?"

Enriquillo had to concede Abiodun's point, so he allowed the dark boy to follow him down the hidden path that led to a waterfall on the other side of the forest.

The trees within the cove were twice as tall as those on other parts of the island, and their high dense canopies only let in small amounts of sunlight. This allowed foliage on the jungle floor to grow green and hardy. There were plants in this section that didn't grow on the mountains or anywhere else in Saint Domingue. The boys even stopped to pick mangos and chop a few pineapples with Enriquillo's fish ax.

"These are bigger than the ones from my village," said Abiodun. He had stuffed his mouth full of pineapple and mango. "And sweeter, too." This made Enriquillo burst out laughing.

"What is so funny," asked his friend.

Enriquillo finally caught his breath.

"Your mouth is so full you look like a blowfish."

Abiodun's confounded expression started him laughing all over again. His response was to run and tackle Enriquillo, and they tussled until they fell into the beautiful blue water of the cove.

"We should probably get out and finish our task," said Enriquillo, as he climbed onto the bank. "Otherwise, mother and the rest of the tribe will go hungry."

They fished and swam for most of that day. The *bejuco* Enriquillo had brought to hang the fish on was almost full along its entire length, and left just enough to tie onto a branch they cut to carry between them.

They were right at the midpoint of the trail into the mountains when they saw the overseer. He was standing at the far side of the trail, in the brush. Abiodun was so shocked he dropped his end of the fish branch.

"It's Etienne," he whispered and began to breathe hard. Enriquillo saw the fear overtaking him again.

Enriquillo had never seen the overseer but had heard stories from Abiodun. This white man didn't look anything like the monster he'd pictured. He was tall and slim but was broad in the shoulders, like he'd once done some work. He was wearing a white shirt that was tucked in, and there was what Enriquillo recognized as a small fire weapon tucked into the front of his pants. And he smiled at Abiodun.

"Pierre," said Etienne. "You've grown since I last saw you."

Abiodun didn't respond but had started to cry.

"No," he whispered.

"I guessed right," said Etienne, as he took a step toward the dark boy. "I knew you hadn't gone very far into the mountains. And that the Indians were hiding you."

Enriquillo didn't like what he saw happening to his friend. Abiodun was frozen. The feet that were faster than his hawk appeared to be sinking into the dirt.

"You don't have to be afraid. Master Bissett—"

"You don't have a master," said Enriquillo, as he came up behind his friend and gave him a shove. Just to make his feet move. "You're free. You've always been free. Remember?"

Abiodun looked at Enriquillo like he had never seen him before, and the words appeared to set something off in him.

"That's right… I don't have a master anymore!"

"What's the matter with you?" replied Etienne, moving closer to him. "You need to come home, boy. All your friends miss you. We—"

"They're not my friends," said Abiodun. "They're property—the master's property. All my friends are free. Like my family, like me!"

Etienne lost his cool in the face of this "free" boy.

"You'll never be free, Pierre. Not ever! No matter what this Indian tells you. Take him!" Soldiers rose up from the thick brush that surrounded the trail. "Take the Indian, too. Alphonse will want him, as well."

Enriquillo saw Abiodun's speed then. One minute he was standing, and the next he was halfway up the trail.

"Cut him off!" cried the overseer. "I'll take care of—" He'd pulled his weapon to point it at Enriquillo, but he was gone, too.

"What in the name of… Cut him off at the cave!"

Enriquillo didn't like the sound of that. They apparently knew about Abiodun's hiding place. He ran as fast as he could up the trail. If only he could fly, Enriquillo was thinking. He'd give up invisibility for flight right now. The soldiers had the ridge outside the cave surrounded when he got there. But Abiodun had climbed up the rocks above the cave. One of the soldiers was aiming his fire spear at his friend's back. Etienne grabbed the man's gun.

"Don't shoot him, you fool! I want him brought back alive, so that others won't even consider trying to escape. Go up there and get him!" The soldier put down his weapon and began to climb after Abiodun.

"I know where he's going," said the overseer. He took the shortcut over the rocks and up the backside of the cliff. That shocked Enriquillo; he thought only the Taíno knew of it.

How long has he been watching us? wondered Enriquillo. He had obviously been wrong. White men did come into the mountains. He was also afraid of what else Etienne knew, about his people's hiding place.

By the time Enriquillo made his way up the rocks, Etienne had reached the cliff.

"I don't want to kill you, Pierre," said the overseer, as he watched the dark boy mount the ledge. "You're too valuable." He backed up and gave Abiodun space.

"That's not true," replied Abiodun, a bit breathless from his climb. "I'm not valuable. Master Bissett has over four hundred slaves, just like me." When he stood up, he actually began to move toward Etienne.

"None of them are like you, Pierre. None of them have tried to escape."

"But they will," replied Abiodun. "After they hear about me, they'll know they can try."

As he ascended the rocks, Enriquillo noticed a peculiar

tone in his friend's voice. He didn't sound afraid anymore—even though the overseer was closer to him.

"There won't be anything to hear, Pierre, because you're coming back. Just like Master Bissett directed."

"He doesn't own me," replied Abiodun. "No man will ever own me again!"

"Have you lost your mind, slave? You're coming with me!"

"You were right, my friend," said Abiodun, looking at Enriquillo as he came up the rocks. "I'm a person. And I can't be owned." He then turned and ran.

"What are you doing?" cried Etienne and ran after him. But Abiodun was already over the edge and seemed to be flying. Enriquillo had started running, too. He wished so much to fly. Why didn't he have that gift instead of invisibility? What good was it? It hadn't helped him save either of his friends. All it had done was hide him from… the overseer was right there in his path. He should have stopped, but something was about to burst inside him and the only thing that would stop it, was to get his hands on Etienne, to rip him apart. For both of his friends, for his whole life of hiding, for even being in his land and hurting those he loved. Instead, Etienne went flying, too—when Enriquillo ran into him. The overseer's face was a mask of shock, like this was obviously some strange mistake, that he was falling along with his slave.

CHAPTER 7

NYIRA KNEW IT was color. She couldn't stop the lion, but she did have the presence of mind to change the color. When she did, the Sahara vanished, and she was looking at the old man again, lying about five feet away. He was on his back like he'd fallen. The carved mask had come off, and Nyira saw his withered face. His eyes were as white as his hair. The medicine man was blind. It didn't seem to slow him down, though. He sprang quickly to his feet and backed away from her.

"That was… It appears I've been taken outside myself," said the old man.

"Those colors hurt," replied Nyira.

"Yes. I see." He reached down and picked up one of the wooden bowls—the one without a flame. "Would you possibly be interested in something to eat?" He held the bowl out to her.

"I didn't come to talk to you!" snapped Nyira. "You eat what's in the bowl."

The old man's hand twisted toward his face, and his mouth opened.

"No!" cried the old man. "I'm not hungry. I don't—"

"Enough!" cried Vandella, as she rushed into the room. "Goodbye, girl!" She ran to the throne and slammed her hand on a spot behind it. Nyira dropped through the floor.

She landed in a body of water. Before the opening above her closed, she heard Vandella say: "I know I promised him I wouldn't take a hand in it. But you couldn't even…" The floor shut above her. Then something grabbed her feet and dragged her under the water.

She tried to kick her legs to push herself up, but the thing was enormous, and it was pulling her down. At first, she was afraid, but something about it was familiar.

Let me go, she said. *I need to get to the surface to breathe.*

Nyira? the thing replied. *What are you doing in here?*

The thing released her leg, and she rose to the surface and swam to the bank at the side of the water.

The lodge had been built right over a canal off the back-water, turning it into an enclosure. The banks on each side of the canal were about seven yards wide, from the central foundation, to possibly five on the opposite shore. The water was clouded by bits of algae, leaves and silt washed in from the backwater. When Nyira climbed onto the bank, it was crowded with crocodiles, and then the huge creature she had conversed with at the fair surfaced.

Reyta? said Nyira.

The crocodile continued to shore and heaved herself onto the bank.

Nyira. I'm so sorry, said Reyta. *I thought you were food. That's how they feed us. They drop things through the opening above. I'm so ashamed; I almost hurt you. You are the only one who has ever said a kind word to me.*

But another crocodile that Nyira sensed from within the

group lumbered toward them. It was almost as massive as Reyta and was not happy.

We should eat this, Reyta, it said. *Why are you speaking to it like it's not our dinner? We are starving! They haven't fed us for weeks. Our mother is weak and won't survive if we don't give her this food.*

Bapha, replied Reyta. *This is not our food. This is my friend.*

If it is your friend, replied Bapha. *Why does it not help us? By allowing us to eat it!*

Eating me won't fill you up, Bapha, replied Nyira. *I'm not very big.*

Before Bapha could reply, something landed on one of the crocodiles lounging on the shore. It was a blaze of some kind. It caught quickly and engulfed the creature in flames. They looked up and saw that the boy, Martolé, stood at an opening in the wall of the foundation. There were a number of warriors with him. They rushed out among the reptiles and began to stab and slash at them.

Run, Nyira! cried Reyta. *The boy takes his sport by killing us!*

"Kill as many as you can!" cried Martolé. I'll use the hides for the chairs in my chamber!" One of the warriors stepped on Bapha's back and drove his spear through the creature's left eye. "And I brought something for you as well, girl!" He held one of the wooden bowls of flame from the medicine man. "From Tongo himself. He taught me how to use it." He blew the flame, and it covered her before she had time to move. Nyira jumped in the water, but it was fueled by it. Reyta came to her aid as she flailed. The massive crocodile opened her mouth and swallowed her. *Do not move so much, Nyira,* said Reyta. *This fire feeds on the water. Be still, and I will smother it.*

But will it not burn you, Reyta? asked Nyira.

Yes. It's very painful. But smothering is the only way to stop it.

Reyta was right. The flame died once she closed her jaws over it.

It's out, Reyta, said Nyira. *Open your mouth, so I can heal the wounds it gave you.*

I'm afraid for you, replied Reyta. *That evil boy is still butchering my brothers.*

You can't keep me in your mouth forever, replied Nyira. *Let me help you stop him. Put me on the bank.*

I don't feel good about this, child. But I'll do as you ask.

Reyta moved to the bank and pushed Nyira out of her mouth.

The boy and the warriors had begun to skin some of the crocodiles they'd killed. But when Martolé saw Nyira lying helpless in the mud, he couldn't resist a chance to finish her.

"Yaako, give me your spear," said Martolé.

The warrior handed the long-bladed weapon to the boy.

"Maybe you should let me, my Prince," said Yaako. "It might be—"

The boy snatched the spear. "Are you saying I can't kill one little girl?" He glared at the huge man, who dropped his eyes.

"No, my Prince. It's just that she—"

"Shut up! Or I'll feed you to these starving crocodiles!"

The boy grasped the spear two-handed and charged at Nyira. When he got within two feet of her, she sat up and tried to make eye contact. The boy quickly turned his head.

"Not this time!" said Martolé. "I'm not as gullible as my mother!"

He raised the spear. Suddenly a huge reptilian tail swung out of the canal and swept him off his feet. He fell into the water.

"Help me," cried Martolé, flailing. "I can't swim! Help me, you fools!" He was screaming at the warriors, but they were afraid to get in the water.

Don't hurt him, Reyta, said Nyira. *I'll try to get him out.* She picked up the long-handled spear and reached it toward the boy.

"Grab it," said Nyira.

"How do I know you won't drown me?" said Martolé.

"Don't be foolish," replied Nyira. "You'll drown anyway. Now take it!"

Martolé grasped the spear, and Nyira began to pull him to the shore.

"You cowards will pay for this!" he yelled at his warriors. "I wi—Auuugh! Auugh!"

Nyira pulled faster, and Martolé made it to the bank. When he emerged, his right ankle was bleeding badly.

"My foot! My foot! What happened to my foot?" Nyira was shocked to see the boy's right foot was gone.

Reyta! I asked you not to hurt him, said Nyira, disappointed.

It wasn't me, replied Reyta.

It was me, said Bapha. He had surfaced, and you could see one of his eyes was missing and he had a foot clamped in his jaws. *That was for my eye, and for mother. She needs something to eat, and this will be better than nothing.* He submerged, clutching Martolé's foot. The warriors ran to the boy and lifted him onto their shoulders.

"Wait!" said Nyira. "Wrap a piece of cloth around his ankle. It will stop the bleeding." Martolé had already passed out from the pain and blood loss.

Reyta came up on the shore as the warriors carried the boy back through the opening in the foundation.

I'm very afraid, Nyira, said Reyta. *Bapha shouldn't have done this. The chief will want blood for the injury to his son.*

That's probably true, said Nyira.

I didn't know how my life would end, but I never wanted to be slaughtered in this canal. I'll never see the river now.

Don't give up yet, Reyta, said Nyira. *We just need a way for you to get out.*

How? We're trapped here.

But you're not always here. How do you get to the market?

The canal has a grate underwater. When they ring the bell and open the grate, I follow the canal around to the ditch in the market.

So it's a grate we have to open?

Yes. I know how to go through it because I've been trained. But my brothers have always been in this space below the stone floor. It's all they know.

Will they follow you out?

I don't know.

We have to try. I'll open the grate. We'd better go now— before Abdullah comes.

How? You're trapped just as we are. There is no way for you to get through the stone floor.

We have to go through the canal.

Can you breathe underwater? Because it's deep.

No, said Nyira. *But you can. Take me in your mouth. Make a pocket of air in your cheek, and I'll go there to breathe.*

Okay. I can try. We don't really have a choice.

The crocodile opened her mouth, and just as Nyira was about to climb in, the foundation door opened again, and warriors poured through.

Run, my brothers! cried Reyta. *Follow me! The child will help us escape!*

The creatures were a little slow to respond, and when Abdullah emerged through the opening, Nyira saw his rage. She jumped into Reyta's mouth, and the creature scooted into the water.

"Kill them all!" shouted Abdullah. "Don't let one escape, or you'll be sorry!"

He swung his machete and hacked off the tail off one creature that was just making it to the water. The rest of the crocodiles began to scatter quickly. Some of them were cut off by warriors before they reached the canal. They were as wide and long as a child's canoe and had the presence of mind to attack the warriors. This allowed some of the smaller creatures a chance to reach the water.

Reyta dove deep and made her way toward the opening, but something strange started to occur. A stone door descended over the opening.

Oh no, Nyira! There's another door I've never seen. They mean to trap us for sure! I need to let you out. You should be able to squeeze through the grate. You're small enough.

No! Wait Reyta. We— The beast pushed Nyira out of her mouth, and she was forced toward the door.

As Nyira made her way to the opening, another large crocodile was in her path. It was Bapha.

This is the last chance I will have, said Bapha. *I was going to eat you. But I see you are trying to free my brothers. But wait!*

He wedged himself under the stone door, keeping it open.

I will hold it as long as I can. It's the best I can offer, child.

Nyira slipped past the beast and searched for a mechanism on the grate. She was about to give up when she spied an algae-covered handle protruding from the lodge foundation. She tried putting all her weight on it but was out of breath. So she went back to Reyta.

I've found the release handle, Reyta. But I need to breathe.

The crocodile opened her mouth, and Nyira climbed in. She only needed a few moments and was out again. The other crocodiles were all gathered at the door. Nyira could sense their fear and confusion. But she had to do her part. The stone door was crushing down upon Bapha as well. She swam under the door again and was able to push the latch down and open the grate.

Tell them to go now, Reyta. I've opened the grate.

The crocodiles began to stream through the opening that led out of the canal and kept going. The river was high, so they were able to swim over the side of the canal and directly into the river.

Nyira, said Reyta. *Bapha and my mother didn't come through. Oh, this is terrible. What am I to do?*

I'll see if I can help. Nyira dove again and saw Bapha, struggling to hold up the stone door.

Bapha, said Nyira. *Your brothers and sister are waiting for you in the river. You can release the door and go to them.*

I won't be coming, said Bapha. *I must stay with mother. She can't come through the opening, and I won't leave her.*

But you know that Abdullah means to…

Yes. I wouldn't do well in the river, anyway. This is the only life I know. They have Reyta. She will be mother now.

He pulled himself from under the door, and it closed. Nyira swam back to the surface to give Reyta the bad news.

Once the crocodiles had escaped into the river, Nyira climbed out of the canal and made her way back to the tent behind the lodge. Abdullah was there when she arrived—looming in the darkness near the tent.

"My son is a cripple! Do you understand that? He will never be a warrior!"

"I didn't hurt him," replied Nyira. "He tried to hurt me. I—"

"You insisted! I warned you to stay away from my wife! But you—" He was so angry, he could hardly speak. "The Dutchmen will be here tomorrow. Why didn't you escape?"

"I have to go with them," replied Nyira. "I believe that was what papa's vision meant."

"I'll be glad. At least I'll receive some value for all the strife you've caused." He stalked off.

CHAPTER 8

ENRIQUILLO GOT NO sleep. His guilt at the loss of another friend kept him awake, and he worried that Etienne had discovered his tribe's cave, along with Abiodun's.

He spent the next few days guarding the mouth of the mother cave.

"It's not possible, Enriquillo," said Agueybana. He had gone outside to keep Enriquillo company in the heat from the jungle. It occurred to him that he was too old to sweat so much. There wasn't much flesh left on his ancient bones as it was, so he had every incentive to coax the boy back into the cool of the village cave.

He brought Enriquillo a gourd of water and a pineapple treat. Higuamota had dipped the dried fruit into some cane syrup she'd boiled down. The pineapple was then skewered on small sticks and roasted over the flame. Enriquillo took the candy and looked at it a long time as if something within the caramelized sugar might provide him the answer he sought. Agueybana finally took the treat and put it in his own mouth.

"You are not a normal child, Enriquillo. But even you should know the purpose of candy."

"I'm not hungry," replied Enriquillo, he was sitting on the ground leaning against the trunk of a palm tree. Periodically he looked up and saw that Taki chased a bird across the lightly clouded blue sky. He reached up and broke a broad green leaf off a nearby fern, and then passed it up under his nose as if he wanted to inhale its scent.

"It wasn't your fault," said Ageybana, and sat on the ground beside the boy. There had been a lot of rain the night before, and the ground was still very wet. "You will answer for the white man before you can enter *Coaybay*. But no one could have known the boy would—"

"Did you?" asked Enriquillo, looking Agueybana squarely in the eyes. "You always know, Agueybana. So did you know he would do it?"

"What does it matter now? Knowing won't always help—"

"I could've stopped him!" cried Enriquillo. "I would've maybe…"

"Fought off Etienne and the soldiers? They were searching for him, Enriquillo. They were never going to stop searching."

"I could've hidden him better."

"You mean like we are hidden? You can become invisible, Enriquillo. Therefore, you can live your life outside. He didn't have that choice."

"He was afraid, and I made him come out anyway."

"You were trying to be his friend," said the *behike*.

"I just wanted a friend," replied Enriquillo. "Someone I could…"

"You helped him be free, Enriquillo. That's what friends are supposed to."

Something dropped out of the sky and landed in Enriquillo's lap. It was the body of a crow that Taki had killed.

"It's time to come back inside, Enrquillo," said Agueybana, his old bones popped as he stood. "The overseer didn't know of our hiding place. If he had, soldiers would be here by now."

CHAPTER 9

THE DUTCHMEN WERE the first white men Nyira had
ever laid eyes on. Her father had spoken of the strangeness of
white men—of their clothing that covered every part of their
bodies, even when the sun was at its highest, but it didn't
prepare her for the actual look of them: pale and thin with
flat hair. These men did not wear *pagne*, and their feet were
clothed in black all the way up their legs. They also kept
long skinny knives at their waists. She only saw them from a
distance when they entered the compound. One of the warriors, who was guarding the slaves and seemed willing to help
them as much as he was able, told her of the white men's
arrival. His name was Chifundo. He told Nyira that he had
once been a slave, too. Only because he was big and looked
fierce, they offered the opportunity to be one of Abdullah's
warriors. The choice was obvious. He had even been able
to facilitate the occasional escape—though they rarely succeeded. Most slaves could not survive on the river—not
without a boat, or a means to return to their village, which
the Mikoni destroyed. That was why he stayed because there
was no other place for him to go. He did not envy her sale to
the Dutch slavers. She would have a better chance escaping

and living in the jungle, where they found her. When she told him it was her destiny, he wished her luck. Perhaps the others were better off if she was with them, but he warned her that white slavers were not as kind as Africans.

The captain of the Dutch slaver was named Antonie Matthias. He was a tall, slim dark-haired man with a silent manner. He didn't do much talking; his first officer named Shelley Rubin did the majority of the negotiating, while the captain stood scowling as if ill-at-ease among so many well-armed natives.

The majority of the slaves were paraded out on the morning of the Dutchmen's arrival. All except Nyira; she was told to stay behind in the tent.

"They want a chance to view their special prize, in private," Benzia told her. Nyira wasn't sure what that meant. It proved to be an accurate assessment.

Abdullah along with a few of the warriors—Chifundo included—came to the tent with some of the Dutchmen. Rubin was a young man—quite a bit younger than Matthias. He was half a head shorter with red curly hair; he stood for a moment gazing at Nyira as she sat on the ground in the corner of the tent.

"So you say she is a sorceress, Abdullah?"

"Yes, captain," replied Abdullah. Nyira was shocked by the big man's deference to the small pink man. His shoulders dipped so, he seemed to be bowing. "She is quite manage-able. But headstrong."

"Is that so?" said Rubin. He started towards her. "Will she talk to me, perhaps?"

"She might," replied Abdullah.

Show them your value, girl. She heard his mind say. *Or*

I may not be able to send the old woman. She has no value to them. And I don't want her.

The Dutchman reached into his pocket and pulled out something.

"Would she accept a sweet, perhaps? Here you go, girl. Come and get it." He had the strangest grin on his face as he handed the item to her. Nyira found him more fascinating than what he had in his hand. She would've preferred to touch his pink face to see if it felt like real skin, and he also had an awful smell to him.

Please take the item, implored Abdullah. *So that you can go with them.*

Nyira got up and took the sweet, and stood gazing at the Dutchman.

"She is a beautiful creature," said the white man. "Her eyes are the strangest green I've ever seen." He reached his hand out to stroke her cheek.

"I wouldn't do that," said Abdullah.

Rubin stopped and pulled his hand away.

Nyira might have allowed it though—just to see what he felt like.

"She is a rare creature," said Rubin. "And she is in the best condition of any of the slaves we've ever purchased from you. In fact, they all are. You have obviously taken very good care of them. That is very smart and profitable, Abdullah. You will see."

"Yes, captain," Abdullah replied. "At great personal expense. My son… It doesn't matter."

"The green eyes are a very good indicator of magical abilities," said Rubin. "And she is a healer as well?"

"She was taught by her father. He was a well-known medicine man in the region she comes from."

"It would be wonderful if we could see a demonstration of her powers."

"I can't promise that. But she is very protective of the other slaves."

The white man looked pleased, and he smiled at Nyira. She didn't return his smile. She'd been warned about the evil Dutchmen hid behind their smiles. Rubin went and received a mumbled word from the brooding Captain Matthias.

"All right, Abdullah. You have sold us. We will take a chance on this quiet little one. But if she doesn't deliver, we will deduct the value from your next shipment."

Abdullah looked very pleased.

On the day she was scheduled to be shipped off with the Dutch slavers, Abdullah barged into the tent where Nyira was housed with the rest of the female slaves.

"All of you get out!" Abdullah ordered, as a couple of warriors followed him, carrying some type of brass platter between the two of them. Another group of warriors started to move the slaves out into the yard in front of the lodge. Nyira started to leave with them.

"Not you, my little sorceress. You stay," said the big man. "I've brought a gift just for you."

Nyira was wary, since there was nothing he could offer she might want, but the warriors strolled toward her and stopped near where she sat on the ground.

"I don't want anything from you," said Nyira. She turned around and faced away from the warriors.

"Oh, now you are being a silly child," replied Abdullah. "Of course you want this."

She could feel him standing very close behind her. It didn't make any sense. He smelled of coconut oil—just like Gnangi. She felt like crying. How dare he ruin her memory of the beloved woman.

"I promise you will not want to miss this. I'll give you a hint. Little girls usually love guessing riddles: It's from a very recent, close friend of yours…"

A recent close friend? What was this evil man talking abou— she jerked around.

"No! You—" Abdullah snatched the cloth from the platter, and Nyira screamed.

Gord's large majestic head stood in the center of the shiny metal. Nyira lunged for the platter, but the warriors snatched it away. "You promised!" she cried. She fought and scratched the warriors. "Please! I must touch him! He was my friend! Oh Gord! Oh Gord I'm sorry!" But she was no match for the large men. She finally gave out, rolled into a ball on the ground and wailed until she had no tears left. After a while, she sat up and looked at Abdullah. "Why? You promised!"

Abdullah had the platter placed on a table next to him. Nyira lunged again, but he blocked her path with his bulk.

"Ah-ah! No touching," said the chief, beaming as if this was the most pleasant game. "He's already sold. And he brought a handsome price, too."

"Why?" whined Nyira. "You promised," she cried, as though it was all she had the strength for.

"I don't make promises to slaves, girl. And any agreement we might've had ended when you hurt my son!"

"He was attacking me! You—" She went for the tray, and when he blocked her, she tried to make eye contact. He quickly turned his head away.

"Oops! Be careful now." He pivoted around and faced away from her. "Or the next head on this platter will be that old woman's."

"No," said Nyira. "I wasn't trying to hurt you. I just saw your eyes. They're just like your other son's."

Abdullah turned and looked at her, and his face was twisted with anguish.

"What… what do you know of my Mustafa?"

"I know he is tall and dark, like you," replied Nyira. "And he has a spear with a red shaft and yellow lines on it." Nyira tilted her head slightly as she spoke—a little smile came to her lips like this was one of her fondest memories. "I also know he is very strong. I felt that when he picked me up."

"Wh—what do you mean… is?" said Abdullah. He went to his knees before the child, as if to try and look into her eyes as she shared her memory. "You mean… my son is alive?"

"When I last saw his eyes, he was," replied Nyira.

Abdullah was practically in tears now.

"But where? How—how can I get to him?" He scooted towards her on his knees, and Nyira backed away—not wanting the man to touch her. "Please… tell me."

"I don't know if they still have him."

"Who? Who has him? How can I get to him? You must tell me!" He rushed her, snatched her up, and began to shake her. "You must tell me! You must! I will do something terrible if you—"

Nyira looked him in the eyes.

"Put—me—down!" She felt only a dull ache in her head now, even though she was very angry.

Abdullah stumbled and fell to his knees, but he still managed to hold on to her.

"Ughhh! The pain!" Tears ran down his face. "You will have to kill me! Ughhn! I must know! Pleeease!"

"Let me go," said Nyira. "And I will tell you where I saw him."

Abdullah put her down.

"You must go to the jungle near my village," said Nyira. "After dark. Stand very still and say the word: Aboo. Then run to the village. They will meet you before you get there."

The Dutchmen had made all their purchases by the end of the day and were ready to transport them to the coast.

CHAPTER 10

BRUNO USUALLY STARTED his day in the eastern fields. He preferred working in the potatoes and stayed away from the sugar cane. It was for the bigger, more violent slaves. The ones who might suddenly go mad from the heat and toil and hack one of the men working next to him, just because he was angry, or just because. He'd lost a friend that way. Arnaud. Arnaud had been young, tall and very, very strong. He could finish half a field by himself, take a small bit of water and work until sundown. Arnaud was loud, had light grey eyes and laughed a lot. Bruno had been in awe of Arnaud's power with a machete in his hands—no one worked faster or longer. There were even bets on who could chop the most by midday. That was how Arnaud lost his life. He had won the contest; he always won. Everyone knew it didn't make sense betting against him. But losers never lost graciously. Bruno should have mentioned this to his friend. He should have said, don't take Christian's bet, my friend. He doesn't like losing. He should have said that.

"Well, he will have to get used to it," Arnaud would have replied. "He should know better than to bet against Arnaud!" Arnaud had started referring to himself in the third person.

Bruno knew where that came from: Etienne, the overseer. Whenever he was comparing himself to someone he considered his inferior. The only difference: Arnaud did it in jest.

Bruno knew that Christian was afraid to lose to Etienne. The overseer always won and then punished you while also taking what little you had. The only thing Christian had worth losing was Madeline, his wife. It was obviously a foolish wager. Etienne had wanted Madeline and tricked Christian into it. Christian even requested a different opponent. However, Etienne was not interested in fair odds; he wanted a sure and decisive victory. That would only come from Arnaud's wide back, massive arms and huge shoulders.

As the mid-morning heat boiled up from the undulating crop, Etienne sat upon his big brown mare and watched the competition begin. A young slave named Benjamin stood next to him, holding a long-handled palm umbrella, to shade him from the sun. Another child named Louis held a pitcher of cold water on a tray. To make matters all the more humiliating, Madeline was stationed next to Etienne on a smaller white pony. She was holding her own umbrella. But Bruno had no misconception about why Christian's wife was given the rare comfort of a horse and shade. It was because Etienne had every expectation that she would no longer be his wife at the end of this event.

Christian was a tall, strong man himself. He was Mandinka, or so he claimed. He was not someone any other slave on the Bissett plantation would challenge. He'd beaten many a man unconscious and dared those watching to report him. No one did. Most of those beatings were behind covetous glances at Madeline. Rightly so—for she was butternut colored with long flowing black hair from her Spanish grandmother, and the most intoxicating hazel eyes. Madeline had a beauty that dared you not to look. Many did and suffered for it.

Halfway through the challenge: to chop a quarter field of cane in three hours. It was an absurd task—but halfway into it, Arnaud got into a rhythm. This was usually manifested by a silly song he had once heard a child sing as he went past the Bissett residence:

Frère Jacques, Frère Jacques,
Dormez-vous? Dormez-vous?
Sonnez les matines! Sonnez les matines!
Ding, dang, dong. Ding, dang, dong.

This development didn't bode well for Christian. He looked back and was horrified to see the boy Louis taking the pitcher of cold water to his Madeline. He began hacking with a frightened frenzy then. Etienne yawned and seemed not to care one way or the other. While Christian wanted to cry, and Arnaud was more than halfway through his portion of the cane. Christian had cut a great deal as well, an impressive feat on any other day. This was not any other day, though. This was the end of his life, his love, every tender moment he'd shared with beautiful Madeline. Tears flowed down Christian's cheeks as he swung his blade like a madman, fighting against the wind. As the hot sun bore down on his wet back, he lost track of where he was within the thick swelter of the cane. He finally chopped until he came clear. The field was done—all the cane was laid down.

"I won!" cried Christian. "I have finished first! I have…" That's when Arnaud strolled past him and headed back to the beginning of the break.

"What are you raving about, you fool!" said Etienne.

"You have blindly stumbled into Arnaud's wake. Look behind you." Christian turned around and saw that he had cut sideways and crossed into Arnaud's cleared crop. His crop was still behind, and only half done.

Christian didn't bother to hide his heartbreak, as Etienne rode away with Madeline trailing behind on the little white pony.

"And don't you leave here until you've finished!" Etienne called back over his shoulder, as he trotted the mare toward the homestead.

Christian went berserk. He flung his blade around like a drunken maniac and screamed at the hot blue sky. And then Arnaud made a gesture—of genuine friendship.

"Don't worry, Christian," he said, stepping up to chop beside him. "I'll help you finish. It's the least I can do." He chopped in earnest as if this was his task all along.

But Christian wasn't in need of friendship, or restitution. He only saw his beautiful one's radiant hair, as the brute Etienne ran his hands through it. Arnaud had already hacked past him, and Christian was looking at his huge sweaty back. There was no other place to direct his rage except at the instrument of his destruction. So he hacked off the top of Arnaud's head and then continued cutting the cane. He knew the overseer would punish him if he didn't finish as he was directed.

He received no punishment for the murder of Arnaud. Etienne actually spoke on his behalf to Alphonse Bissett: that Christian was a strong, productive worker and they could not afford to lose two good slaves.

There was no more Etienne as there was no more Arnaud. The overseer had been gone more than a month now. It made no difference in Bruno's life. He was afraid he had no personality without Arnaud's massive gregarious nature to define him. He kept to himself, as well as was possible on a slave plantation. When the slaves approached the water bucket at midday, he always hung back, not wanting to talk or hear hollow condolences about his friend. He was a good worker and found that he worked better alone.

The new overseer was a man named Bertram Miles. He had not shown himself to be particularly cruel. Not yet, at least. That usually came with time. And he showed no displeasure with Bruno's production. Bruno was managing his grief as well as he could. But then he started to lose his mind.

It started on the second morning of potato season. As Bruno moved up a row, a pineapple appeared in the dirt before him. He didn't know what to make of the fruit but quickly stuffed it into his sack, before anyone saw it. They never gave slaves fruit. He only knew what it was from seeing them as a child in his village. Farmers cultivated the crop and then sold them at the village market. They also grew wild if you wanted to venture deeper into the jungle. He had only been eight when he was stolen by the slavers, as he fished a little inlet that he and his brother Amare had discovered, not more than a quarter mile from his village of Abrolo. So he hadn't had the chance to venture further than his mother allowed him to. If caught with the fruit, they would whip him for stealing. He was sure he could get it back to his shack that he had shared with Arnaud. Everyone assumed he would take a wife. That hadn't happened yet. Within the next hour, three mangos showed up. He had barely stuffed them into his sack before Juliette came over to pick beside him. Juliette was very pretty and always wore little flowers at the ends of her braided hair. He closed his eyes and prayed to whatever cruel god that was granting him these gifts.

"Please stop," he whispered. "I beg you. Don't send any more."

"Who are you praying to?" asked Juliette. She had constantly probed the workings of his mind. He was reluctant to tell her that divine fruit appeared before him. He would need to get the fruit hidden before he emptied his sack. He pretended he had to go pee, and hid it in the jungle next to the field. That's when he saw the half-naked Indian boy. He was sitting beside the palm tree just inside the bush, eating a mango.

"Did you not like the fruit?" the boy asked.

Bruno was shocked that this strange boy knew something he couldn't possibly know.

"What?" said Bruno, and almost dropped the items he was trying to conceal. "Who are you?"

"I'm a friend," said the boy. "You should eat those. Why are you hiding them?"

"Slaves aren't allowed such things," Bruno replied, as he covered the fruit with brush. "How do you know about them?"

"I gave them to you," replied the boy. "Maybe I should've given them to someone else."

"How?" asked Bruno. "I would've seen you. How did you—" The boy evaporated before him, and Bruno ran. He would have screamed, but he was afraid someone might ask him what he was screaming about.

"What's the matter?" asked Juliette. "Why were you running?"

He was winded now and drenched in sweat from the

frying heat. Slaves rarely ran in the fields, because it was too long between water.

"I… I just felt like running," replied Bruno. "I can run if I want to. I just wanted to get back to work quickly."

"Oh," replied Juliette. She didn't question his story. "I will give you half of my water," she said. "You shouldn't run out here."

"No, you won't. I'll be fine. You need your water. Thank you, though."

She decided to change the subject.

"Will you be coming to the *calenda* tonight? Makienda will be singing."

She was so beautiful and so sweet. But what would he do with sweet? He didn't deserve it.

"I… I don't know," Bruno replied, looking down into the rows as if searching for where he'd left off. "I don't think so." He found his hoe and picked it up.

"Oh," Juliette replied, and suddenly looked very sad. She actually dropped her hoe and turned away, as if she wanted to cry. Bruno panicked.

"Wait, no! Don't… don't go. I…" She turned to look at him. Her eyes so hopeful, so… magnificent—the most magnificent brown since his mother. "…I guess I could come. Will you be there?"

"Yes!" Juliette replied, beaming. "I will be there." She took a small flower from the end of one of her braids and placed it in his right hand. She then turned and walked back toward the western fields, where she and her sister, Babette, usually picked.

When Bruno gazed down at the delicate little flower, the

strangest thing occurred. Its sweet scent began to dance joyfully about his nose as if possibly it was an extension of Juliette.

How is it possible that I am given such a gift? he thought, and wondered if the strange Indian boy had had a hand in this, too

CHAPTER 11

NYIRA WAS NOT fond of the ship. Until this structure,
the largest conveyance she had been on was an elephant that
brought a load of spices Papa had purchased from a trader on
the coast. When the creature entered the village, all the children stood back and watched as three-year-old Nyira went
up and spoke to it. Her father had gone into the men's lodge
to arrange payment for the trader. The elephant had made
strange noises and smelled, but finally agreed to ferry her
and a few of the other children around the village. This ship
thing was a hundred times larger, with smells so awful she
was suddenly nauseated, but she recognized it as the same
smell she'd gotten from the smiling white man. There was
also a spirit dwelling upon the vessel, and one of the reasons
she was initially apprehensive to board the three-deck mon-
strosity. There were also a lot more white men.

The spirit had positioned itself at the rail next to the
white men, who proceeded to shout and push the slaves
as they boarded. She stood still and looked at the being. It
wasn't that distinct, as the bright cloudless sky made him
almost transparent.

"Be aware of the big one there behind you," it said. "He enjoys striking with his bludgeon."

"What is your name," Nyira asked.

"I'd be more concerned with that one if I were you."

Nyira turned and saw an enormous, dirty, disheveled white man coming toward her, screaming. As he moved across the craft the slaves were boarding from, the boat dipped a good bit.

"What are you waiting for?" the man bellowed. He was so broad and tall, he blocked out the sun. Nyira smiled at the man, but he still raised the thing he had in his fist. "Don't you laugh at—"

When Nyira made eye contact with him, the anger on his face was replaced by confusion. He looked at what he had in his hand as if he couldn't imagine where it came from.

"What did I come down here for?"

"You were going to help my people onto the ship-beast," Nyira replied.

He turned and gazed at the other slaves, as they struggled to board the large vessel. Instead of helping, he sat down in the boat.

The spirit looked shocked by what it had witnessed and shook its head.

"You are going to be trouble," it said and vanished.

The ship seemed to eat the slaves. They were marched to an opening in the floor and shoved down it. A number of the white men had gathered on the deck. Rubin came toward Nyira when she made it aboard.

"What did you do to Frenchy?" he asked her.

"What is a Frenchy?" replied Nyira, mimicking the man's accent.

"I'm glad you're finally talking to me," said the Dutchman. "Frenchy is that big lump sitting in the boat down there. I was nervous when I saw him approach you. He enjoys hurting."

"He didn't hurt me," replied Nyira, and went past him to the ladder with the rest of the slaves.

"Wait!" said Rubin, blocking her path. "Don't go down there. I have someone I want you to meet." A pudgy, surly looking white boy came up and stood beside the first officer. "This is Piggy—"

"My name is Maximillian!" cried the boy. "I ain't no damn Piggy…" Rubin gave the boy a look that shut him up. Nyira was amazed at how quickly Rubin's face could change from smiling to menacing.

"Anyway," continued the first officer. "Piggy here will make sure you have all the supplies you need for your healing. I have also had them build you a structure here on the deck. It's a healer's house." Nyira looked at the squat clay shed situated to the right of the larboard gangway on the main deck. It had a roof made of reeds. There was also another enormous white man standing beside it, leering at Benzia. He was as tall as the structure and a lot less clean looking.

"What are you looking at, old mom," he snarled.

"Don't pay any attention to him," said Rubin. "That's just Cliegman."

Once again, he had that strange expression. He seemed pleased with himself and expected her to be pleased as well.

"I don't want it," replied Nyira, as she watched Benzia go down the ladder. "I will stay with them." She went down the ladder, too.

The slave deck was in the hold, below the galley, the

gun deck and sleeping quarters for the crew. The vessel was massive, but below deck still seemed cramped. The thing was still long because when Nyira looked left and right, she didn't see an end of it. She met Benzia on the gun deck.

"This reminds me of the mine," the old woman said. "It's just as dim, and the lamps on the wall never provide sufficient light."

"Keep moving!" one of the crewmen pushing the slaves to the ladder yelled. Nyira helped Benzia down to the next level.

The heat and stink of the hold was startling. At first, Nyira thought they were in the wrong section. The area seemed smaller than the deck they had just left. The only air came from small square holes cut into the walls. But these didn't account for the stench and the darkness. Nevertheless, the slaves were shoved into it. The area consisted of a series of tightly grouped wooden bunks, next to shackles hammered into the hull. There were more than she could count, stretching further into the dark to the left and right. This, apparently, was the men's section. As they moved forward, there was a different divider where the women were being kept. Along the way, she noticed large metal tubs with dried excrement. She didn't have to wonder what these were used for. Soon Nyira had to stop and vomit, and many of the females were crying, along with their children, while Benzia was in shock.

"I can't believe they mean to house us in this way," said the old woman.

Nyira saw the spirit stretched out upon one of the bunks.

"It's actually much improved from when I was first chained in here," it said.

Nyira got a better look at him, then. The near darkness brought out his features.

He was a tall, lean African. His face was rounder and his nose flatter than those from her region, so he possibly had been taken from the north. He still had shackles encircling his neck, and there was ritual scarring on his face and chest. As he lay upon the bunk, his legs stretched well past the end of it.

"Even in death," he said. "These things are still not comfortable."

"What's your name?" asked Nyira.

"I was called Lumumba. But that was a couple hundred years ago."

"I am called Nyira. Why are you still here, Lumumba? Why have you not gone to be with your people?" The smile left his face.

"That's not something I'll be discussing with you, child. If you stay out of my way, I'll stay out of yours. You're going to have your hands full with these Dutchmen. They've made some changes to this vessel—to accommodate you, probably. Healers are worth a lot to a ship's cargo. But they still have the shackles, so I wouldn't sleep down here if I were you."

Rubin entered the slave deck.

"Pew!" said the white man. "I didn't realize—. You should come back on deck, child." His features turned red, as he attempted to hold his breath as he spoke. He also had to lean down quite a bit, due to the lower ceiling.

"All my people should be on deck," replied Nyira. "They can't breathe down here. You're having trouble."

Before Rubin could reply, a tall tightly muscled man with a scar on the side of his face entered the slave deck behind him.

"What are you two doing out of shackles? Conrad! Bring the tails and some smaller shackles!"

"That won't be necessary, Nielssen," replied Rubin. "The child will be in the hut on the deck."

"What about the old crone?"

"Benzia stays with me," replied Nyira. She tried to make eye contact with Rubin, but he quickly turned his head. He'd obviously been warned by Abdullah.

"The old woman, too, I guess."

"She can help me," said Nyira.

"It won't be possible to let all of them on the deck at once," said Rubin. "I've taken a smaller cargo this trip so that we can deliver you in better condition. We'll figure something out. Come with me, Nielssen." He went up the ladder.

Nyira found herself busy on the first night of the voyage. One of the male slaves had been knocked unconscious and was bleeding from wounds on his back and shoulders. The man Cliegman dragged the still-shackled bondsman to the door of the hut and dropped him.

"First customer," he snarled and stomped away. Nyira was disoriented and sickened by the up and down motion of the vessel. A few times she ran to the rail and puked over the side. During these moments the boy Piggy was right at her elbow.

"If you're thinking of jumping," he said. "the sharks will be waiting." He stood so close she noted the smell of feces on him. Nyira turned her nose up and backed away.

"What are sharks?" she asked.

"Have you never been on a ship?"

"No."

"They're what waits in the water when the Negroes jump in." She didn't reply and walked back to her healer's hut.

"This is much worse than I ever imagined," said Benzia.

"I didn't imagine anything," replied Nyira.

Two more men were deposited on her doorstep that night—one was already dead. The survivors told of being attacked by the big white man when they asked for water. Nyira went in search of Piggy. She found him on the quarterdeck talking to the helmsman.

"Can you bring water for some of the men?" she asked. The helmsman gave Piggy a look

"Slaves aren't allowed up here," said the boy.

"Why are you letting this creature order you around?" said the helmsman. Piggy's cheeks got red, and Nyira could see he was building up his courage.

"You get back down to your hut, I said!" He snatched up the metal ladle from the water bucket on the deck and ran at her with it. Nyira didn't even flinch as she looked him in the eyes. Piggy stopped in his tracks, turned and went got the water bucket and followed her back to her hut.

"Well blow me down," said the helmsman. "Such a little coward."

Rubin

A week into the passage.

"I have told you, Rubin. My name is Alexandre. Not Frenchy!"

"Well, Alexandre," said Rubin. "You've suddenly become kinder, it seems."

Alexandre looked troubled.

"I haven't! And I will prove it by breaking your arm the next time you address me as Frenchy!"

"So it seems you've decided to use your temper instead of your whip, Alexandre."

"I didn't decide to," replied man, not happy with his admission. "I just can't seem to do it. It doesn't make any sense. Whenever one of them doesn't move fast enough or gives me the evil eye. I just don't know what's happened. But I swear to you, Rubin, if you tell the other crewmen I've gone soft, I'll break both your arms."

"Yes. But will you be able to use your whip on me?"

The big man just glared at Rubin as he walked away, laughing.

On the next day, the first officer approached Nyira while she was down on her hands scrubbing the deck of the ship, with some of the other slaves and crew. He didn't say anything at first. He just stood looking at the child. Nyira stopped and looked back at him.

"Be careful," said Rubin. "Some owners won't like it when you look at them that way."

"What way?" replied Nyira. "I am only looking at you looking at me."

"How did you change Frenchy?"

"He doesn't like you calling him that."

"How do you know that? Can you read thoughts, too?"

She continued to look at him.

"Well, I'll give you some advice after you are sold to the French in Saint Domingue—that's where you're going, by the way. Or did you know that, too? Anyway, don't do any of your... sorcery in front of the priests. I suppose Frenchy was a bit too liberal with his whip. If you promise not to do anything to anyone else, I'll make sure no harm comes to you… and the rest of the cargo. Do we have an agreement?"

"I don't want anything from you."

"Very well. But still, make sure you say something if they aren't getting enough to eat. I don't want the cook turned into a frog or anything like that."

Nyira didn't reply and went back to her scrubbing.

Rubin wasn't sure if the girl was as powerful as the tribesman had claimed. However, something had turned a formerly brutal overseer into little more than a confused human slug. He supposed it was just as well. Damaged goods caused discounts, and the French were shrewd negotiators, always looking to shave a few livre off the top.

CHAPTER 12

THE SKY ON the night of the *calenda* was starless. Bruno made sure to look up because he remembered the way the sky seemed to dance with light on the nights of his village's dances. He then thought that perhaps that wasn't true. It was more likely he was adding things to the memory of his childhood. He couldn't recall a single instant when he looked up and considered the stars. They were just there, like the air and the clouds and the sky. But he didn't have any other way to hold onto it, so he chose to believe he'd looked up at the sky. And as he peered at it now, it was completely black. Like when they razed the ground for the clearing, they pushed the heavens aside as well. Stars wouldn't have mattered anyway. The field was fringed by a number of kerosene lanterns—obviously taken from households throughout the planter community. There were some tar-dipped rag torches as well—protruding from the ground at intervals of five to ten feet around the clearing. The drummers had set up next to a group of the kerosene lanterns. The cloth torches gave off too much smoke and sometimes overwhelmed them.

As he waded through the jungle to reach the area, Bruno felt that perhaps he shouldn't have come. He hadn't been to a tribal gathering since he was taken. What he remembered always made him sad. His father had been the best dancer in his village—among the men. His brother, Amare, had acquired his father's personality and a lot of his rhythm.

When he entered the clearing, the drums seemed to grow in volume. He started to feel sick as if they were somehow connected directly into his head and his stomach. Everyone was moving and jumping and bumping and jostling. He felt a loss of equilibrium, like when he was trapped in the disease-infested hold of the vessel that brought him there. He weaved his way through the dancers and made it to a palm tree. He threw up in the grass behind it. When the drummers picked up their tempo, he thought his head would pop. Everything started to spin, and he sat down in the thick green ferns and palmetto next to the palm tree. He felt a little better and periodically peeped past a palmetto plant. What was he thinking? This was not the place for... Juliette appeared among the gyrating forms of the dancers. He knew he had to stand up then. He didn't want her to see him like that. There was a glow about her. Someone in the crowd said something to her, and she smiled. When he saw that smile, his heart leaped and dragged him to his feet. He was wobbly but standing. He made his feet move toward her.

"Oh," Juliette said when she saw him. "You came." She smiled again—right at him. How could such a smile be? There had to be some magic here. He must be in some kind of dream. She was dressed in a bright yellow, red and green *pagne* that she and her sister produced. Their skill making garments was well known. Babette was right next to her, wearing the identical item. It wasn't right, though. There was no light to it.

"I—I… yes," was all he could manage. He had planned to say more. *Say something more, Bruno!* he admonished himself.

"Your *pagne* is nice," he said. It was just the right thing. Her smile lit up so bright, it nearly blinded him.

"You like it?" she asked, looking down at herself. "I was afraid the colors were too bright."

"I do," replied Bruno.

At that moment, a shout rang out, and all the dancers moved out of the clearing. The trees and brush in the area had been removed long ago, by other slaves that had come before. The clearing was as bald as the plantation yard, and on nights when they needed some release, the slaves frenzied movements raised a dust thick as smoke.

"I got here just in time," said Juliette, taking his hand. He felt a shock go through him. "Makienda will sing now."

Makienda was a tall, slim man. No one knew what plantation he came from. He emerged from the jungle wearing a long orange, green and purple *pagne*, and a wooden monkey mask fringed by feathers. The only information anyone knew about him was he performed at *calendas*. Word of mouth would spread that he would possibly be at an event. Sometimes he would and sometimes he wouldn't. There was never anything definite.

Bruno had heard of this person, but this was the first time he had actually seen him. Makienda didn't waste time and immediately broke into a vigorous dance. And as he began to sing, the crowd took up the song, too. So it wasn't clear to Bruno whether he could really sing. As for his dancing, Bruno thought his father was much better.

Juliette managed to draw Bruno out among the crowd of dancers.

"I don't think I should," he protested, as she took his hand and pulled. "My brother was the dancer in the family; he and my father."

Juliette smiled. "So you grew up dancing then?" She didn't wait for him to answer because while he was mesmerized by her smile, he'd been transported to the center of the clearing. Then the drumming sped up as Makienda began to perform a dance that Bruno had seen his father do, hundreds of times—his brother as well. Amare had even begun to teach it to him. He hadn't quite gotten it when he was stolen away. But the drums seemed to know something about him, something he hadn't known. They caught Juliette, and she began to move with the rhythm. Suddenly Makienda swooped into the center of the circle and was moving toward Juliette as if to dance with her. And Bruno would be outside the vibrations, outside the rhythm. But his body wouldn't let him be a coward, wouldn't let his sadness overtake him. His feet wanted something; his legs did, too. Neither paid attention to the emptiness of his soul. He moved; he jumped—his knees, his feet. All chose joy, chose happiness, chose to move with Juliette, and then something else:

"Why are you crying?" asked Juliette. "You dance too well to be sad."

"I'm not sad," replied Bruno. He was right. It didn't matter what his head might be doing. He'd follow his feet. This really was some kind of magic. Because there was no way he could be dancing, or feeling as happy as he was. So he decided to enjoy it, just as he'd enjoyed the divine fruit. He would accept this gift, too. He just wished Arnaud could see him now. He would… no. No sadness, not now. He would enjoy this dream while he was in it. But Arnaud would've been happy for him. That much he would acknowledge.

The next day, he showed up to the eastern end of the potato field and found Juliette was there already.

"Babette said that I should pick with you now," Juliette said. She didn't say it casually like she was joking. She said it like this was the way it would be, forever. Bruno didn't know how to take this. It now appeared that the other night hadn't been a dream. He had really danced, and Juliette had really been there, for him. And now she wanted to be with him? Forever? But that would mean… he wouldn't have room for sadness anymore. How could he have gotten so lucky? Juliette was by his side from then on. Even the day Christian tried to kill him.

Enriquillo dozed on the front porch of the *bohío*. His mother sat on her *duho*, weaving baskets and chatting with some of the tribe's women. Enriquillo had just come in from fishing along the coast. He'd caught a decent-sized shark and some red snapper. He felt Agueybana sit beside him. He didn't have to look. The old man gave off a strange, not unpleasant tobacco aroma.

Enriquillo knew the purpose of this visit. He didn't want to talk to the *behike*.

"I know why you've been avoiding me, Enriquillo," said

Agueybana. "And I don't understand why you thought it would make a difference."

"I didn't think about whether it would make a difference," replied Enriquillo. "I just had no need of your guidance."

"I suspected as much. You know that what you're doing won't help them."

"No. I don't know."

"They're afraid and away from their home and their people. Your gestures will only confuse them." Enriquillo turned and looked at the *behike*.

"If you knew that I didn't want your guidance, why have you decided to give it?"

"Just because you don't want it, doesn't mean you don't need it."

"You know everything, Agueybana," replied Enriquillo. "So you must also know that I won't give up." He stood up and walked past his mother and the other village women, and went out into the jungle.

CHAPTER 13

BY THE END of first the week of the voyage, Nyira discovered what Lumumba was.

A few of the slaves had started to get sick from the heat and lack of ventilation on the slave deck. Abena's baby, Efuru, was weaker than most of the adult slaves. Nyira noticed the tall spirit hovered near mother and child as the woman tried to breastfeed her baby. The infant began to cough as Lumumba waved his hand over her face.

"What are you doing?" demanded Nyira.

Lumumba's face turned white, and his eyes glowed red.

"Don't bother me, girl. This child is suffering." Efuru seemed to be having trouble breathing.

"Oh please! Someone help!" cried Abena. "My child can't breathe!" The baby thrashed and made chirping sounds. Nyira remembered a remedy her father had once taught her. She rushed up the ladder and found Benzia on the deck, emptying chamber pots for the captain's cabin boy.

"Please, give me some of your grey strands!" said Nyira.

Benzia looked puzzled but sat the pots down and tugged some strands from her scalp.

"What are you doing?" she asked.

"I know what the spirit Lumumba is. He is trying to kill Abena's baby. Have you any salt?"

"A small amount. They don't give us much." The old woman reached into a fabricated pouch at her waist and dropped the few grains into Nyira's hand. The girl ran back down the ladder. She returned a few moments later, carrying Efuru in her arms. Abena was right on her heels. Nyira had tied the salt and grey strands into a tiny bit of cloth and was using it to rub back and forth upon the baby's head as she whispered to her. The child had stopped chirping and was breathing normally.

Lumumba came up onto deck after them. He began to rush and thrash about the ship, knocking over crates. He even picked up a pallet containing forty bags of grain, like it weighed nothing, and dropped it. The boom startled and confused the white men working near it.

"You had no right to steal her from me! She was mine! She is going to die. I can see it. You just refuse to. Babies rarely survive the passage."

"I want her to live!" replied Nyira. "I knew you weren't good. I won't let you hurt her."

Lumumba just looked at her and shook his head.

"You don't even know about life yet. And you think you can stop death? You're a foolish child. I already know her fate. I know all their fates. You'll see. And your sorcery won't be able to do a thing about it."

Efuru died a few days later, just as Lumumba predicted. Nyira could do nothing to prevent it. The next death set off a chain of events that confirmed everything the spirit had told her.

A week after the body of Efuru was flung into the sea,

Abena, still distraught and mourning her loss, waited until she was working repairing sails near the mainmast and jumped into the sea as well. Lumumba had sat on the rail where the woman went over. Nyira sat down on the deck and cried. Benzia held her and rocked her, as only a mother could, and spoke words of encouragement.

After Abena, three more women and four males also leaped over. The captain made a decision. The slaves were once again shackled to their bunks in the hold. The screams from the slave deck were almost intolerable. The next week, three men and six women died of disease on the slave deck. Nyira went and confronted Captain Matthias.

The captain was surprised the girl was able to get past his guards. But the men stationed at his door were no obstacle. Once she looked them in the eyes, they opened the door and ushered her in.

The old man looked like a trapped hyena as she cornered him behind his chart table.

"Why are you doing this?" demanded Nyira

The captain pulled a pistol on her.

"How dare you come in here, slave," he snarled. "I will tell you now I was wary of this 'tribe healer' nonsense. But my nephew convinced the owners of its merits. Were it up to me, you'd all be chained in the hold and be done with it! Now get out, before I'm forced to use this." Nyira decided to heed the man's warning. She hadn't realized how frightened these white men could be, and her only a child.

Rubin came to the hut later that evening.

"You must never go into my uncle's quarters again," Rubin told her. "He is not accustomed to being challenged by a slave."

"I didn't mean to frighten him. I just wanted to tell him that just as many die in the hold as jump off the ship."

"We don't have a choice," said the Dutchman. "He's a businessman. And he has to try and protect the cargo. So they must stay confined for a while. If you can keep them from jumping, then do it. But don't ask us to sacrifice the investment."

Nyira went down into the hold and tried to comfort the slaves as much as possible.

Lumumba appeared on the slave deck, beside the bunk of a man who had sustained terrible wounds to his wrists and ankles as he pulled and fought against the shackles. Nyira touched his head and made him sleep. This at least quieted him while she wrapped his wounds.

"That won't help him," replied the spirit.

"Well, you won't," said Nyira.

The spirit actually looked hurt.

"I can't believe you haven't figured this out yet, child. Your magic and your tears won't save any of them. Only I can. That's why I stay. I have a destiny, too. If I could send them back to where they came from, I would. I don't care if you believe that, but I would! I can't get back to my home, and neither will they. Nor will you. So be prepared, because this is going to get worse."

Once again, the spirit was proven correct.

Ten more slaves perished on the slave deck, and six more deaths were facilitated by the man, Cliegman, as he began to stalk Benzia.

After three weeks, Nyira finally convinced Rubin to allow more of the slaves onto the main deck. But that didn't go as she expected.

They allowed a hundred and twenty-five at a time of the two hundred and fifty remaining cargo. And while Rubin wanted very much to preserve the health and welfare of the goods he had contracted to deliver to Saint Domingue, he also decided to try controlling them better. So the overseers were given a freer hand when the slaves were brought back onto the deck.

CHAPTER 14

WHEN BRUNO WOKE that next morning and left his shack to head for the fields, Christian stopped him. Christian was not a man of many words. And since Bruno was the same, they just stood at the edge of the yard behind the stable that looked out over the fields and stared at one another. When Bruno made an attempt to go past, Christian blocked him. The early morning heat was already causing them to sweat, and the lack of any kind of breeze didn't help.

"What?" Bruno finally said, looking at Christian.

Christian didn't respond and instead gazed out over the eastern field. Juliette could be seen making her way toward them. Bruno was suddenly panicked at what Christian's motive was.

"I have done nothing to you!" cried Bruno.

"No. You haven't," Christian finally said. Without Arnaud to compare or diminish him, Christian was the strongest and most dangerous man on the plantation. "That's why I've decided not to kill you. But I will be taking Juliette for my wife."

Juliette arrived at the yard just as Christian turned to

walk away. He didn't even glance in her direction. Seeing Juliette pushed Bruno's rage to the top of his chest.

"I have done nothing to you!" he screamed at Christian's back. Juliette stopped and looked at Bruno.

"What has happened?" she asked. Bruno could barely look at her. He walked past her toward the eastern field. When she tried to follow him, he said, "No. You must go back to the western fields with Babette."

"But why?" Juliette asked. When she tried to take his hand, he backed away from her.

"You just must, Juliette. Now go." He had to walk away so she wouldn't see him cry. He felt like such a fool, falling for this dream. When he reached the spot where he'd left off the day before, he began to dig with a fury. Another group of mangos appeared in the row before him. He quickly snatched them up and flung them across the field.

"Stop!" he screamed. "I don't want your fruit!"

Someone else informed Juliette of Christian's intentions. Afterwards, she went to Bruno's shack and pushed open the fabricated door. The sun had gone down, but the moon was very bright—almost like it was full. When Juliette stepped into Bruno's one-room abode, the moon through the window illuminated a very bleak scene. The room consisted of a cedar table that Arnaud and Bruno had made together. There were also two decently-made wooden chairs. The shack also contained a couple of wood frame beds, with cornhusk mattresses. But Bruno, whom Juliette could hear breathing, was lying face down on the floor, next to the table. Juliette went to him.

"Bruno. What happened? Are you hurt?"

Bruno didn't get up, nor would he turn over and look at her.

"Go away," said Bruno. "You don't belong here." Juliette could tell he'd been crying.

"Yes I do," replied Juliette. She kneeled down and placed her hand on his back. It was hot. Like the sun at midday. *A fire is burning inside him,* thought Juliette. "Bruno, please," said Juliette. "Please look at me."

"Why," replied Bruno. "What would I see?"

"Someone who loves you."

"That won't help," replied Bruno. "You don't have a choice."

"Yes, I do," said Juliette. "I've already made my choice. I choose you. I don't care what Christian says. He will never have me."

"Even if I'm dead?" asked Bruno. "Because he will kill me."

"I will never give myself to Christian." She laid her head on Bruno's burning back. It was still damp with his sweat. Something strange happened then: A pineapple appeared on the floor next to Juliette.

"Oh, look," cried Juliette. "You get divine fruit, too?"

Bruno turned over and looked at her.

"It's… you mean you get it, too?"

"Yes," replied Juliette, and picked up the fruit. "Let's eat it, Bruno."

"Have you seen the Indian boy, too?"

"No. What Indian boy?"

"Oh. Maybe I was just seeing things."

"Bruno. You've seen the one who sends the divine fruit?

It's been appearing to others, too. Some say it's a miracle, and they've set up shrines to the spirit."

"He's not a spirit," replied Bruno, sitting up. "He's just a boy. He told me he gave me the fruit and then dis… appeared. … I never considered that he might be a god."

That's when Enriquillo appeared, sitting on the edge of the table, his long legs dangling down.

"I'm not a god," said Enriquillo, a bit perturbed. Bruno and Juliette ran to the other side of the room, and cowered between the two beds. "I just wanted to make sure people weren't thinking that."

"Then what are you?" asked Juliette, as she clutched on to Bruno.

"I'm just me," replied Enriquillo. "My name is Enriquillo."

"But you appear out of nowhere," said Bruno. "What else are we to think?"

"Oh…" said Enriquillo. "Now I understand what Agueybana was saying."

"Who?" asked Juliette.

"He is my… nevermind. But I wanted you to know that I was a friend of Abiodun."

"I don't know who that is, either," said Bruno, a bit frustrated. "What do you want from us?"

"He was named Pierre, by the slavers."

"Oh, yes! Pierre," replied Bruno. "Arnaud and I knew him. But he escaped almost a year ago."

"Yes. I helped him. He was hiding in the mountains."

"So he did get away," replied Bruno. "There were rumors he'd been captured and killed. But we knew something wasn't right because Etienne never returned."

"He wasn't captured, and he never gave up, either."

Bruno and Juliette sat silent, as they pondered a slave's successful escape.

"Did you help hide him, too?" asked Juliette.

"I did," said Enriquillo.

"What happened to him?" asked Bruno. "Is he still hiding in the mountains?"

"No…" replied Enriquillo, and paused before he spoke. "When they tried to recapture him, he chose freedom over life as a slave."

"What?" replied Bruno. "What does that mean?"

"I've heard the story," replied Juliette. "I wasn't sure if it was true: Pierre jumped off the mountain, rather than be captured."

"That's true," said Enriquillo. "He refused to be enslaved again."

"… at least he had the choice," said Bruno. "There are those who would welcome that."

"Well, maybe not to die," replied Juliette. "But the freedom to choose."

"Would you be willing to help others," asked Bruno. "Who choose… to be free?"

"It's why I'm here," said Enriquillo. "My people have hidden in the mountains for hundreds of years. I had hoped to help others. Like your friend Pierre."

Juliette looked at Bruno after he asked his question.

"How would we reach you, to let you know?" asked Bruno.

"Just hide a potato in the jungle beside the tree where you first saw me. I'll find you." Enriquillo disappeared then.

Chapter 15

Rubin

It was Cliegman that Rubin knew was going to be the most brutal. While he took the reins off the rest of the overseers, he decided to have a word with the Belgian.

"You must go easy with the old woman. She is to help the tribe healer," he told him.

"You don't tell me how to manage them!" screamed the Belgian. "They are animals, and I'm paid to prepare them for their masters. I will do it in any way I see fit!"

Rubin thought it ironic that the man could label anyone as "animals." He was little more than a giant ball of matted hair. Dirty blond locks hung down his back, thick hair grew on his arms and protruded from any opening in his clothing. He was notorious for not having bathed more than twice since his first expedition into the Congo, more than five years ago. His stink was so overpowering, it became his personality which, Rubin concluded, was why he worked on the slave deck almost exclusively. It was the only area of the ship where those around him didn't complain of his smell.

He was also a terrible drunk. His second favorite hobby was maintaining a consistent inebriation during a crossing.

Rubin supposed that if he was being practical, the old woman was expendable. He had only accepted her because the Mikoni threw her in for free.

The Belgian's usual routine was to get drunk and start berating the slave. It was obviously confusing for them since they clearly didn't speak his language—and more brutal because Cliegman could speak theirs. He was fluent in a number of African dialects. But that wasn't the point—he needed a victim.

When the old woman came onto the deck that morning, to begin the tasks she was capable of, Cliegman started at her right away.

He had stood behind her as she kneeled, scrubbing the deck and emptying chamber pots for the cabin boy.

"You need to move quicker, old mom," Cliegman said. "Or none of the French buyers will be interested in you." The old woman stopped her trek toward the rail for a moment and looked at the Belgian, shook her head as if to convey that she didn't understand what he was saying and then continued on her path. That was more than enough provocation for Cliegman.

"Don't you give me that arrogant look, you old witch!" he yelled.

He snatched the tails from the loop at his waist. His first crack of the thing caught the old woman around the neck. She was spun around, and the chamber pots went flying and spilled on the deck. Cliegman—even in his drunken state—was a master with the tails. He could pluck a grape from the cabin boy's head without a single nick to his face.

Should one of the other slaves try to come to the victim's aid, the Belgian would turn the whip in his direction. That was how it usually went.

Rubin actually saw what happened this time.

This time the child rushed up the ladder from below. When she saw the old woman sprawled on her side, she ran to her aid. Cliegman regarded the girl. He was initially hesitant to use the whip on her. Every member of the crew knew the girl's value, but something about the way the child looked at him, when she realized it was he who'd attacked her friend, set the big man off. When he raised the tails to strike, the girl rose up and made eye contact while pointing at him. The huge man staggered and looked like he would topple over. Instead, he righted himself as if given assistance from an outside force. Cliegman kept his hand up like it couldn't come down on its own. He also had a perplexed look, as if something had struck him on the head. He lumbered and weaved toward the rail. He was halfway there before Rubin realized what he intended to do. He got a handhold onto the starboard shrouds and lifted his right leg.

No one was really watching the man. Seeing the Belgian use the tails on some innocent victim was nothing new for the crew. Rubin cried out, "Lars! Put hands on Cliegman!"

Lars was closest to him as he was doing some repairs on the quarter-deck behind the helmsman. But the Swede didn't really understand the urgency of Rubin's order. Lars just looked at him.

"What…?" He was holding a paintbrush and bucket of paint. Cliegman had already pulled himself up onto the starboard shroud and was climbing it. So it was up to Rubin. He ran to the girl.

"Stop it," Rubin said. He didn't yell. But his voice was forceful. The child still focused on Cliegman. "Let him go!" He took a step toward her and took out his pistol. "Let him go, I said!" He fired into the air. Nyira took her focus off the Belgian and glared at him.

"It won't change anything," said Rubin.

"Yes it will," replied the child. "He won't hurt anyone anymore. He wants to jump, anyway. Look at him."

She was standing over the old woman, who moaned and writhed in agony at her feet.

"No, it won't. I will simply hire someone else, who will be just as cruel or worse." Rubin heard Cliegman cry out then.

"What the blazes! How did I get up here?"

Lars had made it to him by that time and had climbed up to retrieve the confused overseer.

"Oh quit your complainin', ya' stinkin' lump. You must've had too much to drink again, and thought ya' could fly."

Rubin noticed the morning breeze then. It was hot coming in off the coast of Saint Domingue. He remembered there was a French woman there that he had walked along the beach with on his last visit. And if this girl didn't make him jump off this ship, and be food for the sharks, he would get to spend more time with her. But he couldn't focus on that now.

The child turned her head to the side as if to ask him a question—and then she did ask it. Inside his head.

Will you use the fire thing on me?

Rubin stepped back and shook his head.

"What? What—don't you do that to me! Speak to me with your mouth. I don't want your... sorcery in my head!"

Nyira kneeled down to continue giving aid to Benzia.

Rubin was suddenly very frightened and knew he had to get this creature off his ship.

"Peter!" he bellowed to a crewman who had just come up the ladder. "Take the old woman to the ship's doctor. And have some of the slaves clean... No, have some of the crew clean up this mess!" He rushed to the ladder himself but took a last look at the girl before he went below. She seemed to have already lost interest in him and was intensely focused on the old woman.

Nyira went below when they took Benzia to the white doctor. They laid the old woman on a cot, and then just left her there.

"I can't do anything for her," said the white medical officer. "She isn't worth anything anyway."

Nyira went to Benzia's side. The tails were a vicious weapon, and apparently, the evil Cliegman had added some type of metal to the tips of the thing. Benzia's throat had been cut. The old woman could look at her, but she couldn't speak.

"Benzia, I am sorry," said Nyira. She had to listen to the old woman's mind.

What are you sorry about? You didn't do anything.

"I should have been watching. I could've stopped him."

And were you going to be on the plantation, when someone whipped me there for being too slow? I wasn't even supposed to make it this far. My life was fine. I have lived long enough.

"No you haven't," said Nyira. "I will make—"

Stop child. Please just stop. You are very special. And you need to concentrate on the ones you can save, and on yourself. I have enjoyed knowing you, but my friend is here now.

"Who…?" She looked up and saw Lumumba standing in the doorway.

"I didn't come to fight with you," said the spirit. "So if you want a little more time with her, I'll step outside."

No. Don't go, said Benzia. *It's time. I am tired.*

Nyira just stood back and cried, as Lumumba stepped up and took hold of the old woman's hand. It was over very quickly, and Benzia was gone.

Nyira spent the night next to the body, and insisted on washing and dressing her friend's wounds.

"It won't matter," said Piggy, when they came to get Benzia's body. "She is going into the wa—"

"Shut up!" said Rubin to the stupid youth. "Or you may be going in as well."

When Nyira was finished, she wrapped the old woman in some clean sailcloth. She was dressed neater in death than she ever was in life. The seamen came in and handled the body with reverence, as Rubin had directed. They then slung Benzia out into the sea.

CHAPTER 16

THERE WAS NO way for them to choose how it happened: André, a moody, angry field hand bashed in the head of Henri Bissett. Henri was Alphonse's younger brother. The slaves knew about it right away, because Henri had been trying to whip André, and had taken him into the stable to tie him to the center beam. André had simply not been inclined to be punished that day and had gotten hold of a blacksmith's hammer left out by Big Giles. André didn't often think when he did something, especially when he was angry—he'd been furious at something his wife Clarissa had done that morning and had attacked her in the fields. When André ran out of the stable and Henri did not, all the slaves knew. They also knew that Alphonse would want blood for the death of his kin, and not just André's blood either. By the time the rest of the overseers discovered Henri's body, André had disappeared.

Bruno was yet on edge over Christian's intentions toward Juliette and was a little frustrated with her. She refused to take the threat seriously and insisted on coming to his shack every single night after she left the western fields.

"I am being reasonable," she told him. He was trying to make her understand that Christian cared nothing for love. "But I do," she replied, as she spooned more of the stew she had made him onto his plate. She wanted him to take better care of himself. So she had cooked for him and also washed his clothes in the little creek out behind the slave quarters. He only had two shirts and one pair of britches, so she made some for him. Although he preferred items that were plain, so he could wear them in the field, she forced a bit of color on him.

"You can wear them when we attend the next *calenda*," she told him.

"Juliette, please," Bruno implored her. "We are in danger! At any moment, Christian could kick down my door and hack off my head."

"You are worrying too much," replied Juliette. "Christian knows I don't love him. Here, have some more stew. I think I've made too much."

Bruno didn't want to sound like he was afraid, but the danger was very real. It didn't matter anymore what happened to him. That's when he knew he was in love. He wasn't afraid for himself. He was afraid that after Christian killed him, he might do the same to Juliette. It was obvious that he didn't really want her, but was exacting retribution upon the person who had been closest to Arnaud. He wanted to relax and accept Juliette's argument: that Christian was only mourning the loss of Madeline, and it was just an idle threat. Bruno wished it were true. Juliette had brought so much to his life, such as color and warmth to his home. There were fresh wildflowers on his table and pretty accents all over the room. It brought back memories of how his mother had been such a vibrant and loving presence in his family's hut. There were spices sprinkled all over the beds and on the floor. He tried to tell her that it was too much, that he must not allow himself this and have it taken away. He picked up the bundle of fragrant flowers tied in a bunch at the center of the cedar table.

"These are not mine!" he cried, and sat down in the chair at the table, placed his head on it and groaned. "How can you not hear me?"

Juliette stopped sweeping the floor for a moment and looked at the man she loved.

How can I love someone who is in such pain? she asked herself. But she knew the answer.

"I don't care, Bruno," she replied. Bruno raised his head and looked at her. "You seem to think you're the only one who's in pain. I came here just like you, in the same ship. And yes, my sister is with me. But we both saw the slavers kill our mother and father, then take us away. And we're stuck here. But I…" She dropped her broom and sat on one of the beds, and then broke down. Bruno wasn't used to seeing her cry, or sad at all. He went and sat beside her and held her. This was oh so dangerous. At least he had someone to… die for.

"I understand that you are worried," said Juliette, with her head on his shoulder. "Christian may well come and try to take me. I just choose to focus on what I can do. I can be here with you. I can cook for you. I can give my heart to you." They were still holding each other when someone kicked Bruno's door in.

"I didn't have anywhere else to go," said André. Bruno had insisted he hide beneath one of the beds. In case someone happened by and saw him through the window.

"So you decided to put my life in jeopardy, too?" asked Bruno. He had started to reconstruct the flimsy framework of his shattered door.

"That wasn't…" André paused to finish off the plate of stew Juliette had provided. She seemed pleased that it wouldn't go to waste. "I never intended that. I just heard a rumor that—"

"What rumor?" demanded Bruno.

"That you know a means of escape," replied André.

"What! That is… How could such a rumor have started? No one could know such a thing!"

Juliette suddenly looked guilty.

"I am sorry, my love," she said, as she handed him another piece of board to hammer in place. "I told Babette—"

"Ow!" cried Bruno. He had missed the nail he was aiming for. He quickly felt much better when Juliette took his hand and began to massage it. "And why did you kick down my door?" he snapped at André.

"I… I don't know. I guess I was afraid you wouldn't be home. I also needed someplace to hide. I couldn't trust anyone else."

"You didn't think, André! You never…" Bruno seemed to get more furious as he thought about it.

"I had no other choice, Bruno. They're going to kill me if they find me."

"You killed the master's brother. And now you've killed us!" Bruno moved toward him with the hammer in his hand.

"Bruno, please," said Juliette, wrapping her arms around him. "We have to help him."

"Who's going to help us? You think no one saw him kick down my door?"

"I'm sorry. I didn't know what else to do," replied André.

"I'll take the potato to the tree," said Juliette. "It's dark now. You finish the door." She headed outside.

"There's one more thing," said André. "My family will have to come, too."

Bruno leaned his head against the remains of his shaky door. Juliette put her hand on his shoulder.

"That's right," she said. "If he escapes and leaves them, the master will take his revenge on them."

Bruno walked over to André and shoved the hammer toward him.

"Why don't you take this and bash me over the head, André," said Bruno. "It will be a lot quicker and less painful than what the master will do to me for hiding you."

"I'd best get to that tree," said Juliette. "Hopefully he gets the message tonight."

"Yes," said André. "We won't have a chance once the sun comes up."

Juliette took off at a quick trot toward the eastern fields. Bruno was sorry he ever broached the escape question with the Indian boy.

Juliette returned an hour and a half later. Bruno had begun to worry when he heard a light knock on the repaired door. When he opened it, Juliette looked very excited.

"Bruno, I brought…" There was no one beside her. "Where did he go? He was just right—"

"I'm over here," said Enriquillo, as he appeared on the bed above André.

André was in shock.

"You are the divine one!" He scrambled to his knees and bowed before the boy. "Oh, great and powerful one—"

"Tell him to stop that!" said Enriquillo, scrambling away as if he'd been stung by a bee. "Why is he doing that?"

"That's what happens when you appear out of nowhere," said Bruno.

"Then I will stop it! Tell him to get up!"

"I'm sorry," said André. "Have I offended him?"

"Yes. Get up," said Bruno, exasperated. "He doesn't wish to be worshipped."

André looked confused. "But he—"

"He's just a boy. So get up. We don't have much time."

Bruno wasn't happy with the idea, but Juliette had to go across the property alone again.

"And something else, Bruno," she said.

"What?"

"You are not going to like it."

"Then I'm sure I won't. What is it, Juliette?"

"You and André must hide in the jungle, right now!"

"Oh, yes. I know what she means," said André. "I'm sorry, Bruno."

"I'll tell you when we're hidden," replied Juliette. "We must go now, Bruno!"

"Okay! Okay! Let's go!"

"Don't worry," said Enriquillo. "I know the best hiding place."

The boy led them along a barely visible trail through the bush. The foliage was dense and vines growing along the ground were thick as ropes. Enriquillo picked up one of them and started pulling it; the vine ran all the way into the upper branches of a giant elm tree. "We will have to climb," he said.

"But before we do," said Bruno. "Now, Juliette. Why did I have to leave my home?"

"Because I realized that if André came to you seeking escape—"

"Others will too," continued Bruno. "...and they will bring the overseers."

"Looking for me," said André.

"All because of me," replied Juliette.

"But if we climb," said Enriquillo. "We can see if someone comes."

The boy was right. Once they reached the upper branches, they had a view of the property along the eastern fields. They also saw torches hovering in the area near Bruno's cabin. There was no way to tell if they were slaves or overseers.

"Well that settles it," said Bruno. "You can't go now, Juliette. It's too dangerous."

"I have to go, Bruno. If they find her, the master will kill her and the children."

"I'll go with her," said Enriquillo.

"And what can you do if someone attacks her?" asked Bruno.

"I will make sure they don't."

"Let's go while it's still dark," said Juliette.

"Yes. I can protect you better in the dark," said Enriquillo.

"With what weapon?" asked Bruno.

"A vine is all I'll need."

"That is foolish, boy! What can—"

"We must go, Bruno. Or the daylight will catch us," said Juliette.

Bruno felt like a coward watching his woman climb down the tree to embark on a journey she might not return from, accompanied by a boy armed with nothing but a vine.

They made better time along the edge of fields and staying near the jungle.

"We need to stop for a moment," said Juliette.

"Why?" said Enriquillo.

"We must decide what we can do to protect ourselves."

"Well, no one will see me. So I don't—"

"How will that help me, Enriquillo? I am the one who is in danger. What can you do with a vine? I must know if we are to have a chance."

"I can also make sounds that will frighten them?"

"What kind of sounds? Can you make the sounds of a lion?"

"What is a lion?"

"It's a fierce beast in the land I come from."

Enriquillo thought for a moment.

"I think I know a way you can show me."

"What? I can't show you a lion. Not unless we can go back to my home."

"No. There is another way. It is something only our medicine man has done. I will make an attempt at it. You must sleep for a moment and think of this lion, and I will peek into your dream."

"I don't know if I can sleep now," said Juliette. "I'm too worried to be tired."

"Don't worry. I can help you," said Enriquillo. "It will only take a few moments, and when I see this lion, I can make it be seen by others."

"That is… magic," said Juliette.

"No. It's something our *behike* does to take evil from our dreams."

"Where does he put it when he takes it away?"

"I don't know. I've never asked him. But sit here beside this tree, and I will try and see this lion that will protect you."

Juliette sat, but could not relax.

"I won't be able to sleep like this."

"Yes you will," said Enriquillo. He placed his hand at the base of her skull, and she dozed off. He couldn't venture very far into her dream but was amazed at the incredible things he saw in that brief glimpse. He awakened her after a few moments.

"Did you see it?" asked Juliette.

"I think so," replied Enriquillo. "You have incredible creatures in your homeland."

"Yes. I hope they can keep us alive tonight."

They picked up their pace, but only got so far before they had to use the road into the slave quarters. Just as Juliette feared, a couple of men stopped her.

"Where are you going on this night, woman?" This was a slim, wiry slave named Anthony. He was a known informer for the overseers. There was also a second younger male with him. A boy of sixteen, named Octavius. He was Anthony's son.

"Good evening, miss Juliette," said Octavius. He smiled

at her in a way that his father could see he had eyes for the woman. Anthony backhanded him.

"Keep your grinning to yourself, boy."

"Let me pass, sir," said Juliette, trying to go past him.

"You're Bruno's Juliette? That picks and keeps house with him?"

"What about it? I need to be getting home."

"No, not yet. I hear your Bruno knows of an escape route."

"Well, that doesn't make any sense," replied Juliette. "We would escape ourselves."

"That might be true. Or you could be helping others. Maybe you know where that murderer, André, is hiding. The master is offering five livre and a job in the house for the one that finds him."

"I don't know anything about a murderer," said Juliette. She tried to push her way by him. He backhanded her this time.

"You will be sorry for that," said Juliette. She didn't look as afraid as Anthony expected.

"I don't think your Bruno is much to be feared."

"It's not Bruno. I have a spirit guarding me. And if you don't let me pass, I will call it upon you." She reached down and picked up a hand full of dust from the road. Anthony was curious, but Octavius looked worried.

"Papa, maybe we should let her—"

"Shut up, boy! If you want your teeth!" He looked at Juliette and smiled. "I want to see this magic you have, woman. Then I'm going to show you what happens to witches in my village!" Juliette tossed the dust in the air.

"I call the divine one!" Before the dust cleared, a deformed creature stood in the shadow cast by Anthony's torch. Octavius screamed and ran. The thing stood regarding Anthony, who froze in shock. Juliette was confused and afraid herself. This was not what she'd called. It wasn't a lion. It stood upright like a man, with a leopard's head but the body was some type of ape and one leg like a hyena. The thing let out a scream and charged Anthony. Juliette screamed too, and ran in the same direction as Octavius, while Anthony just collapsed.

When Juliette looked back, the thing was still chasing her, so she kept running.

"Why are you running," called Enriquillo. He had become himself again. Juliette stopped and looked at him.

"That thing was chasing me. It was horrible."

Enriquillo looked confused. "It was your lion thing. I did the best I could. It scared the men away."

"That was not something you saw in my dreams!"

"I saw lots of things in your dreams. Was it not the lion you wanted?"

Juliette laughed. "How foolish of me. I should have described what a lion looked like."

"But it did protect you," said Enriquillo.

"Yes. Thank, you. It did protect me. Now let's go find my sister."

Enriquillo remained invisible while Juliette talked with Babette. Unfortunately, Babette did not know where Clarissa was hiding. However, she knew that Ona Ma would know. Ona Ma was soot-colored and a cook in the Bissett household. She also acted as grandmother to all the female slaves with children. Her shack was a shrine to her home in

Africa. She had hand-carved masks and various deities situated around the one room. Even the chairs she sat on were ceremonial. There were altars too, laden with discarded food items and dried fruit from the masters table. Ona Ma was also a thin woman, and so was not the commonly wide, respected old woman of Babette and Juliette's village. But Ona Ma would not tell where Clarissa was hiding.

"And I will deny it if you tell someone that I know."

"But if we don't find her before sunup," said Juliette. "It will be too late to get them away." The old woman was still suspicious.

"I would die if something happened to poor Clarissa and her children. For all I know, you someone trying to get the livre the master offering."

Juliette thought for a moment. "All right, Ona Ma. What if I told you the divine one himself will help them escape?" The old woman just stared at Juliette.

"That means nothing. Anyone coul—" A mango appeared on the floor beside Ona Ma's left foot. The old woman fainted. Juliette caught her before her head hit the floor. It took her and Babette five minutes to revive Ona Ma. All during this time, Babette looked hard at her younger sister.

"I never thought you'd keep anything from me," Babette said.

"I didn't," said Juliette, as they carried Ona Ma to her bed. "There was no time to tell you. We have to find Clarissa and her children. So we can get them to safety."

"Will I get to meet him?"

Ona Ma opened her eyes once they laid her down. The old woman began to sing an old tribal song that Juliette recognized, for praising the gods.

"I don't think now is the best time, Babette. If she faints again, we may not be able to revive her."

Once they got Ona Ma calmed down, she told Juliette that Clarissa and the children were hiding in the jungle behind the *calenda* grounds. And if someone she knew called to her, she would light a torch and come out.

When they got to the halfway point, between the *calenda* grounds and the Elm tree where Bruno and André waited, Juliette made a choice.

"I must go to the *calenda* grounds, Enriquillo. Go and tell Bruno and André I will meet them there."

"Your Bruno will be angry if I come back without you."

"Yes. I know. But tell him I will be waiting for him to come and dance."

When Bruno caught sight of Enriquillo without Juliette, he jumped from the tree—he grabbed the vine only as an afterthought. He was at a full run when he hit the ground.

"What happened? Where's Juliette? Did they capture her?" He was breathless.

"She—"

"Is she hurt! Oh god! I should never have let her—"

"She's at the *calenda* field."

André slid from the tree a lot slower, using the vine.

"What? Why aren't you with her? What—" Bruno took off without an answer.

"Bruno, wait!" hollered André. "Where is he going?"

"Juliette said for him to meet her at the *calenda* field."

"Why?"

"Because that's where the old woman said your wife was hiding with your children." André set off after Bruno. Without a torch, he quickly lost track of him in the tall ferns, thick brambles, and high grasses. Bruno was running like a man going to put out a fire. If André hadn't known where he was going, he never would have found him. Enriquillo brought up the rear. He arrived at the field just after André.

"Juliette!" screamed Bruno. "I'm here! You can come out now!" No answer. When Enriquillo arrived, he told them what the old woman said would bring André's wife out. Bruno tried that, too—and still got no answer. He was pacing so fast he was raising dust in the dry, hard dirt. The quarter moon highlighted the sweat on his brow and the whites of his eyes as he continued to howl Juliette's name. He finally wheeled around and charged at Enriquillo.

"Did she say anything else, Enriquillo? Maybe she's hiding somewhere. Did she possibly say something else?"

"Yes, she did," replied the boy.

"What? Tell me!"

"She said for you to come and dance."

"What!" Bruno looked like he could kill the boy, so André stepped in.

"Why don't you let me try, Bruno."

André was right; once he gave a call they saw a torch, and it was coming toward them. When the persons emerged from the bush, it wasn't Clarissa. It was two men and a woman. One of the men was Christian, and the woman was Juliette.

"Your wife is safe, André," came Christian's deep voice. "I have been protecting her. And I thank you for sending me mine." He raised his and Juliette's hand together.

"Bruno, stay back! I'll be fine," said Juliette. Her tone made it sound like this was nothing, as if she'd just sprained her ankle out in the fields. Bruno knew she thought he would be afraid. That wasn't true anymore. He had already decided that he would never concede anything again, especially what he felt for her.

"You will not take her, Christian," said Bruno, stepping up to face the larger man. "You don't really want her. You just want a reason to kill me, isn't that right?"

Christian's torchlit silhouette cast a massive shadow over the *calenda* field. He let go of Juliette, gave his torch to the other man, and stepped up to face Bruno.

"You're a fool," replied Christian. "But it won't matter when you're dead."

"Why?" asked Bruno. "My death won't bring back Madeline's love."

André came up and touched Bruno on the shoulder. "Here, my friend," he said. "You might need this." He placed a machete in Bruno's hands. He saw Christian's eyes light up at the sight of the blade. That's when Bruno knew he would die.

"I guess it's a good thing I brought my own," said the big man, unstrapping the weapon from his belt. Bruno had a notion to go and hack André's hands off. He always thought of the worst thing to do in any situation. He was not unfamiliar with the blade—he'd worked the cane field for a long time, too. The handle was hot from where André held it, but it still felt light and sure. That was important because he had to bring it up quickly to block Christian's sudden attack with a downward slice. Bruno had the strangest thought. He was thankful that Christian wasn't as strong as Arnaud, because that blow would have shattered his blade and split him in two. He was quick enough to keep his feet moving and fend off Christian's wild lunges and swipes. While this battle was taking place, Enriquillo and André snuck into the bush and found Clarissa and the children.

At first, she was afraid of her husband.

"No. Clarissa. I'm no longer angry. We must escape. The divine one will help us." Enriquillo appeared then, and if it wasn't for the way the woman cried out and fell to her knees before him, he would have admonished André.

"Yes. We must go," said Enriquillo, trying to sound wise, like Agueybana—even if it felt silly. When they came into the field again, Christian was still slashing at Bruno in earnest, frustrated he hadn't been able to kill him already. Once again, André caused a mishap. When they came out into the open, and he saw that Bruno was holding his own.

"Ah hee! Kill him, Bruno!" André hollered. Bruno, distracted just enough, tripped over an obscured root and fell. Christian quickly took advantage. As Bruno scrambled to his feet, Christian's blade came down and hacked off the first two fingers from his left hand.

"Oh Bruno!" cried Juliette, as if it was she who had been cut.

"I'm fine," said Bruno, to reassure her.

The wound still weakened him, and even though he showed no sign of surrender, Christian was emboldened by the blood. He soon caught Bruno across the shoulder, and again in the thigh. Suddenly he was on the ground. That was the last thing he remembered.

André told Bruno that Juliette had saved his life. She'd agreed to stay with Christian if he let Bruno live. Christian, apparently satisfied with the victory and her offer, let them take Bruno away.

CHAPTER 17

NYIRA DIDN'T SPEAK as she sat in the wagon. She was waiting for the black woman with the basket to return. The white man who'd purchased her kept looking back at her in the bed of the wagon as if he wasn't sure how she'd gotten there.

"What was I thinking," he said. Nyira gave him a little smile and sat very still. She would've hidden behind one of the male slaves if she thought it would help. She knew the man was considering taking her back and wasn't sure what she could do. She had a feeling that if she could hold on until the woman came back, she would be safe. Once she laid eyes on her, she would not let her go—or so she hoped. Nyira could tell by the way she moved that she had not had any children of her own, and by the thoughts in her mind that she was only thinking of the list of items she was to purchase that day. Not having her own mother, she had observed this from the women of her village. A mother's thoughts never strayed far from the welfare of her children. Gnangi had had ten children and knew where each of them was and what they were doing at any time of the day. None of them lived in Mael, so this was quite a feat. When the auctioneer stepped out of his building and was locking the door, the overseer stepped off the wagon and approached him. Nyira was suddenly distraught. She had to stop herself from running between the two men and saying: No! Don't do this! I'm staying! She considered running away, rather than being given back and sold again. Even though she had no idea where she would go, but she could see the jungle and wasn't shackled. She got down from the wagon and began to survey the area.

"But I don't know why I bought her," she heard the white man say. Nyira's heart was in her throat. There was a crowd at what looked like a market not fifty yards away. Maybe she could hide in the—

"Hi," said the woman from the other side of the wagon. Nyira liked the look in her eyes, and she had a pretty smile. "Do you belong to us now?" Nyira ran to the woman and grabbed her by the hand.

"Hurry," she said, as she pulled the woman around the wagon toward the two white men. "I think he means to give me back."

"What? Why?" asked the woman, looking at her strangely. "And how do you know that?"

"Well… I… I heard them talking."

"But why did he buy you? He came here to get field hands."

"I—I don't know. He just… he just did, and I… I would so much like to stay with you."

"Oh really," she smiled at Nyira. "That is very sweet. I suppose I could use some help with the sho—"

"Yes! Please go and tell him!" The two men walked toward the wagon.

"You're not thinking of taking her back?" asked the woman.

"It appears Mr. Franscescu has—"

"I will be keeping her!" the overseer suddenly said, and went and sat behind the reins of the wagon. "Let's go, Esmerelda." Esmerelda smiled at the auctioneer and climbed up next to the overseer.

"I guess he has changed his mind again," replied the auctioneer. Nyira jumped on the back as the wagon pulled away. She smiled and waved at the auctioneer. He waved back, even though he looked completely befuddled.

Nyira had never seen lodges like those in this village. All of them were enormous and appeared made of a strange kind of hard clay. One structure was composed of steps that went all the way into the sky and was the color of elephant's tusk. Another was big and tall and light grey, with colorful windows all around it. It displayed pictures of white people with wings. The village itself was a hundred times larger than the Mikoni, and there were white people everywhere. She never imagined there were this many in the whole world. But when the black woman, who was named Esmerelda, looked in the back of the wagon at her and smiled, she felt safe.

They rode for what seemed like hours (only because Nyira was anxious to get wherever they were going). They finally pulled up to a large lodge that wasn't as tall as the Mikoni, but still enormous, with a lot of steps leading up to the porch. On that porch were white woman and black women. All of them seemed to be waiting for them to arrive. Nyira noticed all the fields around this lodge were green and stretched far out into the distance. She wondered who the chief was here.

The overseer took the male slaves from the wagon, but before he left, he looked at Nyira again.

"I guess you'll know what to do with this one?" he said to Esmerelda.

"Yes, master Luigi, I know exactly what to do with her." She bent down and looked at Nyira. "I know you can speak my language because you came from where I'm from. What is your name, child?"

"I am Nyira," Nyira said, smiling.

"Well, I am sorry to tell you Nyira, that you will be getting a new name from these white people."

"Why? What is wrong with my own name?"

"They own you now, and they like to name everything that they own."

"Did they give you a new name, too?" asked Nyira. Esmerelda was taken aback by the child's directness.

"I am not used to children. I forgot how straight to the point they can be." A white woman came down the steps toward Nyira and Esmerelda. She looked directly at Nyira.

"Oh, she is beautiful, Relda. And her eyes are amazing."

Esmerelda spoke in Nyira's language, telling her that this was Constance, the major's daughter. Nyira already knew this, of course. She looked at Constance and smiled. "So you speak her language, too, Relda. That is wonderful. Father told me I would get to name the next female slave we bought. So let's see... I think... Camille is a nice name. What do you think, Relda?"

"I think it's a fine name, Miss Constance." Nyira wasn't so sure, but she smiled anyway.

"I think you'd better—"

"Just a moment!" said another short older woman who

was coming down the steps. Esmerelda told Nyira that this was Josephine Mallet, the household manager. Miss Mallet stood looking at Nyira for a moment. "I wasn't aware we needed house slaves. Are you responsible for this, Esmerelda?"

"No, Miss Josephine. She was in the wagon when I returned from the market." Nyira was starting to get nervous again. She gave the uncomfortable woman a smile, and she looked shocked. "What is she smiling at? Can she understand me?"

"She understands a few words, from the ship, ma'am. But mostly no. Maybe she just likes the sound of your voice." Josephine snorted and turned up her nose at this idea.

"I doubt it," she said and marched back up the stairs to the house. "Get her cleaned up and in a clean uniform, Esmerelda!" she said as she went through the front door.

"I know you are used to *pagne* where we come from," said Esmerelda, as she laid out a small dress and pair of shoes on the chair next to the tub. "Here they are called dresses."

"Is it not permitted to bathe in the river?" asked Nyira.

"No. The rivers are not as nice here as in the Congo."

"The Congo River was not nice either. There were snakes, but it was closer." Nyira kept looking at herself in the full-length mirror next to the tub. "So you say that image is me? I have seen my face in the river, but never all of me like this." She walked over and touched her face. "I think I like my face," she smiled at herself.

"All right. You can look at yourself later. Into the tub and wash up. We have some chores for you to start on."

Nyira played in the water and splashed so much that

Esmerelda had to get her started with using soap and scrubbing her face and behind her ears. She also gave her an oil that smelled familiar.

"It's made from coconuts. We have them here. We don't have leopards or hippos or elephants, but we do have a few other things, like the jungle."

"Do they have gorillas? I like gorillas."

"No. No gorillas here. I doubt any of these people have ever seen one." Nyira looked disappointed. "But there are other things here that will keep you busy."

"Like what?"

"You can help me with the cooking."

"I would rather go into the jungle."

"I'm afraid those days are over. No more jungle for you."

Once Nyira finished bathing, she regarded the dark blue dress with a white collar.

"Is there nothing with more color?"

"These are what those who work within the house wear."

"And the black things are for my feet? Why do they cover themselves so? It's hot here, too."

"I really don't know. It's just their way."

Nyira's first chore was to gather eggs from the large chicken coop in the yard behind the kitchen. She was handed a big basket by Daphne, the assistant kitchen maid.

"Does she understand French yet?" Daphne asked Esmerelda.

"She understands some. I think the Dutch spoke it to them on the ship."

"YOU MUST TAKE THIS OUT TO THE COOP IN THE YARD AND BRING BACK SOME EGGS!"

"Why is she so loud?" asked Nyira.

"She thinks you don't understand her." Nyira laughed as she went out the door with the basket.

"Why is she so happy?" asked Daphne.

"I think she's just happy to be off that ship."

Nyira liked the idea of one place where all the chickens could lay eggs. Normally she had to search the fields and bush around the village to discover where the hens had hidden them. The yard was large, consisting of a number of fruit trees, and a giant palm tree situated behind the back veranda and leaning a bit over the manor's rear roof. There was also a duck pond at the far eastern edge of the yard. Nyira picked a pear as she went through the makeshift orchard. She could hear the chickens clucking as she approached the large coop. She hoped they wouldn't mind her disturbing them as they sat on their nests and—something flew at her face. She instinctively threw her arms up. When she brought them down, they were slashed, as if by a small knife, and a black rooster with a large orange cone strutted between her and the coop. There was blood on the white cuffs of her new dress now. Before she could back away, it launched itself at her again, but she was ready this time and fanned her right hand in the air. The bird dropped to the ground—it was now solid stone. Nyira heard a cry from the veranda. When she turned around, Esmerelda was sprinting toward her. She stopped cold when Nyira looked at her.

"Child, look at me. See me. Can you see I mean you no threat?" Nyira's green eyes had a hot glow. When she focused them on Esmerelda, it went away. Then she saw what she did to the chicken.

"Oh! I'm so sorry. It came at me so suddenly. I acted without thinking."

"Put the rooster in the basket," said Esmerelda.

"What? Why? It was an accident, I—"

"Put the rooster in the basket and follow me, child." Esmerelda walked past the chicken coop and took the shovel that was leaning against it and walked into the bush behind the yard. Nyira did as she was told and followed the woman into the jungle. They went about fifty yards into the twisted vines, ferns, palmetto and tall weeds. Once she stopped, Esmerelda began to dig. It took about ten minutes, and when she was done, she took the rooster and dropped it into the hole and covered it again.

"Now I don't know how you did what you did, but you must promise me that you will never do anything like that again."

"I—I promise I will never harm the chickens again." Esmerelda kneeled down and looked into the child's eyes.

"That's not what I mean, Nyira."

"I don't understand."

"All right, I will say it more plain: what you did is a crime in the eyes of the priests and church of these white people."

"What are priest and church?"

"They are part of what rule this land. And if they were to discover what you did, they would burn you to death on a pile of logs."

"Why? I didn't—"

"Not for what you did, but what you are. And since I hid it and informed no one, they would kill me, too." Nyira could think of nothing in reply. When Esmerelda started back toward the yard, she followed her. "And one last thing: You must tell no one about this."

"I—I promise."

"I didn't think it would be that hard," said Daphne when Esmerelda and Nyira entered the kitchen.

"What are you talking about?" asked Esmerelda.

"I didn't think the child would need help gathering a few eggs."

"Oh, no. I was just telling her about the hawk that sometimes comes and snatches a chicken."

Instead of the servant's quarters at the back of the manor house, Esmerelda thought it best to keep the child close.

"My husband Claude and I have a small cottage right before the western cane fields. Would you like to come and stay with us?"

"Will your husband not mind?" asked Nyira

"I don't think so. He is big and silent, but a good man—a good husband."

"Thank you, yes. I would be happy to."

"If you are quiet and cause no trouble, you will get on well with my Claude."

Nyira was sitting on the floor beside the fireplace in the three-room cottage when a shadow covered the front door. Though it wasn't a shadow, it was the massive Claude. He filled the door so that it looked like he might not be able to squeeze through it.

"Say hello to our guest, Claude!" cried Esmerelda, as if she had to speak louder in order to engage her husband's attention. The man grunted once and stumbled over to the chair beside the fireplace. He nearly stepped on Nyira to get there. She scampered quickly out of his path. When he dropped himself into it, it groaned as it took his weight. Nyira was surprised it held. The big man let out a sigh and leaned forward to place his head in his hands. After Claude had sat for about ten minutes, he finally noticed Nyira.

"There is a green-eyed child here," he declared.

"Yes. I introduced her as you came in. Her name is Camille. They bought her this morning." The man frowned as he gazed at Nyira.

"They say that green eyes are an indication of magic, child." He stared at her. Nyira wasn't sure if he was asking a question or making a statement.

"Well, I am—"

"Time for supper! Camille, come and help me!" Esmerelda moved quickly into the kitchen.

"Did I do something wrong?" asked Nyira.

"Shhh," said Esmerelda. She leaned close to the girl's ear. "You are not to do magic, and you are also not allowed to discuss it. Especially with my Claude. Do you understand?"

"I… yes, I suppose."

Nyira worked well the whole week, helping Esmerelda prepare desserts and finding that she very much enjoyed cooking. Because she got to lick the remains of the cake batter or have a piece of fruit while she was cutting it to go into a pie. She had only one slip up when Daphne was trying to reach a jar of preserves in the top of the pantry. She left for a moment to go and get a chair to stand on. When she returned, Nyira handed her the jar. Daphne stared at the small child.

"How did you get this down from there without a chair? Even on one, you would be too short." When Esmerelda looked up from the butter churn, she quickly realized what had happened.

"I—I allowed her to stand on my shoulders," said Esmerelda. "I didn't realize it was for you. Otherwise, I would have waited. I guess she was just trying to be helpful." Daphne took the preserves, but before carrying them into the dining room, gazed suspiciously at Nyira.

"You have got to control yourself, child," said Esmerelda.

"I'm sorry. She just looked like she needed help."

"All right, let's be clear. Don't help anyone anymore. No matter what, Nyira. If you can make it to the end of the week without a mistake, I will take you shopping on Friday."

"I can go to the market with you?"

"If you can control yourself, yes."

"Oh! I will! I promise not to help anyone for the rest of the week!"

"We shall see. For you, that will be easier said than done."

"You will see. I promise."

She made it without a single slip up. When Diego, the groom, brought the carriage up to the house that morning, Constance decided to go as well.

"I have my recital practice with Madame Fournette, this morning. I will ride with you and Camille, Relda." Esmerelda did not like having Constance in the carriage. The girl was so critical that Esmerelda found she couldn't always concentrate when she was so close. And with Nyira only one little slip up away from being reported to the archdeacon, she would have rather she not.

"You must be very quiet while Constance is in the carriage, child. I don't trust her; she's always up to something and is very mean and vindictive. So be careful."

This market, to Nyira's relief, had no shrunken heads or men wanting to be set on fire. There were also no live animals—it appeared to be primarily food. Although there was a juggler and a fortune-teller. The fortune-teller was a shriveled old woman who was caramel-colored and had large dark eyes. She wore a scarf over her grey hair, with a bit of net covering that. Nyira stopped and stood staring into the old crone's ancient yellow eyes.

"Give me your hand, child," said the old woman. "Why do you cry? Are you troubled?"

"What is the matter, Nyira?" asked Esmerelda.

"Nothing," said Nyira. "She can't help me anyway. Can I go and look at the man with the flying balls?"

"Yes. But don't be gone too long. We have a good bit to buy before we leave." Nyira raced over to where a small crowd stood watching the juggler. She soon realized after watching for about five minutes, that this was not a very good juggler. He didn't have anyone to jump over his head or run through his legs, like the last juggler invited to her village market. Nor did the balls burst into flames or change shapes to a hippopotamus or a zebra. This man just had regular balls that he threw in the air. Just another thing about this place that she found disappointing. She finally just strolled through the market, gazing at lots of vegetables and lots of fish, and lots of white people. It was a bigger gathering and more food, but nothing interesting until she saw the half-naked boy.

She followed him with her eyes as he moved through the crowd. He was reaching and picking up items—as if he was trying to make up his mind, and no one took notice of him. When he got closer to where Esmerelda stood, Nyira went toward her. He didn't look like a slave; he wasn't dark. He was red, actually, with a strange flattened forehead, and his clothing—what clothing he was wearing—was similar to what the boys of her village wore: a loincloth, but there was a large gold earring dangling from his left ear. Nyira could tell from the way the boy moved through the crowd, that no one else could see him.

"What are you doing," whispered Esmerelda.

"I'm looking at the boy from the forest," replied Nyira.

"What boy?"

"He's invisible."

"That is very convenient, child. But you're not here to play with invisible boys." Esmerelda placed a basket filled with fish and other seafood into her hands.

"Habari," Nyira said to the boy as he came closer. He stopped then and looked at her. His face lit up with a smile, and he came toward her.

"Tau," he replied.

"I'm Nyira." She pointed to herself.

"Enriquillo, the third," he replied, pointing to himself.

"Where are the two others?" asked Nyira.

"They reside in *Coaybay*. Are you the dark princess?"

"Yes," said Nyira, smiling. "My papa always called me Princess."

"My mother had a dream that I would meet a dark prin-

cess. She said I would marry her and make her my *co-cacique.*
Have you a husband?"

"I am eight."

"Who are you talking to, child?" asked Esmerelda. "People are starting to notice. And what language are you speaking."

"I'm speaking the language of the forest boy. My husband."

"We must get back to the carriage," said the cook, taking her by the arm. "Tell your invisible husband goodbye."

Esmerelda

Esmerelda looked at the girl as if she had lost her mind. Though by what she had already witnessed from the child, she knew for sure she was a sorceress, so she couldn't discount anything she did or said.

"I must go now, Enriquillo," said Nyira. "Ask your mother to let you into her dreams tonight and I will see you again there."

When they got in the carriage, Esmerelda said, "Now, what have we agreed?"

"That I must not turn anyone or anything to stone," replied Nyira.

"And what else, Nyira? This is very important."

"That Claude nor any of the slaves shall witness my powers. I don't understand this. The people of my village all knew what I was."

"Because they won't understand," replied Esmerelda. "And they would be afraid of you."

"Why would they be afraid? I would never harm them."

"People fear anything they don't understand. My

Claude is no different. He spends too much time with the priests to allow a sorceress under his roof. He might even try to harm you."

"But I love Claude—even though he is grumpy sometimes."

"And Claude loves you, too, child. But the priest's teachings make men do very strange and dangerous things on behalf of their god. Just remember: don't talk to invisible boys when Claude is present. Do you understand?"

"Yes, Nolwazie, I understand."

"And my real name will not be spoken aloud. I only told you because I knew your name. It's a secret Claude doesn't even know. He's been a slave in this land for most of his life and chooses to know nothing of his people. The priests would have him believe such knowledge is evil."

As they pulled up near the Cabildo where Constance waited, Nyira became quiet as the girl entered the carriage.

"Might I drive today, Relda?" Constance inquired when she was seated.

"I have been instructed by Miss Josephine that that is not permitted." She didn't look at the girl, knowing she wouldn't be happy with her answer.

"If you do not, I will tell the archdeacon what Camille does to the chickens."

"You can't speak of—" Esmerelda grabbed the girl's arm before she realized what she was doing. Constance began to cry. She was a girl of fifteen and the size of a woman, but she was very delicate and petulant.

"I will also inform Madame that you have been rough with me!" When Constance displayed her arm, her pale skin bore the marks where she'd been handled. Esmerelda realized she was in an untenable position, so she handed the reins over to the girl.

Constance snatched the reins and slapped them forcefully, which caused the carriage to plunge through the middle of Port-à-Piment too quickly. She was barely able to steer the team around a priest, who was just crossing from the chapel toward his quarters on the other side of the square. Esmerelda saw that it was the archdeacon, Phillipe Dominic, and he knew well the markings of Major Dugard's carriages. She would be in for a scolding from Miss Josephine for this. She just hoped Constance didn't kill them before they made it back to the plantation. When Esmerelda looked in the rear of the carriage at Nyira, the child didn't appear frightened. She also did something that Esmerelda still hadn't gotten used to. She spoke to her with her mind.

Would you like me to slow the horses? You look uncomfortable.

Yes. I would also like it if you didn't do… this.

Do what?

This in my head talking.

How else was I going to ask you if you wanted me to slow the horses?

All right. Slow them a bit. But don't make it too obvious.

As you wish.

The horses gradually slowed their pace. Not a lot, but enough that they were more controlled. When they got within half a mile of the plantation, they were only at a brisk trot and stopped smartly once they reached the front yard of the manor house.

"I'm getting better at this," declared Constance. "You worried needlessly, Relda." She hopped out of the vehicle, leaving Esmerelda to the task of getting the horses to the stables. When Esmerelda looked up, Josephine was standing on the veranda, watching.

"I would have a word, Esmerelda," said the household manager. "Once you have returned the horses to the stables." Esmerelda had hoped to delay the berating, because it would be renewed once the archdeacon gave his report.

When they entered the stable grounds, Diego was there. He smiled as he took hold of the team of horses. Diego was a tall skinny boy of about eleven; he had taken an instant liking to the young Nyira.

"Comment allez-vous aujourd'hui, mademoiselle?"

"Je vais bien, mon bon monsieur."

"I'm glad you are improving your French," snapped Esmerelda. "Now let this boy be about his task so that we may get to the house."

"Can I not stay and help Diego with the horses?" asked Nyira.

"No. We have the fish and shellfish to clean. Or do you plan to do that by magic?"

"I would if you allowed it. Shall I?" The little girl waved her left hand as if to cast a spell over the basket she held.

"No child! I didn't mean it! Promise me you'll never do such a thing!"

Nyira laughed. "You are so funny Nol— I mean, Esmerelda."

Diego obviously didn't understand them, but he seemed fascinated by the exchange. He could understand a word here and there. She had taught him a few when he was smaller, and he knew never to repeat them around anyone.

"I'm not funny," replied Esmerelda. "I'm tired already, and we haven't even begun. Get back to work, Diego!"

Esmerelda took Nyira by the arm and pulled her toward the house. They entered the kitchen at the rear of the residence after climbing the wooden steps to the back veranda. Esmerelda hoped Josephine would put off their talk until she was able to at least start the midday meal. But there was no hope of that, as the short, trunk shaped woman was standing near the giant fireplace when they entered the kitchen. The fire was only low burning coals, but before Josephine could move toward Esmerelda, her face furious, the blaze sprang up and caught the tail of her shawl. The little woman quickly found herself occupied with putting out her garment, and Esmerelda rushed to help. Once the fire was out, Ms. Mallet's face was in full blush at her sudden vulnerability.

"Thank you, Esmerelda," she said, barely able to look her in the eyes. She quickly exited the kitchen. Esmerelda turned to look at Nyira, who was still standing in the entryway from the back veranda, smiling.

"Don't be so smug, girl! If she had been harmed…" Nyira's smile vanished. "You never think!"

She left Nyira in the kitchen to consider what she'd done, while she went to the dining room to receive the scolding she was due from Josephine.

Nyira took the basket of fish and seafood and placed it on the block table in the middle of the room. Sometimes she wasn't sure what to make of Nolwazie. Even when she was right, she was wrong. The fire wouldn't have harmed Josephine—she wouldn't have allowed that. Esmerelda should know that. But still, she seemed to resent Nyira's help when she most needed it.

CHAPTER 18

WHEN ENRIQUILLO RETURNED to the village cave, he went to the wall near the entryway to draw the picture of his encounter with the dark princess.

"So you've seen her, my son?" asked Higuamota.

Higuamota was a square-faced woman with long black hair set in two braids off her shoulders. She was beautiful in the way of an older princess. Although not past forty, her full cheeks had taken on the sag of sadness. She also tended to squint a bit, a product of living in the cave and having to adjust her already weak eyesight to less sunlight. Her lips were full, but her chin often trembled when she spoke. She was taller than the average Taíno woman, which also marked her royal bloodline. She rarely stood amongst her people anymore, preferring to recline on the front porch of the *bohio* and talk to Agueybana.

"It was just as you said, Mother," replied Enriquillo. "She was the only one able to see me. She said I should request entry into your dreams tonight. There we shall meet again."

"You are not schooled in the navigations of dreams, Enriquillo. You will need guidance from Agueybana, and he is yet healing the dark one you brought."

"The *behike* doesn't like my dreams."

"Agueybana says your dreams are full of monsters, and that you have no butterflies in your soul, like other children your age."

Enriquillo went to the second chamber out of the central village enclosure. The *behike* often took those who were gravely ill into the dark region. To keep the spirits of death away, one needed to pit them against others spirits. The chamber spirits wouldn't allow anything to interfere with the *behike*'s healing ritual. Enriquillo waited a moment.

"You can come in, Enriquillo," said the *behike*. The boy went cautiously, aware of the sacred nature of the *behike*'s ceremony.

"I have healed his wounds," said Agueybana, "but I can do nothing for his heart. That may kill him." Enriquillo went and sat beside Bruno as he lay on the cotton pallet next to the fire.

"You! Get away from me!" said Bruno, when he saw the boy. "Your fruit and your freedom didn't help Juliette."

After they brought Bruno to the *behike*, Enriquillo led André and his family higher into the mountains.

Enriquillo had no answer for Bruno, and he knew from experience that he would have to find the answer on his own. As he left the chamber, he saw Higuamota lounged near the village fire on a *duho* stool she had placed there. He went and sat beside her, and laid his head in her lap.

"Will you go to the valley and pick yams for meal, my son?" she asked, stroking his head. "I'm not feeling strong for walking tonight."

Enriquillo stepped outside the cave entrance and picked up a bundle of vegetables.

"I found these at the market, mother."

"You didn't steal these, did you?"

"I will replace them with fish. The mounted police have found the hidden valley and destroyed the crops there. Uncle Jaceux is searching for a new plot to replant. He also captured one of their warriors."

Higuamota looked stricken. "They haven't discovered our home, have they?"

"Uncle doesn't believe so. Their *behike* walked the man's dreams and saw nothing about our hiding place. Uncle will release him on the path to the town."

"How is my brother's village?"

"They moved again after the crops were discovered. Once they have re-settled, he will send a warrior to tell us its new location."

"I miss my big-go. I haven't heard him laugh in a long time."

Higuamota then fell silent by the fire.

Enriqillo wouldn't say so aloud, but there were nights when he awoke to his mother's tears. He knew she would give anything to walk along the beach in the sunshine or travel the coastline of her homeland in a canoe.

The cave they resided in was as large as a city. It had had a considerable amount of rock and stalactites removed by Agueybana's magic. The floor of the cave was smooth like the open square of an outside village, with a stone-lined *batey* court constructed at the center. Enriquillo and Higuamota's large dwelling was the focus of the community with each of the respective ni-taíno members of the court arrayed around in successive order of position.

Higuamota was now the sole *cacique* after Enriquillo's

father died when a mounted police unit stormed the cove where the tribe's garden was planted at the time. She was so heartbroken at the loss of her husband that Agueybana had assumed most of the decision-making in the tribe.

As Enriquillo approached, the old man sat still as a stone on the porch of the *cacique's* dwelling, waiting.

Everyone Agueybana knew as a young man was now dead, so there was no discerning his age. He was thin, brown and wrinkled as a dried tobacco leaf. Though he was still strong enough to take the *cohoba* and sit all night spouting his visions, as his pupils oscillated between brown and dark red. His hair was still black, and so were his fingernails, as if they'd been dipped in blood, and dried. Higuamota had sat at his knee as a child and still did so when her melancholy overtook her. Enriquillo just wished the old man wouldn't tell her of his horrible dreams because it didn't help her spirit.

Enriquillo went back and sat by his mother. He wasn't looking forward to approaching the old man. Perhaps there was another path into her dreams.

"You must go now, Enriquillo," said Higuamota. "Soon we sleep, and you can't walk in my dreams without guidance."

The boy got up and trudged over to the old man, who did not look at him for a while.

"Time for more monsters," Agueybana sighed.

CHAPTER 19

ARCHDEACON PHILLIPE DOMINIC had to brush the dust off his cowl as he continued toward the priest's quarters. He was lucky that he still had quick reflexes or they would be taking his carcass to the chapel. He saw the girl Constance was at the reins of the carriage. The slave Esmerelda was sitting beside her. It was obvious from the woman's expression that she'd relinquished the reins against her will. He was not a fan of fast horses or anything of such excess. He would have a word with the major about his child's recklessness, for all the good it would do. He had a notion to let it go, but it was what people expected of him. His back had begun to ache, so he braced himself against the small statue of Saint Fidelis.

"Pardon, my presumption, your grace," he said. He caught his breath at just the right moment.

"Come on, Phillipe." A tall cheerful-faced priest stepped past him and went to open the front door of the Cabildo. The archdeacon had to pick up his pace. Artemus was a quick stepper, with his long legs. He moved to the doorway and grasped it.

"Thank you, Father Reyes. I'm a bit winded. I was almost run over by a child."

"You must remember, Phillipe: children are not the only ones to be careful of in this square. You just need to look before you step out."

The archdeacon had heard this lecture before.

"Yes. As I've told you, Artemus, there are not many carriages in the parish I come from."

"And as I've told you, Phillipe, you are no longer there. So look before you walk."

Father Reyes went ahead of him so he could start getting dressed for morning mass.

As he made his way toward his office, he heard Artemus warn the secretary, Philomena:

"You should probably put that away. Phillipe is coming."

"But I just made a full—"

When the archdeacon entered the room, the secretary hid a cup behind her back.

The archdeacon just stood and looked at the plump middle-aged woman. He was still breathing a little hard, and put his hand on the corner of her desk, to steady him.

"I think I would like a cup of tea, Philomena," said Phillipe.

She was a fair-skinned woman with bright red hair and freckles. Not what he would call attractive, but her smile was a wonder to behold.

"Really, Father?" She pulled the cup from behind her. "I just happen to have some—"

"No, not really," said the priest. "And you shouldn't be having it either. Plain water is better."

Father Reyes shook his head.

"Let's go, Phillipe." He offered his arm to his fellow cleric. "I'm surprised you fell for that ruse, Philomena."

Philomena had turned beet red.

Father Reyes practically dragged the archdeacon behind him as they made their way toward the archdeacon's chambers.

"You should be ashamed of yourself, Phillipe," said Father Reyes. "She hasn't taken our vows."

"Yes. I suppose I should be. I will confess that I can't help it," said the priest, smiling. "She just makes it so easy."

"So am I to take it this is your confession?"

"No," replied the archdeacon. "And I will leave it at that."

The sanctuary was already full by the time the archdeacon had donned his vestments. He made it in time to step behind the altar servers as they entered. The parishioners were singing along with the entrance chant. When he reached his chair, he led them by saying:

"In the name of the Father and the Son and of the Holy Spirit…" He then signified the presence of the Lord to the community. By the time he got to the Penitential Rite, he noticed Major Dugard in one of the middle pews, and he was reminded of a strange incident he'd witnessed in the slave market the previous week.

The archdeacon often went down to the market when the slave ships came in. He wasn't interested in the dynamics involved in bidding on and purchasing of the slaves; he just found beings that'd just arrived from the Dark Continent fascinating. And sometimes the traders would share stories of strange lands they'd visited and the dangerous beasts they'd encountered. Phillipe had even considered a life as a seaman.

His childhood afflictions soon ended that dream. Sailors had to be lithe and strong—or at the very least, able to stand upright for more than a few moments at a time. He imagined life aboard ship would be cruel for one such as him—just as life in the parish school had been. Children were inherently evil. This was not a notion he shared with the parishioners who confessed to sometimes wishing an exasperating child had never been born, but every bit of information he'd been given concerning children had confirmed his belief.

There had been something very peculiar about the girl brought to shore from the Dutch vessel that day. Phillipe found the Dutchmen very unsavory. It wasn't one specific thing, and not just the fact that they trafficked in human beings—though that was part of it. They just seemed a bit too cheerful for men engaged in such a gruesome enterprise. There had been instances, despite their gleeful nature, where their slaves had obviously been mistreated.

He was not a Jesuit, and so not diametrically opposed to the institution of slavery, though the Dugard model proved the merits of humane treatment. The slaves from the ship the child came from were different, though. For one thing, they had sustained no real injuries, and even more amazing, they were not shackled—not one of them. The girl, as she stepped onto the dock, seemed to be leading them. She walked ahead of the slavers, as well. The French auctioneer had not known what to make of this absurd sight. The bondsmen and women looked more like patrons coming to the market, rather than items to be sold within it.

The auctioneer, Gilles Moreau, approached the Dutch first officer when he came into the square.

"Rubin. Has there been some kind of accident? You have a smaller cargo this time."

"No. Not at all, Gilles," replied the Dutchman. "I just thought I'd bring them in in better condition this time."

The archdeacon had seen this man before, and this was the smallest cargo he had ever delivered.

"So you didn't stop on the Ivory Coast this trip?"

"We just went to the Congo. I don't think the buyers will be disappointed. The quality will speak for itself."

Luigi Francescu, the Dugard overseer, had ridden in at the reins of a large wagon. Esmerelda, the Dugard's head cook, had been sitting in the bed behind him. Most of the people and quite a few slaves of Port-a-Piment didn't care for Francescu. He'd used his whip on not a few of them during various encounters, including gambling disputes. Esmerelda was as highly regarded as a house slave could be in the city. Her decision not to sit next to the Corsican would only enhance people's opinion of her.

The wagon traveled through the market. The girl stood near the auctioneer as he sorted and assessed the stock. They were then moved inside the facility, to be bid on by overseers and various other landowners and their representatives. It was only a split second of recognition, but the child saw Esmerelda and smiled when they made eye contact. The archdeacon only noted it because slaves brought to the auction house were never in such a bright mood. It just felt... odd. Like he'd witnessed a connection he wasn't meant to see.

The convening proceedings were just as odd.

The overseer came into the auction house and began to peruse the various individuals offered for sale. The archdeacon saw him walk past the girl. As he moved through the slaves, the child placed herself in his path, and smiled at him, as if he were someone she had once known and was glad to see again. Luigi seemed confused for a moment like there was a thought in his mind he couldn't quite grasp. It was only a momentary pause on the part of the overseer. After he had made his decision, he moved out from among the slaves and waited for the auction to begin. Once it did, there was no doubt which slave Luigi was focusing his bidding on. He bought other slaves, but he purchased the girl first.

CHAPTER 20

AGUEYBANA PATTED HIS lap.

"Come Enriquillo, lay your head here." As the boy approached, he noticed the macana leaning on the porch next to the old man.

"Why do you need the war club?"

"You ask too many question when we should be getting started. The club is for the monsters. I'm going to create a pathway for you into your mother's dream, but I will also have to hold off the creatures in your dreams."

"You wouldn't have to if you allowed me to dream my own dream. I have control of the monsters. I defeat them every night."

"That's why I will need the macana. Your creatures won't know me. Now lie down. This will be unpleasant enough without you stalling."

The boy laid his head across the old man's skinny, wrinkled thighs. Enriquillo was at first afraid he wouldn't be able to gain sleep—the old man's lap felt like lying upon old sticks, but Agueybana placed his right hand at the base of the boy's skull, and he felt himself begin to doze. In his half slumber, he saw the *behike* standing at the beginning of a rise leading into a valley.

Now you must go and lie down beside your mother, Enriquillo.

Enriquillo felt himself get up and sleepwalk into their *caney* where his mother was waiting, though it felt like he was outside his body.

Higuamota was standing beside the big hammock that had been his father's. It was long and wide and weaved throughout with multicolored cotton fabric. But the rope that secured it to the two corresponding beams within the structure was red interlaced with colored shells and bits of gold. No one had slept in it since his father's death. He could still make out the shape of his father's body within the cloth. Higuamota climbed into the bed and made room for him.

"Fear not, my son. I will make a wonderful dream for you and your *cacica*. Just lie down and let your soul rest."

The boy did as he was told and his mother wrapped him in her embrace. One good thing about this dream, his mother seemed happier than he'd seen her in quite some time.

CHAPTER 21

NYIRA TOOK A knife from the bottom drawer of the kitchen dresser and began to clean the fish. As she did, she thought about Enriquillo. He had come from the dense jungle at the base of the mountains. The jungle around her village was much larger. She didn't realize how much she would miss the river until there was no river. She wasn't sure what her father's destiny for her was, but she sensed it had something to do with Enriquillo. She wished there were gorillas in Enriquillo's jungle.

She still mourned her friend, Gord, and missed being able to just walk into the bush and be at peace with herself. She wondered what type spirits she might encounter in this bush. She even missed Aboo and its brothers, and longed for the warmth of it dark, thick form, curling around her, the rumble of its purr. There was something so fulfilling about sitting quietly in the jungle.

"Nyira!" cried Esmerelda. "What are you doing, child?"

Nyira came out of her reverie to discover the knife she'd been holding had continued to clean the fish as she sat daydreaming. It floated just above the table as it worked, making sure to stack the fish in a neat pile.

Esmerelda started to approach the knife but stopped.

"Make it stop! Make it stop at once! You promised!"

Nyira quickly took hold of the knife. "I'm sorry, Nolwazie—I mean Esmerelda. I was thinking about my home. I swear I didn't do it on purpose."

"How am I to train you? How am I to teach you if I can't leave you to a task?"

"What is going on in here?" This was mistress of the house, Madame Dugard. Simone Dugard was a tall, pale woman with large dark eyes and an elegant chin. Her thick eyebrows had grown into two dramatic arches, which gave her face the look of constant surprise. This was exaggerated by her right hand, which she often held pressed to her chest.

Esmerelda and Nyira froze. Madame didn't usually engage the household slaves. That was Josephine's job. She apparently had been disturbed from the nap she often took in the drawing room off the kitchen. Esmerelda didn't appear capable of addressing Madame, so Nyira took it upon herself to break the tension, and pulled a live—yet wriggling—little carp out of her mouth, laid it onto the block table, and curtsied to Madame Dugard. Madame's face registered surprise mixed with disgust.

"I have never seen such a thing," cried Simone. "How was it possible?"

Esmerelda quickly stepped in.

"Please excuse her impertinence, Madame. She is still learning her manners." She placed herself between Nyira and the flustered white woman.

"How did she pull a live fish from her mouth? What kind of sorcery is this?"

"It is a child's trick, Madame, something common

among our people. There is no sorcery. It's more of a crude way to say hello. I will make sure she doesn't do it again."

"I—but what if I would like her to do it again? Could she?" She sounded like an infatuated child.

"I don't believe so, Madame. She is still learning her manners. It was a mistake." She began to move Nyira out of the kitchen and onto the back veranda.

"I will assign her some chores in the stables. I apologize for any trouble she has caused." They were already halfway down the back steps, and Simone was at the door of the kitchen, watching Nyira very strangely. Esmerelda chose not to look back as she practically carried the child away from the woman's sight.

Esmerelda burst through the doors of the stables, dragging the girl behind her. She searched three stalls before she found one empty and pushed the child into it.

"You have no idea of what you've done," Esmerelda said as she knelt to look the child in the eyes. "You don't want to be labeled as a slave who does tricks. You could be sold to someone who would make you do things that you might not like doing. I'm trying to keep you from being singled out. So from now on, you will work here in the stables with Diego. Just for the next month or two. We need to keep you out of Madame's sight, out of Josephine's sight as well. And please promise you will not do anything else to call attention to yourself."

"I promise, Nolwazie." Esmerelda let that pass.

That evening—in the small brown cottage, after Claude said the blessing over the meal, Nyira asked him about God.

Claude Dugard was very guarded with his words. He looked at Esmerelda as if to ask her assistance. Esmerelda gave a look of fatigue, which said everything.

"I don't know… what are you asking, girl?"

"I was just wondering, does praying to him make the food taste better?"

"What?" replied Claude. Esmerelda lowered her head and placed her hand over her smile.

"Because we seem not able to eat until you have done so."

"No," Claude replied. "But it makes… it just makes it seem better. Perhaps the archdeacon can explain it better."

"No!" replied Esmerelda. "That will not be necessary."

"But if she doesn't understand the word of our Lord, the priest wi—"

"I will explain it to her. I have studied the book and I will help her. There is no need to trouble the archdeacon with this." Claude frowned as he looked at her—clearly dissatisfied with this determination—but he never argued with her. He finally stood up from the table, and for a moment appeared to want to say something to the girl, but instead trudged over to his chair near the fireplace. He picked up the Bible the priest had given him and began to thumb through the pages. The field hands were not permitted to read. What few words Claude knew, he learned from her. But he held the book as the priest held it. That apparently made him feel better.

CHAPTER 22

THE BOY'S DREAM was stronger than the *behike* had ever imagined.

As Agueybana moved over the ridge, he found that he was already in the world of Enriquillo's dream. It was a strange realm with a purple sky and yellow moon. The moon was too large, thought the *behike*. Either that or it was much closer to the ground than in the waking world. It also seemed to be watching him. There was a hunger about it as if it might attack and eat him if he didn't keep an eye on it.

The region below him was dry, with a lot of brush and a grove of large strange looking trees that were heavy with leaves. He couldn't get a good concept of their size from where he stood. As he moved down the trail onto the dry plain, he realized that they were giants. He had the sense that the trees were large enough to block out the sky. When he got closer, that is exactly what happened.

Now, where are the monsters I'm to be clubbing? thought the *behike*.

It was not long before he had his answer. When he walked into the grove of trees, a creature he couldn't have conceived dropped to the ground out of the branches. It was a huge dark thing over seven feet tall. It was heavily muscled and broad in the shoulders. Its head looked like some strange mutation of a French ox and what the French called wolves. He had only seen their depiction upon flags flown within the mounted police divisions. The thing was something other than the French image. Its fangs were as long as spearheads and just as broad. It also had eyes as red as blood and glowing.

"Where is the boy?" asked the creature. "It is my turn to fight him."

"The boy is elsewhere," said Agueybana, hefting the club onto his shoulder. "He is in a part of this dream that you shall not travel to."

The beast smiled, and its teeth were so white they gave off their own glow.

"Is that so, old man?" The thing made a feint to the left of the *behike* as if to get by him. "We will see about that."

Agueybana made himself grow to the size of the creature.

"Yes we will," he said.

The thing lunged and swiped at the *behike*'s legs. He dodged its claw, though not quite fast enough, and was tripped up and almost lost his club when he hit the ground.

"I am Aurelius," said the beast, grinning, pleased with itself. "I just want you to know who will be killing you."

Agueybana got to his feet quickly and swung the macana with a two-handed grip. He caught Aurelius right in the snout and sent him sprawling.

"You talk too much, monster," said the *behike*.

Aurelius sprang to his feet, enraged and charged the *behike*. The thing was fast. Agueybana just barely got the club up as the beast sunk its teeth into it.

"I hope you will not get tired, human. My brothers will have their turns next."

By the ancestors, thought Agueybana. *This will be a very long nightmare. Hopefully, the boy wakes up soon.*

Agueybana promised himself that he would spend the rest of the week teaching Enriquillo how to navigate through his mother's dreams. There was no way he wanted a repeat of this experience. The *behike* fought twenty different monsters in the boy's nightmare.

It is no wonder Enriquillo is never at peace. Agueybana didn't want to know what would happen to him or Enriquillo if he lost one of his many battles. This was the longest dream he'd ever experienced.

After he came over the rise, Enriquillo was looking down into a world he didn't recognize, with trees as tall as mountains, and some almost as wide as his village cave. The foliage was so dense that there didn't appear to be any way to enter. He spotted what looked like a small hairy child right at the jungle edge, eating a piece of fruit.

"Hello," said Enriquillo, as he moved toward the child. "Can you tell me where I am?" The child gave a shriek, showed its teeth and then disappeared into the forest. Enriquillo decided that since this was a dream, he should just jump in. As he waded in, he smelled the strangest heaviness, and the heat was unlike any he had experienced. It felt like the trees and plants on the jungle floor—wherever it was—were crowding in on him. The plants were too numerous for him to count, many of them higher than his head, but it didn't stop there. There was another layer covering anything and everything—

trees, plants, and the ground—in a green velvet blanket. When he touched it, it was soft and moist. He wasn't sure where he was going, but he felt that if he kept moving, he might meet someone who could help him find his way. He heard a cackle overhead, and when he looked up saw the strangest looking bird. It was white with a plume on its head, and then there came another bird on the branch just above, and this one had a wide bill and colorful body and started to perform a bizarre dance as Enriquillo stood gazing at it. As he observed this creature, twenty more fluttered down, of different colors, all vying for his attention. He then heard a familiar voice.

"You won't get far if you stand there." He turned to his left and saw her up in one of the tall trees. There were furry little children all around her. She was sharing fruit with them.

"Who are those children you're eating with?" Enriquillo asked.

"They're not children, silly," Nyira chuckled. "They're monkeys."

"What are monkeys? I've never heard of such a thing. Are we still in my mother's dream?"

"No," said Nyira, as she climbed down from the mahogany tree. "I am sorry. I've been so homesick lately."

"Yes. I met someone else recently who said the same thing. I can't imagine what that must be like. You don't seem sad, though. My friend was sad."

"No. I'm never sad in my dreams. Because everyone I miss, I see them there."

This idea struck Enriquillo like a bolt of lightning. "What… you mean you can just…?"

"Dream them. Yes. Whatever you want can be in your dreams."

"I've never dreamed that way… I—I don't know if I could." Nyira came up and took his hand.

"Yes, you can. You just have to try. First, we must get to the river!" She turned and ran into the bush.

"Wait!" cried Enriquillo. "I need to make sure I don't get lost in here."

"What?" said Nyira, as she stopped to stare at him. "You can't get lost. You're in my dream, and I will make sure you always know where you are. Now let's go!" She took his hand and practically dragged him through brush, down slippery trails over extruding giant roots, bulging out of the ground like massive green shoulders. As they ran, she snatched fruit hanging from the trees and tossed it to him.

"Here, eat that."

"What is it?"

"Don't worry. Just bite it."

"It's amazing! What's it called?"

"Monkey fruit!"

"What! Those little children can grow their own fruit? That's incredible!"

Nyira squealed with laughter. "You are so funny, Enriquillo!"

They made their way out of the thick jungle and entered into a grassy clearing.

"What is—look out!" cried Enriquillo. "Run! It's coming at us!" He tried to drag Nyira back into the cover of the bush.

"No. Stop!" said Nyira. She pulled her hand away.

"But—but that monster!"

"That's not a monster. That's my friend. His name is Gord. He's a gorilla."

"What is a… all right. I'll stop asking. This is your dream."

Gord stopped a few yards from the two children and sat staring at Enriquillo.

"That is the strangest looking human I've ever seen," said Gord. "What happened to his head?"

"There's nothing wrong with… he talks?"

"Yes, he talks. He's always been able to talk."

"I guess I need to get used to this kind of dream because, in my dreams, he's a monster."

"Maybe you should try seeing someone you know," suggested Nyira. Enriquillo just frowned at her.

"What? How would that work?"

"You don't have to think about it," replied Nyira. "Sit down." She sat on the ground as if to show him how to do it. He just stood for a moment looking confused. So she took his hand and pulled him down. "Come on, just try. This is supposed to be fun."

"Maybe something's wrong with his head," said Gord, and gave a chuckle, which came out as a growling, wheezing huff. Enriquillo couldn't take his eyes off the massive creature. But he finally sat down.

"Good," replied Nyira, taking his hands in hers. "Now all you have to do is relax, and want."

"Want?"

"Yes. Just want to see them and you will."

"Anyone?" asked Enriquillo. "Anyone I want to see?"

"In a dream, you can see anyone or anything you choose," said Nyira and smiled at him. He only had to look into her wonderful green eyes to believe her. So he relaxed and wanted.

"Enriquillo! What are you doing, you lazy crow!" came Arak's voice. "Come on." His friend slapped him on the shoulder as he ran past, heading for the river. "Man this is a big cove!" and dove on the run. "WHOOOEEE!"

"Arak!" cried Enriquillo, and jumped up to chase after his friend. Arak was already coming up for air by the time Enriquillo got to the bank. "Arak… you're here."

As Arak treaded water near the shore, he looked curiously at his friend.

"Why do you stand with your mouth open, my friend? Jump in!"

When it dawned on Enriquillo that he could and should, he took the plunge.

"Come on," said Arak. "I'll race you to that big rock." They took off and were even stroke for stroke. As they drew closer to the large gray boulder in the middle of river, it raised its head and opened its mouth.

"By the ancestors! Look out!" cried Enriquillo. They turned around and raced back to the shore.

"Where is this place?" asked Arak. "The rocks move." They climbed out of the water to catch their breath.

"I can't help you, my friend," replied Enriquillo. "We are in her dream." He pointed to Nyira.

"Who is she?" asked Arak. "You've started playing with girls? You've missed me a lot."

"Yes… I have," replied Enriquillo. "I can't even tell you how much…" He sat down and began to sob.

Nyira and Gord had followed the boys to the river. "Why are you crying?" asked Nyira.

"This is a new kind of dream for me," replied Enriquillo. "So I'm learning."

"Are they at least happy tears?"

"Some of them are."

"Well I have a surprise," said Nyira. She immediately turned into a red, yellow and green bird. "In dreams, you can be whatever you want, as well!"

Enriquillo perked up again when he discovered he could also transform into any creature he chose.

"I think I want to be a gorilla," said Enriquillo. He immediately was.

"Well, human," replied Gord. "Your looks have much improved. And I have the perfect game." Arak joined them and transformed as well. They then climbed into the trees and raced through the high canopies, with Nyira holding on to Gord's back, just like the old days.

When they stopped for a moment to climb a banana tree and eat a few, they were jostled by an impact against the tree.

"Wow!" said Arak. "What is that? It's the size of a mountain."

"That's called an elephant," replied Nyira. "They're very big but friendly."

"I want to be one of those," said Enriquillo, and in the next moment, he was racing through the bush, with all his friends on his back. "I really like this kind of dreaming. I'm having more fun than I've ever had!" They had stopped in a grove of coconut trees. Enriquillo discovered that they fell easily if he slammed into the trunk. He picked one up with his trunk and tried to smack it on the ground.

"That won't work," replied Nyira. "I use a rock. Like this." She smashed the coconut shell, picked it up and placed it in Enriqullo's trunk. "Elephants usually like this," she said.

Enriquillo, the elephant, trumpeted his delight. He began to slam repeatedly against the coconut tree, which caused a rain of fruit. The other members of the group had to run for cover.

"Hey!" shouted Nyira. "That's enough! We won't be able to eat all these! Even an elephant couldn't." Nyira tried to help Enriquillo hold a rock in his trunk, but it was still awkward.

"It'll be easier if you turn back into yourself," she said. "Hands are more efficient." So Enriquillo changed back and sat down to the task of cracking coconuts and drinking the milk.

"Thank you, Nyira," he said. "This is a wonderful dream."

"You just needed to want," replied Nyira. Enriquillo laid himself down in the thick grass of the clearing and gazed up at the sky.

"This is such a beautiful sky," he said. "I love the blue and orange around the edges of the clouds. I've never noticed the sky in a dream before."

"You don't look at the sky?" said Nyira, incredulous. "What do you do in your dreams?"

"Fight monsters," replied Enriquillo. "And run a lot. I am always running."

"That doesn't sound like much fun. Do they ever catch you?"

"No. I'm very fast in my dreams. That gives me an idea!" He sat up quickly. "My friend Abiodun was very fast. I think I would like to race him."

"Who's that?" asked Nyira.

"He was my sad, homesick friend."

"Where was he from?"

"I am from the West," said a voice from the bush, behind them.

A tall, powerfully muscled boy dressed in a long kente

robe and carrying a gold-tipped spear and shield covered in zebra skin, stepped out of the bush. The robe was secured at the shoulder, by a gold lion brooch. Nyira stood up as he approached. Abiodun was also wearing a gold lion's tooth necklace.

"You are Mandinka," replied Nyira.

"Yes."

"And a prince. Pleased to meet you, your highness."

Enriquillo was shocked.

"Abiodun, you never said you were a prince."

"It didn't matter when I was a slave."

"You were a slave, too?" asked Nyira.

"That's how Enriquillo and I met. He freed me," replied Abiodun. "And once again you've brought me to a wonderful place, my friend."

"Yes," replied Enriquillo. "It's her dream. But I'm having fun too. Can we race?"

"I would like to race, too!" said Arak.

"This is my friend, Arak," said Enriquillo.

"Dreams are wonderful," said Abiodun. "Let's all race."

Nyira sat and watched as the boys lined up at the beginning of the clearing. Gord stood to the side, intending to call the race.

"HAAA!" roared Gord, which was obviously gorilla for go! And they were off. It was very close, but apparently, Arak was as good a runner as he was a swimmer, because he won. All three of the boys collapsed in the grass and commenced to roughhousing.

When they had worn themselves out, they harvested more monkey fruit, bananas and many other delicacies of Nyira's jungle and had a sumptuous feast.

CHAPTER 23

THE FIRST DAY of the following month was to be Enriquillo's eleventh birthday. He knew his mother had planned a village feast, but the night before he was anxious and couldn't sleep, so he dragged one of the canoes from their hiding place at the edge of the jungle, intending to go paddling on the ocean. He wanted to be awake when he turned eleven. He considered going to look for Nyira and have her share the moment with him. She was surely asleep at that hour. Her dream had been so powerful that he half expected to see Arak waiting for him at the spot on the beach where they usually cast off.

The moon was huge that night—as bright as a giant torch—and the stars were out too. This was a good omen. The tide was out. He would have to drag the canoe a few yards to meet the waves. The sea was calm and had a dark glossy solidity as if he could walk out onto the water and gaze down into the depths. Before he made it to the surf, he saw someone else had come out to walk along the shore as well.

Enriquillo stood for a moment and watched the person, looking to see if they were carrying a fire spear. As they came closer, he didn't see one. The person looked familiar, or rather what they wore did. They were clothed in the hooded black garment preferred by those the white men called priests. Usually, during the heat of the summer, they kept their heads uncovered. This individual had his hood up. Perhaps it was too big for him since the garment dragged the ground as he walked. The priest appeared headed directly for him. Enriquillo had no desire to encounter a white man this evening and again began to drag his boat toward the waves. Something strange happened in the sky then: brightness like a burning hot coal streaked past the stars. He wondered if that was the moment, signifying his passage into eleven. He felt an odd tingling upon his skin, radiating up his arms. It was warm, but not hot, and it kept going all the way to his toes. He was practically naked and could see his skin emitted a kind of glow, like low moonlight. It was unsettling, but not painful.

This is definitely eleven, he thought to himself. He'd been so self-absorbed that he'd forgotten the priest. The white man had gotten much closer now. As he drew near Enriquillo discovered, that whoever it was wearing the hooded garment, it wasn't a white man. Suddenly the being rushed him, and when the hood fell off, he saw that it wasn't human either. It was a giant toad-like creature with huge bulging eyes and long jagged teeth. Enriquillo instinctively threw his arm up to shield himself, and when the thing tried to take a bite out of it, it let out a scream and was jolted about ten feet. Enriquillo had felt something hot go through him, but no pain.

"What kind of demon are you?" he asked it. He then had the distinct feeling that he could kill it if he chose to. Something outside him was compelling him to do just that. He dropped his boat and moved toward the thing. The creature seemed to discern the danger it was in. It scrambled to its feet and stumbled away through the jungle.

What just happened? And how did I know what to do?

If this was a dream, it was… He didn't know what it would mean. He would maybe talk to Nyira about it.

CHAPTER 24

THE MINISTRY FOR the slaves was always a difficult detail. A number of his subordinate priests were assigned this duty. Although when the Montoya plantation had a report of witchcraft he, as the archdeacon, was required to investigate. He didn't relish going out to many of the plantations. Most of the slaves had a palpable air of desperation and fear about them, particularly after a punishment. Most of the Spanish nobles had long since sold out to their French counterparts. But Montoya, a former General in the Spanish brigades, wouldn't concede his holdings to anyone, especially the French. The Spaniard's property had slaves that were much more of a mix. There were families of Indians from the first Spanish settlers, still held by the Montoyas. The archdeacon was fluent in Spanish. It helped that he had Artemus to practice with, whose family was actually Spanish.

The Spanish manor was as large as a palace. The pillars of the front veranda were in the style of Roman columns.

Phillipe saw a woman in the front yard of the property as he pulled up in the parish carriage. Her clothes were torn off to expose her back. The flies were feasting on the shredded ribbons of bloody flesh. The archdeacon sat for a moment and watched. If she really was a witch, this was the least she deserved. The job of interrogation was rightly with the clerics. The whole procedure here had not been set up properly. It appeared no one was assigned to watch the woman, to observe if a spirit exited or entered her body. He had to be careful what he said here—these Castilians were rather unpredictable. He hoped the woman really was a witch because it had been almost a year since the last burning. He had not been Archdeacon then, so it wasn't credited to his administration. Father Barineau had been moved up to the diocese, and now worked under the bishop.

When he got out of the carriage, the overseer, Meritricio Gonzales, approached from the side of the house. The man was medium height and rather rotund. They ate well, these Spaniards.

"Good evening, your grace," said the overseer; he affected a slight bow as he approached.

"I'm not a bishop," said the archdeacon, rather crossly. "Father will do fine." He stood looking at the woman in the stocks. He could hear her moans now that he'd come closer.

"Is this the slave accused of witchcraft?" asked the archdeacon.

"Yes, Father," hissed Meritricio. "This is the vile creature."

"Is there a place I might question her? She will need to be removed from this contraption, of course."

The overseer looked flustered as if the priest's request was unheard of.

"But she has been condemned, Father. I—I don't understand."

The archdeacon simply stared at the man as he considered his statement.

"By whom?" asked Phillipe.

"I don't understand…"

"I can't imagine why. It is a very simple question. Who has condemned this slave?"

"The General, Father. We have already had her trial."

"That is nonsense, sir! Only the Church is ordained to declare a witch. Remove this woman from these restraints!"

Meritricio turned the color of a man who'd been slapped. Phillipe had the notion to do just that if he were physically able. The nerve of these… The overseer went toward the manor and disappeared around the side of the house.

The archdeacon began to feel an ache in his lower back. He would've steadied himself on the implement the slave was being held in, but was repulsed by all the flies. He trudged back to the carriage and got himself inside to wait for the man's return.

After Phillipe had sat in the carriage for about ten minutes, two male slaves came around the side of the house and began to unfasten the irons holding the woman within the device. The overseer returned just as they finished. He walked up to the carriage.

"The General has instructed me to take her to the barn, Father. You will be able to interview her there."

"Will she be provided clothes to cover her nakedness?"

"Yes, Father. I will see to it personally. Give us a few moments to make everything ready." He called to one of the male slaves. When the man got to him, Meritricio gave him an order that sent him running back toward the western part of the property.

When the archdeacon entered the barn, the slave was secured to a chair by leg shackles and was dressed in a dirty sack-like garment that covered her from the neck down. There were also four men and two women in the room, only one was not a slave—Meritricio.

"I will need a chair as well, Mr. Gonzales."

This made the overseer snarl something at one of the male slaves. The boy looked stricken and ran from the room. He returned a few moments later carrying one of the chairs the Father saw on the veranda of the manor. It wasn't comfortable, but Phillipe didn't think this inquiry would take very long.

The woman was not an African slave; she had some African features, but she was obviously combined with another race. Her hair was not wooly like some of the Negroes; it was thick and long and wavy. He had seen the offspring of an owner or an overseer and a slave. This woman was that but had a few other elements in her blood as well. What he found most compelling was that she was stunning. Her name was Almira—the overseer provided this information. She still appeared to be in a lot of pain and was leaning forward with her hands clasped in her lap, and she was mumbling. As he came closer and sat down before her, Phillipe was shocked to realize it was a prayer.

CHAPTER 25

ENRIQUILLO FOUND NYIRA in the stables the next morning. She was helping to muck out the horse stalls when he strolled in. Victor, a young slave of about nine, was working with her.

"Hi," he said, standing right next to her. "I would like you to come to our village cave, to meet my mother." Nyira tried to be nonchalant because she knew Victor couldn't see or hear him.

"Not now," she replied under her breath.

"What?" said Victor. "Not now what?" He looked confused.

"It was my mother who dreamed we would meet," said Enriquillo. "She very much wants to meet you."

"Just wait," she mumbled. "I'm busy now." Enriquillo was hurt.

"But the stuff you're doing smells awful! It can't possibly be more fun than coming with me! My mother will have a feast for my dark princess."

"Go away. I can't now."

"But if I go away," replied Victor, perplexed, "you'll have to finish this by yourself."

"I'm sorry, Victor," said Nyira. "I didn't mean to be rude, but I can finish this by myself."

"But Diego will—"

"I will tell Diego. He won't mind."

"Oh… okay." He perked up as he considered what he might do with his sudden free time, but still stood there, unable to choose.

"I believe there is a kickball game behind the barn," said Nyira.

Victor smiled, dropped his shovel and fled in the direction of the barn.

"I don't understand," said Enriquillo. "I thought we had fun in our dreams."

Nyira put down her shovel and led him into the next clean stall.

"I can't leave now. I promised Nolwazie I wouldn't draw attention to myself."

"But no one is here. Who would know?"

"I have to stay. I promised. She has to teach me."

"You have to be taught this? It doesn't look very difficult."

"More than this, Enriquillo. I also have to learn how not to be seen."

"Can you be invisible? I would teach you, but I don't know how it works."

"No. That's exactly what I can't do," said Nyira. "I can't use my powers."

"But what good is having them, if you can't use them?"

"It scares Nolwazie. And I don't want to be sold to someone to do tricks."

"If they try to sell you, I can help you run away."

"Maybe someday. But Nolwazie would be blamed if I ran away now."

"That is why you should escape. And she should, too."

"I still must wait. Papa told me to hear my heart, and I will see the right time. It's not time yet. I also can't just start speaking to someone that no one else can see. Only the priests are allowed to do that."

"You should be careful of those priests," said Enriquillo. "They're dangerous."

"Yes. I know."

"So can we go and meet my mother now?"

"I can't just leave. I'll come tonight, when everyone is asleep."

"Okay," he replied, but still looked a bit sullen.

"I also have to finish this awful smelling stuff. Unless you would like to stay and help me."

"No—I—I'd better go," said Enriquillo. He left the stable quickly.

"Just like a boy," said Nyira, shaking her head, and went back to mucking.

Nyira snuck out of the cottage after Claude and Esmerelda went to sleep. Her pallet was in the front room—not too far from the door. She opened it slowly, and it made the slightest squeak. Enriquillo was waiting at the stables.

"Shhh," she whispered, holding a finger to his lips. They hurried to the jungle behind the property.

"I wanted to get away from the property before you started to speak," Nyira said. "How far is your village?"

"We can't go now," said Enriquillo. "Something has happened, and my friends need our help."

"What friends?"

"They are farther into the mountain."

"Friends from your tribe?"

"They're from your tribe, actually. I helped them escape."

"There are slaves hiding in the mountains?"

"Yes. And a number of them are hurt and needs a healer. Will you come?"

"Yes, but what about Agueybana? Your medicine man?"

"How do you know about him?"

"While you were in my dreams, I met him in yours. He needed help with your monsters."

"He doesn't agree with what I'm doing. He believes it will endanger the tribe."

"And you still want to help?"

"I have to, after meeting Abiodun. I can't imagine being stolen away from my people."

"I wish I couldn't." She sat down beside an elm tree and sobbed for a while. Enriquillo sat down beside her. She leaned her head on his should. She hadn't really leaned on anyone since Gord. "You will be a brave *cacique*," she said and gave him a hug.

"So will you, my *cacica*. Now we must go. Mounted police search this area for runaways."

They traveled along the base of the mountain, by a trail through the jungle the Taíno had established over six hundred years before. There was no way to see it. You had to be led. There was a quarter moon. Nyira found the jungle canopy was not as thick. She actually saw her hands in front of her face, and was surprised that she felt out of her element, almost lost. Even the breeze smelled different. She realized that that was because of the ocean.

"Bruno's camp is about ten miles into the mountains. We won't have to go that far."

"Why not?"

"The injured are taken to a lower camp. To tend their wounds."

The lower camp was only two miles into the mountains. When they arrived, Nyira saw five injured runaways. The camp wasn't high enough for it to be cold, but the air was cool and thinner compared to the dense humidity of the jungle. One of the injured slaves was a man named Peter. Peter had been struck on the head and stabbed in the shoulder. Nyira was shocked at the injuries. The others had stab wounds as well. One was already dead.

This was not as bad as the ship, though there she had had an agreement with death—for sickness. One of the injured was a woman. Nyira went to her first. She looked afraid of the child.

"What's your name?"

"I'm called Yiella. Are you the sorceress from the ship?"

"You were on the Dutch ship?"

"No. But a woman I worked beside was. She described you exactly, right down to your green eyes."

"What happened to you, Yiella?"

"The Mandinka, Christian, attacked us. He thought we were trying to help his wife escape."

"She's not his wife!" declared another slim slave who was not injured. "He stole her from me!"

"You're Bruno," said Nyira, looking at him. Bruno had stepped away from tending to one of the other injured men. Nyira recognized him by the two missing fingers. Enriquillo had told her about the battle.

"Yes," said Bruno. "And it's my fault they got hurt."

"What did you do," asked Enriquillo. Before he could answer, there came a surprise out of the darkness.

"Nyira!" cried Esmerelda. The cook stumbled breathless into the camp and collapsed. "Are you going to escape?"

Nyira was speechless for a moment.

"Nolwazie… what are you? How did—"

"I heard you go out the door."

"I promise I'm not. I came with Enriquillo. Why did you come so far? You should've said something."

"I didn't know what to say. I was shocked. I thought you were happy with Claude and me." She leaned forward and placed her head in her hands. "Oh, I'm so tired. I don't know what to do! I can't get back!" She began to cry. Nyira went and embraced her.

"Nolwazie, I'm sorry. Don't cry. We'll get you back. Can you get her water, Enriquillo? She looks thirsty."

Bruno stepped forward and handed Esmerelda a large drinking gourd.

"Is there no way we can convince you to stay, Nolwazie? You're already here." He smiled, and Nyira could see that he fancied her.

"I… no. I have Claude. He would be lost without me. I have to go back."

"We will," said Nyira. "But I must clean and wrap their wounds first. Enriquillo, can you get me some plants from along the trail? The blue and the yellow flowers, some leaves from the star fruit tree and palmetto leaves. Also, some bark from the pine tree. Nolwazie, would you be willing to part with a section of your dress?"

Esmerelda was hesitant.

"I made this dress," she cried. "It's one of my favorites…" Then she looked around at the other individuals present, many from plantations nowhere near as hospitable as the Dugards. What clothes they wore were rags. Some of them were lying on the ground, bleeding badly. "So you know how to help them, Nyira?" She stood up, turned around, and tore the lower section of her dress and handed it to the girl.

"Thank you, Nolwazie." She tore a section and dropped it into the small pot Bruno handed to Nolwazie. Who then filled it with water from the drinking gourd, and set it on the fire.

"Yes. I can help them," replied Nyira. "Papa let me help him when he saw I understood as well as his older apprentice."

"I don't understand what you're doing here," said Esmerelda. "Are you going to be helping these people, from now on?"

Nyira paused and then looked at Enriquillo.

"I guess I am. Will you help me, Nolwazie?"

"Oh, child… I—I don't know. You've already changed my life so much. Let me think about it."

When Nyira finished binding and cleaning everyone's wounds, she looked at Enriquillo again.

"Agueybana could've healed these people. We'll need his help, too. I can ask him if you won't."

"I can try," said Enriquillo, not sounding happy about it. "He knows we need him. He knows everything."

"He also knows you don't want to ask him." She turned and headed out of the camp with Esmerelda.

"Don't you want me to guide you back along the trail?"

"No. I remember the way."

On the walk back, Esmerelda asked:

"Why are you doing this, Nyira? Don't you have enough to occupy you on the plantation?"

"I won't put you in danger, Nolwazie. So you don't have to help. But I have to. Papa told me to listen to my heart. I think he sent me here."

Esmerelda had to sit down after a while. She braced her hand against a palm tree and lowered herself down into the grass.

"I haven't been in a jungle since I was a little girl. It doesn't feel quite the same as the Congo."

"It's not, Nolwazie. You wouldn't be able to see if we were in the Congo. And you would know not to sit down."

"I know. But I'm tired. How is it you know your heart? You're a child, brought here like the rest of us."

"I gave up my freedom to save my friend, and I haven't felt like a child since my village was burned and papa killed. But I want to be a family with you and Claude, though. I promise to keep you from danger."

"I want that, too. You can't control danger, Nyira. I'm not a sorceress, but I'm sure about that."

"We'd better get moving again. Enriquillo said soldiers sometimes search this area for runaway slaves."

"Are there that many?"

"More every day. You saw Bruno's group. And I doubt all of them are friendly." She helped Esmerelda to her feet, and they moved on along the trail.

CHAPTER 26

EARLIER THAT EVENING, Bruno took André and a new member of the camp—Julio—on a rescue mission. Julio had been the husband of the slave Almira. Once Meritricio killed his wife, Julio knew it was just a matter of time before the overseer focused his animosity on him. The General and he had blamed Almira for the death of the child fathered by the overseer. It was an accident. Almira tripped over the last step to the veranda and dropped the baby, while on her way to give it to the plantation wet-nurse. They blamed Julio, too—by association.

Julio had heard of the slave Pierre's escape and was encouraged. He was not a dark slave. He was brown-skinned, tall and solidly built. His greatest flaw was he only had one eye—due to an accident in the cane fields. Because of the eye, he was more afraid for his life. A man needed two eyes when he knew his days were numbered. Julio worked in the plantation's massive stables, tending the stock and stacking hay and loading grain into the feed loft.

It was lucky he wasn't crushed under the hundred bags of grain dropped by Pablo, one of the overseer's slave hench-men. The grain had instead landed on Miguel, who stood where Julio had been, just a moment before. Pablo looked very disappointed after the incident. There was no other way to describe his expression. His eyes were already dark, and his long hair and Indian features only enhanced his menacing nature. Julio could practically hear the man's eyes say: *I am sorry I didn't kill you.* He knew then, that if he wanted to live, he had to take his chances in the mountains. André had discovered him hiding in the jungle as he returned from a fishing trip to the secret cove. Once Bruno heard Julio's story, he knew he had to try and rescue his love.

They made it through the jungle bordering the town without encountering a mounted police unit. Thankfully, the sun was just setting, so they didn't need a torch to see by. When they entered the bush fronting the western fields of the Bissett property, Bruno got quiet.

"Bruno," André whispered. "Are you okay? What should we do now?" Bruno's heart had sped up for a moment until he realized that André had the most to lose if they got caught.

"I'm okay," said Bruno. "Just a few nerves at being back here."

"Yes. I know. So I hope you understand if I let the two of you go on without me."

"I understand. I guess it's just you and me, Jul—"

"Wait! Someone's coming," said André. "It looks like… I think I know her."

Yiella was leaving her potato in the jungle that evening. Her husband was Francis. One of the overseers had begun making advances upon her. This, Yiella knew, would lead to a yellow child. When she saw Bruno and André, she knew their intentions.

"She may not want to come," said Yiella. She was a

beauty in her own right, and if she stayed, none of her children would be by her husband.

"Why would she not want to come?" asked Bruno.

"Because she knows Christian will kill you the next time."

"It's his mistake he didn't do it when he had the chance," replied Bruno. "Tell her I will return at full dark."

"Tell Bruno that I intend to keep my promise," Juliette told Yiella. That would have been the end of it, except someone overheard Yiella deliver Bruno's message to his love, and conveyed it to the Mandinka. As Yiella, Francis, and three other slaves waited in the jungle, Christian and a group of slaves who owed him money attacked them.

Bruno saw it as an act of cowardice because Christian hadn't waited for him.

"It's bad luck to fight a man you almost killed," said André. "The gods may not smile upon him a second time."

"I don't care about his luck," snapped Bruno.

Word of Julio's escape emboldened others. In response, a slave-hunting platoon was established. More slaves attempted escape, but hardly any got away. Not because the platoons were so effective. Most of them wandered aimlessly in the jungle. The escapees never planned. And since the jungles of Saint Domingue bore no resemblance to the African Congo, hardly any made it to the mountains. The few that did joined Bruno's band. Bruno never saw himself as a leader. But he found that he could be ruthless when he had to be. This first occurred when one disagreeable man who was about to be expelled, threatened to expose the camp's location. Bruno dispatched André and Julio with a couple of machetes to make sure he didn't.

By the end of three months in the mountains, Bruno had a band of over thirty men with machetes.

One day a scout spotted a slave-hunting platoon of about twenty soldiers, making camp in the valley about two miles from Bruno's upper camp.

"I think they're searching for us," said André.

"And they're getting close," replied Julio.

"You said they were just making camp, Emile?" asked Bruno.

"Yes. About two miles below us, in the valley," said the excited youth.

"The general would wait until they were asleep," said Julio. "But if they are allowed to awaken, they may find us."

"Then it's best that they don't," said Bruno. "Let's give them about five hours of rest."

"Then we rush the camp," said André.

"If we take out the sentries first, we won't need to rush," replied Julio. "We could take our time." Julio was right. Bruno really liked this new Spaniard.

Once the sentries were down, they could go from tent to tent. The only soldier to see them was one man who went out into the jungle to have a pee. He got a look at André who walked toward him with a grin on his face and a machete on his shoulder.

"Good night soldier," said André. The man stumbled backward with his pants around his ankles and fell into Julio, who cut his throat. When it was done, they had acquired twenty muskets, fifteen flintlock pistols and a cache of ammunition and other tools and supplies. It was also Julio's idea that they shouldn't keep the horses.

"Why not?" complained André. "We could use some horses."

"We need to cover our tracks," replied Julio. If we tie the bodies to the horses and send them down the mountain, they won't know where we attacked them. We don't want them to know how close they came."

Bruno decided it was time to sit down and plan what they would do next. Their first priority was more food—because hungry men were often angrier with their leaders. André stated the obvious: "Why not go to the Bissett and take some corn and potatoes?"

"But not all together," replied Julio. "The soldiers usually go out in small groups."

"Yes. They move faster that way," said André.

The first operation was easy. The crop was still in the fields. All the men had to do was pick it. The women in the camp had fashioned large baskets from palmetto and palm fronds. The baskets were full within half an hour. A sugar cane crop was also available. The former slaves drew the line at that. They had access to fish and other seafood along the coast. When they discovered how easy it was to attack the crops, livestock was the next target.

"We'll have to go into the property to take anything large," said Julio. "That will be dangerous."

"All of this is dangerous," replied Bruno, in his brooding tone. Leading was taking its toll on him.

CHAPTER 27

WHEN THE ARCHDEACON came to the Dugard property, he was usually there to provide religious counsel to the Major and Madame, also to inquire about Constance possibly becoming a nun. He derived a cruel satisfaction at how pale the girl's features became when the subject came up. She often made a hasty exit from the room whenever he had had a few glasses of wine and became jovial. It wasn't his best quality.

On this particular evening, Esmerelda gave a little chuckle at the Father's jest. This drew an evil eye from Constance.

"You're amused, Relda," replied Constance, acidly. "I wonder if Camille could perhaps show the Father the way to turn chickens into stones. That would perhaps amuse him." Esmerelda nearly spilled the plate of pastries she'd been serving around the dining table.

"Of what blasphemy does the girl speak?" asked the Father, looking at Madame Dugard.

"The child has some minor ability with trickery," replied Madame. "I myself witnessed her produce a live fish from her mouth."

The archdeacon's face was rather placid as the possibility of an actual witch bounced around in his mind. It seemed unlikely, but after the Montoya incident, he would make sure such proceedings were handled properly. The girl Constance surely didn't consider all the unpleasant ramifications of such a serious charge, and probably made her remark out of spite. There was no getting around it now though.

Esmerelda was speechless.

"Is this true, Esmerelda?" asked the archdeacon. "Have you and Claude been hiding a sorceress?" His tone was just slightly mirthful, but there was no levity in his inquiry.

"I assure you, Father, Claude and I wouldn't take such a thing lightly. The child is very playful and learns quickly the tasks that I set for her. But she is no sorceress."

"I see," replied the Father. "You understand that I will have to question the girl? That is the requirement of such a charge."

CHAPTER 28

"HE WISHES TO see chicken turned to stone?" asked Nyira. Esmerelda had gone to the stables, where she was working, forking hay into the various horses' stalls. Esmerelda sat down upon an upended milk pail to compose her words.

"Please listen to me, child." She got up and took the pitchfork away from the girl, and made her come and sit beside her on the floor. "He doesn't want to see any magic. Remember the agreement we made about Claude and the rest of the household?"

"That I shouldn't show them anything? No magic or cures? I've kept it, Nolwazie."

"Well, now you must be doubly on your guard, for if you show this man even the slightest display of your magic, he will burn you."

"For what reason? I've never said a harsh word to the archdeacon. And he always smiles when he sees me and I take his horse to the stables."

"How can I make you understand, Nyra? It is a function of his faith."

"It's a part of his faith to kill me?"

"Not just you, but all who are like you. They consider

you to be evil. The whole of his world is the murder of those like you, and any who might shield you."

"So you and Claude…?" Suddenly the girl's face registered the magnitude of her dilemma.

"And such a thing is accepted?"

"Yes."

"But yet, I'm considered evil?"

"Tell him nothing," replied Esmerelda. "Show him nothing. In fact, try not to speak at all unless you have to."

CHAPTER 29

ENRIQUILLO WAS PLEASANTLY surprised at the vibrancy of Bruno's high camp. Women were tending cook fires, while men erected dwellings along the edge of the clearing and even further out into the valley. They chopped down trees with axes and other tools captured in raids or brought by recently escaped individuals. There were also Africans hacking a clearing out of the thick towering rain forest foliage.

"You have become *cacique*," said Enriquillo. He'd strolled confidently through the camp. Some of the warriors eyed him dangerously and reached for their machetes. André set them straight about the divine one. Some weren't initially convinced. He looked just like any other boy to them. "He's not," replied André. "You'll find out soon enough."

Bruno was also uncomfortable with the title of chief, even as he reclined in the colorful cotton hammock provided by the women of Enriquillo's tribe. There was also a *duho* stool made by a Taíno artisan. Enriquillo also heard the sounds of drums from far out in the valley.

"I can't be King," grumbled Bruno. "No man is complete… without a queen."

"I see a number of women in your camp," replied Enriquillo, as he plopped down on the ground and took a mango from the pile near Bruno. "Surely there is one you can choose." Someone had also gifted Bruno a kerosene lamp they'd brought with them. His face looked aggrieved in the light.

"No. There isn't."

"You're not happy being free?" asked Enriquillo.

"It's not that simple," replied Bruno, as he brought his knees up and laid his chin on them. "I enjoy my freedom, but happiness has nothing to do with it."

"I don't understand."

"When I was a slave, I was happy with Juliette beside me. And if I could have her back, I'd give up my freedom."

"That doesn't make sense," replied Enriquillo.

"I told you it wasn't simple. You have special abilities, but you're still a child. There's no magic to make you understand. But you will, one day."

Enriquillo took a bite of his mango and sat quietly, as he considered Bruno's words.

"You're wrong," he finally said. "I know sadness very well. My mother is the same way. She would give up her life if she could be with my father."

"Maybe one day I can meet your mother," replied Bruno.

"I don't think so. She doesn't care for visitors, and rarely leaves our cave."

"I'm sorry if your mother truly feels the way I do."

"Agueybana couldn't heal your sadness or my mother's," said Enriquillo.

"I do have something you can help me with," said Bruno.

"What's that?"

"We need someone to sneak onto the Bissett property and bring out a few pigs and cattle. Our numbers are growing too fast to rely on just fish and fruit."

"Okay. I can open the pens and shoo them toward you."

"That will be fine. We'll graze them up here in the high valleys. Let us know when you're ready."

CHAPTER 30

THE CHICKEN WALKED around inside the church chamber where the archdeacon had arranged for the inquiry. Nyira regarded the bird with curiosity.

"Will it hatch its eggs in your chamber, Father?" The archdeacon and the council he'd gathered to witness his interrogation shook their heads and scowled at the child's question.

When Phillipe had heard Constance's accusation, it made sense, given his first encounter with the child.

"It is not here to lay eggs, child," replied the archdeacon. "It's here to attack you. What will you do?"

"I would run," replied Nyira. "I always run when the rooster chases me. This is not a rooster, Father."

"The child has a point," replied Father Reyes. "Roosters are much more threatening than a mere chicken. Perhaps you should have brought a larger chicken, Phillipe."

Father Reyes had not agreed with the archdeacon's assessment and decision to proceed with the tribunal. He suggested that the girl Constance had simply sought to lash out at the slave Esmerelda, to keep her in her place. He had positioned himself as counter to the archdeacon's prosecuting intentions.

The rest of the council gave a bit of a snicker at Father Reyes's remark, and looked side-eyed at the archdeacon, to see if he took the humor of the comment. He had not.

The archdeacon was not happy about this development and was also piqued at this chicken—for not being threatening enough and contributing to the less than serious tone this proceeding had taken. He decided to make sure it would be that evening's dinner. He was also growing impatient with this silly slave child. Constance, who was a bit silly herself, had led him to believe this girl had some sort of magical powers. The discovery of an actual witch would surely raise his stature in the eyes of the diocese. But the child was making a fool of him. What had he been thinking listening to a young woman who wasn't even smart enough to get herself married by this time?

"Perhaps the girl was mistaken," continued Father Reyes. "Maybe the child actually flies." The other priests began to laugh at this comment. Artemus was in rare form today. He also gave the archdeacon a viciously ingenious idea.

"In that case, we must go to the bell tower!" This wiped the smile from Father Reyes's face.

"You cannot be serious, Phillipe."

"Oh but I am," replied the archdeacon. "Thank you for your idea, Father Reyes."

"You will not lay this insanity at my feet!"

"I am trying to perform an inquiry, Artemus. It is you who have allowed this child to make a mockery of these proceedings!"

"I can't believe you intend to kill this child to spite me, Phillipe. Where is your compassion?"

"I believe the child is concealing her evil powers, Artemus. And I intend to—"

"And destroy Major Dugard's property."

"Monsieur Dugard trusts my judgment in this matter."

"I wish I could. For even a slave deserves the protection of our Lord."

"You dare paint my motives as contrary to our faith! I will speak to the bishop of your blasphemy."

"Indeed. We should speak with his Excellency. He should be made aware of your murderous ambitions!"

"Nevertheless! We proceed to the tower!"

The detached bell tower rose over forty feet above the plaza. Like an old tooth, it was still white but had yellowed to the shade of dark ivory. It was a remnant of the Spanish regime and was constructed of limestone. The steps were also of limestone and were chipped and worn uneven with use. Nyira had never had to ascend more than twelve or fifteen steps, those leading to the Dugard veranda behind the kitchen. She found herself growing a bit light-headed from the breeze that was magnified as it snaked through the open squared windows that corresponded to every fifth or sixth step. She was also strangely exhilarated by the height. When they had gone halfway, she noticed a beautiful mural painted on the stairwell wall. It was of a woman holding a child and there appeared to be light coming out of her head. The woman didn't look particularly pleased with her child, and Nyira wanted to ask who the woman in the picture was, but the somber nature of the procession didn't lend itself to inquiry. The mounted police were so close behind her, she was likely to get pushed if she tried to slow down. And

Father Reyes was not close enough for her question to fall on sympathetic ears.

As they ascended the last few steps, they entered into what appeared to be a bird sanctuary. There were a number of pigeons that apparently had been fed by someone because they were not startled at the sight of people coming into their space. One of the birds lit upon the archdeacon's shoulder. He looked at the creature and smiled, making a strange little sound with his lips. This picture created an off-kilter image in Nyira's mind, composed of tenderness merged with malice; she couldn't reconcile it.

As Nyira gazed out over the distance, she could see what might be the valley not far from Enriquillo's cave, and the undulating surf of the shore.

There was silence as the archdeacon regarded her, and then he looked at the pigeon. He flicked the bird from his shoulder, which made it fly at Nyira's face.

"It's attacking you, child!" Nyira just caught the bird on her finger and looked at the priest. Something in her green gaze unsettled the archdeacon.

"Guards! Do your duty!"

Two guards snatched Nyira up and tossed her from the tower. Luckily, she made eye contact with one of the guards. He held her by the arm as she dangled over the edge.

"All right, Phillipe!" cried Father Reyes. "I'm sorry! In the name of our Lord, do not sacrifice this child to prove a point. Though her life may not hold much value to her master, it's your soul for which I fear! I see no sorceress in this dark creature, just an innocent child who has no understanding of her dire circumstances. She shouldn't die because of our foolish pride. Search your heart!"

"I'm to be spared, Nol—I mean Esmerelda," cried Nyira, still clinging to a beaming Father Reyes as he charged into the anteroom. "The archdeacon decided not to toss me from the bell tower!" She didn't mention what she had to do to the guards. She decided it was better not to scare Nolwazie.

Esmerelda was already crying when she took the girl in her arms.

"Hush," said Esmerelda, as she stood Nyira on her feet and pulled her out into the square leading from the church offices. "We must get back to the manor at once. The major has a hunt today, and the horses must be prepared." They made their way to the carriage positioned near the stables just behind the building.

"But Diego has always prepared the horses for hunts," said Nyira. "He has only taught me a par—" Esmerelda placed an index finger over the child's lips.

"Shhh…" was all she said. She took the horse's reins and headed out of the square.

When they were a half mile out of town, Esmerelda finally spoke.

"I didn't want you to say anything that might renew the archdeacon's inquiry. Many have lost their lives with a random remark when they thought the inquisition ended. Your joy could have given you away. And then we would all be doomed."

"I'm sorry, Nolwazie. I made sure to control myself. Although I thought I might have to fly when the archdeacon ordered the guards to throw me from the tower." Esmerelda was shocked at the idea.

"Then I'm glad they didn't!"

"I'm only playing, Nolwazie."

"But… can you fly?"

Nyira smiled.

"Yes," said the girl. "Every night in my dreams."

Esmerelda let out a sigh of relief. She didn't even want to think of the consequences if someone saw the child fly.

"I know that I will one day. I don't know why, but one day I may have to."

CHAPTER 31

A WEEK FOLLOWING Nyira's tribunal, the mounted police captured Enriquillo's uncle, Jaceux.

His uncle had always seemed a tall man to the young Enriquillo, but seeing him in chains escorted by the strutting troop made him shrink. Invisible, he came abreast of his mother's brother as they marched him into the square of Port-a-Piment. The boy found that he now appeared to be a full head taller than his uncle, who was smiling as if bound for a great feast, rather than a public death.

"Uncle, whence comes your joy?" asked Enriquillo. "They mean to give you death."

"They are fools, nephew! I will live forever. You will protect our people, now. Look at how you stand. You are a giant. You could crush them with just the flick of your wrist. I'm happy."

"What is this savage rambling about?" asked the sergeant escorting him to the gallows. "And why does he look so pleased with himself?" The Taíno interpreter could not look Jaceux in the eyes. It was believed that if you betrayed him, he would kill you in your dreams.

"He says you are fools," said the interpreter. "And he

spoke to someone named Enriquillo. He called him nephew."
When the chief regarded the thin, raggedly dressed Taíno
man, the interpreter began to tremble.

"Alonso. I don't blame you," replied Jaceux. "Fear not.
I will speak to our elders in *Coaybay*. Your dreams will be
safe." Alonso began to cry.

"You honor me, great *cacique*," cried the man. "Say the
word, and I will throw myself upon these devils and try to
free you."

"No. Save your life, my brother. Sing our names to these
people so that our memories won't die. Say the names of our
elders, so their names remain a time longer."

Alonso began to sing then; it was a Taíno areito that
he'd learned from his father and his uncles. It included the
names of all who had died and now included Jaceux's name
as well.

The procession led the chief and his few captured warriors up the steps of the gallows erected on the square in
front of the Cabildo.

"Please, uncle!" implored a distraught Enriquillo.
"Don't leave me. If you give the order, I will set fire to these
buildings. I can declare war on them with the warriors we
have left."

"You don't need to fight, nephew. You need to live for
my sister and our people and the dark princess. You must
live so we all can live. I order you to return to the cave and
celebrate with our people."

A mounted police captain stood on the platform at the
top of the gallows steps as they walked Jaceux up them.
When they'd positioned he and his four captured warriors
before the nooses, the man read the charges to the crowd.

"Jaceux, in the name of the French crown, you and the whole of your rebels have, in absentia, been convicted of kidnapping, assault, and insurrection. The sentence for which is death, to be carried out immediately."

Enriquillo walked solemnly out of the square, past the market. He actually saw Nyira as she sorted through vegetables and fruits while Esmerelda negotiated with the fishmonger. He would've liked to have stopped and had a word with his beloved, but he didn't want her to see him cry. At least she wasn't among the crowd gathering in the square to watch the execution. He needed to think of a way to tell his mother that her bi-go was gone. Then a thought struck him: who would show him all the secret coves within the mountains? The boy turned back, to go and ask his uncle. He heard the crowd in the square raise their voices, and when they quieted, he knew Jaceaux was dead.

When he reached the cave, he went to a wall just past the entrance and spent over four hours drawing the history of his uncle as he evaded the French soldiers and maintained the stability of his village and people and became a mentor to his young nephew.

Higuamota went to her son and watched him as he progressed through the story. When he got to the part where he needed to draw the gallows, he couldn't hold himself, he was so overcome. That's when his mother took him in her arms. He was already as tall as she and ten pounds heavier, but she picked him up like he was still five years old.

"We must not be sad, my son," said Higuamota. "Agueybana told me of my brother's coming death last night while you slept. I didn't have the courage to tell you. I was also afraid you would try to intervene, and I might have lost you as well. We must celebrate. Is that not what my bi-go said?"

"Yes," replied Enriquillo. "But first I must cry, mother."

"Then cry, my son. Just leave room to celebrate. My brother goes to the elders. That is a happy thing."

"I will try, mother. I just wish it were night so that I could dream with my dark princess. I saw her today as I left the town. She was in the market. I couldn't bear to speak to her with such sadness in my soul."

The villagers from Jaceux's tribe began to arrive for the celebration later that evening. They brought food and carved gifts to their *cacique*'s sister and then there were ball games played in the village *batey*. Once the celebration was about to end, Agueybana led both tribes in an areito about Jaceux's deeds and a ceremonial dance around the large chamber.

The laughing and jubilation was too much for Enriquillo. He took a torch and other provisions and left the main chamber of the tribe and went farther into the cave. He didn't stop at the boundaries; he chose to walk where only *behike* or shaman would go. At the boundary to the dark realm, he lit the small torch.

There were drawings along the walls of strange beasts and men dancing and fighting with evil spirits. He took no heed to the warnings of danger written in pictographs along some of the chambers.

After a while, as Enriquillo continued his off path journey, he no longer saw the signs of doom on the walls. Instead, there were skeletons—small and adult size. He at one point came upon a number of them, and they appeared to have been a family. There was the smaller woman with her hair flowing behind her, and a larger male whose hair was equally as long, and the two children. The farther he went, the warmer it got. He knew that he was traveling down into the earth. Agueybana had told him that as you get closer and closer to *Coaybay*, the earth got hotter.

Once Enriquillo had walked for what seemed like seven days, his torch went out. He sat down to rest and to have a bit of the dried fish he carried in the pouch at his waist. He finally went to sleep. It seemed he slept for days.

When he awoke the sun was on his face, and there was the smell of food cooking.

He saw his uncle Jaceux crouched next to a *barbacoa* roasting what looked like a *hutia* he'd killed.

"Uncle!" cried Enriquillo, and jumped up to embrace Jaceaux.

"Did you not remember what I told you, nephew?"

"…I—yes, uncle." The boy was confused. He'd never seen his uncle angry before.

"You must return to our people, Enriquillo. You can't just walk to *Coaybay*."

The boy looked around.

"This is *Coaybay*? I didn't realize there was so much sun here."

"No, nephew. This is not *Coaybay*. This is the boundary before. You are in pre-death: The land of the *Kopai*. You must agree to turn back now, or you won't see my sister or your dark princess ever again."

"But it's beautiful here, uncle. Why can I not visit you here? That way I can talk with you from time to time."

"That's not the way of this land, Enriquillo. You remember the bones you saw along your path?"

"Yes, uncle."

"They are the remains of those who chose to stay too long, who wouldn't allow their dead to sleep. So the *Kopai* kept them. I will feed you now nephew, but you must be about your way—lest you leave my sister broken hearted, and she soon joins us here. You've spent your life protecting her. What would she have if you didn't return?"

Enriquillo knew that his uncle was right. Higuamota's only reason for living was him. So the boy sat down to a wonderful meal of fried yams and hutia with his uncle. Jaceux also gave him enough to take with him so he wouldn't be hungry on his trip back.

"Speak to me in your dreams, Enriquillo. That way I can spend time with you and your dark princess." He embraced the boy and sent him on his way.

CHAPTER 32

THE WEEK AFTER Enriquillo's visit with Jaceaux, someone left a potato in the jungle on the Bissett property. When he went to retrieve it, he found Juliette crying.

"What has happened?" asked Enriquillo. "Are you ready to escape?"

"Yes," said Juliette. "But first I will need your healer to come to Bruno's old cabin."

"I will have to go and get her."

"Please hurry. They are badly hurt."

When they returned, Nyira brought enough cloth and herbs to bind a few people's wounds. Esmerelda came, too. Partly to make sure Nyira came back with her. When they entered Bruno's cabin, they found three hacked up people, one on the floor and two on the beds. The victim on the bed near the wall surprised Enriquillo.

"You didn't tell me one of the injured was Christian," said Enriquillo.

"I hoped it wouldn't matter."

As Nyira and Esmerelda prepared the bandages and boiled water for the herbs, they noticed something about Juliette.

"You didn't move them here yourself, did you?" asked Esmerelda

"My sister Babette helped me."

"When will your baby come?" asked Nyira.

"In the summer, I think," replied Juliette.

Esmerelda pushed one of the chairs from the table over to her. "You need to sit down and rest."

"No. I'm fine. I need to help."

"Be careful, or your baby won't make it till summer," said Esmerelda.

"So you weren't trying to escape?" asked Enriquillo.

"Not at first. But now we have to, or they will kill him."

"As will Bruno. If he sees him."

"Then you must take us to another part of the mountains."

"He will still come and search for you."

"Make sure to hide us well, divine one."

"It may not be necessary," said Esmerelda. "He's bled too much."

"Is this the man who almost killed Bruno?" asked Nyira.

"Yes," replied Juliette. "He's my husband. Can you help him?"

"I can try. Papa once told me that if the soul stays, the body will live."

"How can you do that?"

"It takes a lot of energy. Papa would sleep for a week after he did it."

Once they cleaned Christian's wounds, Nyira sat down beside him on the bed. She remained still and quiet for almost half an hour. When she closed her eyes, Christian's body floated up from the bed. Juliette gasped. As he began to rotate, the cuts and gashes in his flesh disappeared.

"What are you doing, Nyira?" asked Esmerelda.

"I am healing his outside wounds," Nyira replied. "So his soul will feel safe. Then I will go inside." She laid hands on Christian and brought him back down to the bed and placed her head on his chest.

... Nyira found herself wading through the forest near the Congo River. It had been a number of years, but the heat and foliage was just as thick, and the call of the cockatoo reminded her of the many hours she spent here, hiding from the women of her village. Who were always in search of her for tasks that little girls were supposed to do. Unfortunately, this visit was not for play. She heard someone breathing and moving around in the bush nearby.

"I hear you," said Nyira. "I won't hurt you. Please come out."

"You can't possibly hear me, girl," replied a small voice. "I am a warrior and quieter than a leopard. You must leave. I'm hunting and must go soon."

"What is your name, mighty warrior?"

"I am Mohamadou. I will be chief. I must kill a lion and take its hide to my village as proof of my skill."

"Perhaps I can help, Mohamadou. I have keen vision and sharp hearing."

"You must leave, girl! I don't need a woman to help the future chief."

"I cannot leave, Mohamadou. I seek counsel with the future chief. Please, it is very important."

The boy walked out of the bush wearing a dirty, tattered rag around his waist. He was holding the remains of a broken spear that looked like he'd found it somewhere. It had no spearhead, only a midsection where it had been broken off and formed a point. He was not more than six and appeared severely beaten. Nyira could also see the child's ribs. She reached into the basket she was carrying and brought out some fried yams she had prepared. She knew that spirits were often hungry. Her father had taught her that you should come prepared with food to offer.

"I have an offering to the chief," she said, kneeling as she presented the yams. The boy snatched them and stuffed them in his mouth so quickly half of them ended up on his nose and cheeks. When he finished, she laid a cloth on the ground and placed Ndakala and kwanga in banana leaves. She said nothing and simply sat and watched the small child eat. Once he had finished and looked satisfied Nyira said:

"Are you sated, my chief?"

"I am, woman. What is it you wish to speak to me about?"

"First allow me to add salve to your wounds." The boy turned and offered his back.

Nyira was shocked at the damage.

"Has someone attacked you, my chief?"

"Never mind how I sustained my wounds, woman. I am a warrior. I will be leaving soon, so it doesn't matter." Nyira coated some of the salve she had brought onto the boy's bloodied narrow back.

"I would hope to convince my chief to stay. I'm very afraid in this forest, and will need protection when I gather food."

"I understand, but I believe there are better places," replied the boy. "Perhaps we can find a new forest."

Nyira began to cry.

"What is troubling you, woman? Why do you cry?"

"I am sad, my chief. I know that I must go where my

chief bids me. But my family is poor and will not be able to leave with me. My father is not well. I know creatures in this jungle are fierce. If my chief can't protect me here, I will go where you command." The boy turned and looked at her.

"What do you mean, I can't protect you? I am a great warrior. I fear nothing here or in any forest."

"I have no doubt, my chief. But I will flee this land as you will me. We must go where we are safe." The boy stood up; his eyes blazed with renewed fury and defiance.

"I am lord of this land, and I will decide when to leave and when to stay. You will be safe here. All my people will be safe. Nothing will challenge my rule!"

"By your word, my chief. My family and I thank you. Shall I prepare another meal?"

"Yes," said the boy. "I will need my strength. And then you may go about the forest and gather what you need for your family. Nothing will interfere with you here. I swear it."

Nyira disappeared into the bush, as the boy stood holding his broken little spear, guarding his jungle.

Enriquillo led Christian and Juliette and the rest of their group into the western mountains.

"You must hide yourself well," he said. "There are some good caves in this region. The slave platoons will be searching for you as well. I would say only come out at night until you know the area."

"Will you keep our location from Bruno?" asked Christian.

"Yes, just as your wife requested. I will come back later and guide you to some of the freshwater coves."

"I never thought I would see the jungle again," replied Christian. "Not like this."

"It's not like the jungle you came from," said Enriquillo. "There are no leopards."

"How do you know about leopards?" asked Christian, surprised.

"Your wife showed me. I must leave. But remember: only come down to the valley at night, to hunt and fish."

"Thank you and your healer for saving my life."

It wasn't long before a few escapees, more familiar with Christian, chose to join his band. Christian had no problem being called chief. Enriquillo hoped that they wouldn't cross paths, but knew that wasn't realistic.

CHAPTER 33

THREE NIGHTS FOLLOWING Christian and Juliette's escape, Enriquillo slipped into the stockyard on the Bissett property and let out four large sows and three boars. He also managed to retrieve two milk cows from the barn. He herded the animals toward the jungle at the edge of the property. André and three other runaways met him in the middle of the potato fields. The pigs were content, as they fed on the crop. The cows didn't seem to care one way or the other. There was a moderate amount of moonlight. Bruno and twelve more of his men were waiting in the jungle. The pigs didn't want to leave the potatoes until the men got ropes around their necks. Before they were able to get the animals up the trail toward camp, they heard a familiar voice.

"I would appreciate one of those pigs," said Christian. Bruno got quiet and drew his machete.

"You will have to take it," replied Bruno. "What do you want with a pig? You're the king of the property."

"Things have changed, Bruno. I had to leave to protect my family."

"What family? Show yourself."

"You outnumber us. I'd heard you sometimes came back to get food. I don't want to fight."

"Then what do you want?"

"There aren't many of us. We can help each other. My wife—"

"She's not your wife! Show yourself!" He began to hack wildly at the surrounding bush.

"Juliette has made me see," continued Christian. "We need to work together to survive."

"Where is she?" demanded Bruno. "Release her and I will consider sparing you."

"If you leave one of the pigs, I will release her," replied Christian.

"Where?" asked Bruno. "Where will you release her?"

"Leave the pig, and I will let the boy bring her to you."

Bruno glared at Enriquillo. "I should've known you'd know where they were. Leave them a pig!" ordered Bruno, and stalked off into the jungle. Three hours later, Enriquillo and Juliette entered Bruno's camp.

Her hair was no longer in the long flowered braids; it was short and her garment was just a plain brown frock. Someone brought her the *duho* stool that Bruno sometimes sat on. Bruno did not approach her but hid himself away in the *bohio*, as if he was still shy. Yiella brought her a gourd of water.

"Thank you, Yiella," said Juliette and embraced her. "It's good to see you again."

"You look different," replied Yiella. "Being a mother will do that."

"Yes. I suppose so. I'm still getting used to it."

"Why?" said Bruno. He'd come up behind the women as they talked.

"I—I don't understand what you're asking," replied Juliette. "You said you—"

"Why didn't you let me die...?" He didn't care if his men saw he was crying.

"Oh, Bruno, I couldn't." She took a step toward him, but he moved back. "I loved you..."

"I told you not to! I told you!"

"I couldn't," cried Juliette. "I just..."

"I had everything I wanted. I wasn't afraid because I knew you loved me. That was enough for me. Now what have I got?"

"But you have all these people who need you." She took a step toward him again. "Don't you—"

"Go away!" he shouted. "Go back to... just go away." He turned away and headed back to the *bohio*.

"I'm sorry," cried Juliette. "I love—"

"Don't say it!" cried Bruno, drawing out his machete and putting it to his own neck. "If you do, I will cut my throat. Then you will get to watch me die anyway. Go away, please!"

"We can go back now if you wish," said Enriquillo, and went to take her hand. Juliette's response was to look at him and then faint. Bruno ran to her and picked her up.

"We can take her to my hut," said Yiella. "I'll make sure she's comfortable."

"No," said Bruno. "It was me that upset her. She can sleep in the hammock."

"But where will you sleep?"

"I won't. I don't sleep much these days anyway. I will stay awake and watch over her as she used to watch over me."

He carried Juliette to his *bohio*. "Send one of the children to fetch André and Julio from their positions at the edge of the valley."

"Is she well?" asked André when he entered the *bohio*.

"She's resting," replied Bruno. André smiled.

"Well, now you can cheer up. You have her back."

"No, I don't. That's why I sent for you and Julio. She will be going back to her husband. But I don't want her to walk."

"What? Why are you giving her back? He stole her."

"No, he didn't. She doesn't belong to me. And she will not walk back."

"You want us to steal a horse?" asked Julio.

"Even a mule would be fine. Something she can ride back to her husband on. Take three men and some rifles."

They entered the property along the eastern fields, through the cane crop. During the day it was being harvested, but so far the field hands had barely made a dent. Its stalks were still densely packed, and as they crawled along the ground among them, the heat that was trapped below the leaves rose up and assaulted them. By the time they reached the edge of the fields behind the slave quarters, they were dripping with sweat. They moved quickly through this district and hoped no one noticed them—but knew that that was a slim possibility. There were hundreds of shacks because Bissett held one of the largest slave populations on Saint Domingue. Over five hundred slaves lived in the quarters, and another hundred and fifty lived in the manor house and stables, to work the dairy, stockyard, and stables. Someone was always awake in the quarters. Nothing was ever formally stated that they should be, but somebody always watched and knew what had happened the night before. André just hoped it wasn't one of the overseer's spies, or someone trying to gain favor with an overseer.

"We need to pick up the pace now," he said when they left the quarters. "In case somebody was watching and sent word." They also wore dark clothing dyed with blueberries, just so they wouldn't be betrayed by the moonlight.

When they reached the stables, André and Julio went in. André had hacked off a few stalks of cane. "For the horse," he said. "To keep it quiet as we walk it through the fields."

The three other men with the rifles waited along each side of the building, watching for someone coming up from behind. Most of the horses were asleep, but one brown mare in the third stall came and poked her head out. She recognized André and gave him a little whinny and bobbed her head. André peeled a piece of sugar cane and fed it to her. "This is Josephine," he told Julio. "She was always a light sleeper."

"Well, at least she won't fight you," said Julio. "Let's take her." They led the horse out of the stables, along the same path Enriquillo had taken when he took the white colt. Josephine was a deep dark brown so the moon couldn't give them away—besides, the clouds kept it at bay.

When they reached the western edge of the cane fields, they came out at the beach and walked Josephine about two miles along the shore. The beach ended at an embankment leading up to the road into town. It was their intention to cross the road and head back to the jungle, but as they came over the rise a troop of mounted police were just passing.

For a moment, the two groups froze as they registered what was happening. On instinct, André jumped onto Josephine's back. That's when one of the mounted policemen shouted:

"Don't move! Put down your weapons!" Josephine seemed to sense the urgency and took off before André had a chance to mount her completely—he was hanging over the side. This position actually made him a harder target, and then one of the three armed runaways fired upon the troopers. Josephine had already barreled past the troop and was in full gallop when they began to return fire. André took the shortcut through the bush at the edge of town. Once he was upright, he let Josephine have her head, feeling that if anyone got in his way or tried to stop them, they'd be run over.

Julio had taken cover quickly when the mounted police began to surround his position. When the runaway named Gaston was killed, he knew they were in trouble. He had been their best sharpshooter. There were just too many troopers with endless amounts of ammunition. When they killed the second runaway named Leland, he considered taking up a rifle, but Pasqual went down soon after. That's when Julio dropped to the ground and showed no resistance. It wasn't until they placed him in irons that he realized he would probably not stay in jail long, that the Montoya plantation would soon come to retrieve him. That is when he wished he had fought to the death.

When André rode into the camp alone, Bruno had a good idea of what had occurred.

"I was worried that somebody from the quarters would sound us out," said André. "But we just had bad luck running in those troopers like that."

Losing Julio did not improve Bruno's mood. He had been the most capable man in his camp. It was Julio that had taught the men how to load and shoot the captured rifles.

"What are we going to do, Bruno?" asked André. "We can't let them get away with taking Julio."

"Shut up and let me think," Bruno told him. He sat quiet for a long time looking out over the valley. Finally, he said: "You and six others take some rifles and get Juliette back to her husband. I'll tell you what we'll do when you return."

When André got back that evening, he had a message from Christian.

"He wants to enter the camp and talk," said André. "He waits in the forest for your answer." Bruno made him wait over an hour, as he turned the hatred he felt for him over in his mind. He finally told André to bring him in.

"Them," replied André. "He has four of his men with him."

"Of course he does," replied Bruno. "Why should they allow their chief to put himself in danger?"

Bruno sat on the front porch of his *bohio* and watched Christian approach. He had already heard the story of how Nyira had brought him back from the brink of death and healed his flesh. As he thought about this, he looked at his own wound, inflicted by this man. The *behike* was only able to heal the outside, and Juliette had ensured that nothing would heal the inside. The torches along Christian's path cast a wide shadow and brought back the memory of their battle. He only had to pick up the rifle sitting next to him and exact his revenge upon Juliette's husband. He felt that was the best way to refer to him, so that he wouldn't want to kill him. It would hurt Juliette. That's what he could tell himself. It was the best he could do.

When Christian got within five yards of the *bohio*, he stopped and looked at Bruno. All his men laid down their machetes when he told them to.

"They won't help us against guns anyway," said Christian.

"What do you want?" demanded Bruno.

"First, let me extend my deepest thanks for the hospitality to my… Juliette."

"That is why you walked all this way?"

"No. I came because I want to help you take revenge for Julio." Bruno looked at André.

"Did you not want me to tell him?" asked André.

"I haven't yet decided what I'll do."

"I know exactly what we should do," said Christian.

"What would that be?"

"We should steal Josephine and Pierre Paul."

"You want us to sneak onto the property and take Mistress Bissett's personal maid and the household manager?"

"We don't have to go to the property. She and Pierre go to the market every Monday morning. No one will expect such a thing."

"Bissett will have the mounted police searching for those two."

"Yes. We will also set the cane field on fire. It will distract them."

"No one will be guarding them," said Bruno. "So why set the cane on fire?"

"Because I want to, and it will make Bissett very unhappy."

CHAPTER 34

NYIRA'S REPUTATION AS a healer had reached other plantations. Esmerelda, acting as her shield, was the means by which a request was conveyed. She came to Nyira in the stables that evening as she brushed down three of the major's horses. Since the healing of Christian, she knew this latest task would be very hard on the child. A stable slave on the Orbon plantation had fallen forty feet from the grain loft, breaking his neck and back.

"Someone has asked for help," said Nyira when she saw Esmerelda standing quietly in the doorway of the stables. The sun went down over her left shoulder, giving her a haunted shadowy aura.

"It doesn't mean we should, Nyira. Some people are meant to die."

"So you don't want me to help people?"

"It's not that, child. We just have to be careful. If you continue these miracles, you will be at risk. We both will."

"Can we still help Bruno and Christian?"

"It's fine if you want to help those in the mountains. You're only one person. Even the priest's god can't save everyone."

"So we will turn down this person who asked you tonight?"

"Yes. I know it might seem harsh. But too many saw him fall, and know he won't live."

"And if I—"

"Questions will be asked. And you know by whom."

"Then you will tell them I can't help them?"

"I will say you only use herbs to heal."

"As you wish, Nolwazie. I promised to keep you from danger."

"And I told you, that danger doesn't adhere to the whims of a child."

Nyira did her best to abide by Esmerelda's cautions. She hadn't told her that she'd already healed a few broken limbs on the stable boys. The boys were amazed at their friend's abilities, and as children will do, they made up a game around Nyira's healing powers. They called it: Fix Me. The rules of it, to Nyira's chagrin, involved the boys injuring themselves. It was exhilarating to watch her fit them back together.

"You must tell them to stop," she told Diego. "If Nolwazie finds out, she will be angry and very frightened."

The frolicking reached dangerous levels when one boy named Stephen dove from the rafters into a bed of hay and ended up impaled through the chest by a pitchfork. When Nyira extracted the implement without leaving a scratch, she knew something terrible would have to happen to make them stop.

The game, while upsetting to her, was infinitely entertaining for the boys. She had gotten angry with Diego, because instead of dissuading them from these gruesome acts, he was amused, too.

On the day that Nyira was away at the market with Esmerelda, the grooms devised a playfully horrifying surprise on her return. As Nyira and Esmerelda pulled up to the manor in the carriage, the archdeacon pulled up beside them.

"Good day Esmerelda, Camille," replied the Father. He only exchanged a quick smile, as he expected a cool reception from the two slaves. Esmerelda stepped out of the carriage first.

"Good day to you too, Father," she replied, maintaining as cordial a tone as was possible under the circumstances. "Camille. Why don't you take the Father's carriage to the stables first? I will get the food into the pantry and get started on the meat and fish."

"Yes ma'am," replied Nyira, giving the archdeacon a glowing smile. It only served to unnerve him, and he got out of his carriage without his hat and bible. As he mounted the steps to the front veranda, Nyira turned the carriage toward the stable. The archdeacon suddenly realized he was naked of head and of word.

"Oh my goodness. I have forgotten myself," he said and headed off to the stables to retrieve his bible. Nyira, on the other hand, was just pulling the carriage inside. As she did so, she heard a scream from the rear of the stables and witnessed a terrifying sight. One of the younger boys, Jolie, was running toward her, clutching something in his right hand. It was his severed left arm, and he was impaled through the chest on a pitchfork. Nyira jumped out of the carriage and ran for the boy, as the archdeacon came in right behind her.

"I seemed to have forgotten my… what in the name

of the Lord has happened?" The boy was flailing, as blood spurted everywhere from his various wounds, especially the stump of his shoulder. The archdeacon noticed that he seemed to want something from the girl. Though she could do nothing, as the child's blood was all over her and he collapsed in her arms.

"One of you boys, go and get the house manager!" ordered the archdeacon to the stunned stable boys.

"Nyira! We were just playing," cried Stephen. "Help him, please!"

"Are you mad, boy?" cried the archdeacon. "How is she to help him? Go quickly and alert the manager to get a doctor!" Diego took off. The other boys stood around in horrid silence. The first person to arrive was Esmerelda. Diego had told her what happened. She acted very quickly rounding up all the grooms and herding them as a group into the yard behind the barns.

"Is Jolie going to die, Miss Esmerelda?" asked a confused boy.

"I don't know, child. He's very badly injured." Stephen began to cry.

"It was my fault," he said. "We were playing. I wanted to surprise Nyira."

"Surprise her how?" asked Esmerelda.

"She asked us to stop," said the boy. "She said you would be angry and scared."

"What was I to be afraid of, Stephen?"

"That she was fixing us. It was a game."

"You must all come with me," Esmerelda told them. She took them to her cottage and sat them down in the front room, to explain why their game was very dangerous to Nyira and to them.

"The archdeacon tried to kill Nyira?" asked Stephen, confused.

"Yes," Esmerelda confirmed. "And if you speak of this game again, you will be condemned as well."

"But we were just playing. We didn't do anything wrong," said Stephen.

"Your game has probably killed one of your friends. What more proof do you need? If the archdeacon had not been there, she could have saved Jolie. Never speak of this again. Or we will all burn."

They buried little Jolie in the slave graveyard on the property. The archdeacon said a few words and decried the dangers of rough play that led to sin. Nyira cried through the whole ceremony. Esmerelda wanted to tell her to stop, lest the archdeacon become more suspicious. She knew the guilt the child felt, but she had no control over the situation. Esmerelda decided it was time to take Nyira back into the manor house, so that she could keep a closer watch over her.

CHAPTER 35

ENRIQUILLO PONDERED HIS decision for a week. During that time, he avoided Agueybana's dream walks. When the mounted police captured and executed two more warriors from Jaceux's tribe, he sent a message to Guayo, Jaceux's former second in command.

"Taíno-ti nephew of my *cacique*," Guayo said embracing the boy. Jaceux had maintained a number of lower camps throughout the forest. These were where he'd planted orchards of traditional Taíno fruits. Fifty warriors lounged in the grove where Enriquillo sat down to talk with Guayo. The trees were so thick that midday appeared to be late evening.

"It's good to see you, uncle," said Enriquillo. *Guaxeri* brought platters of fruit and roasted fish and iguana. They sat them down between the boy and the commander.

"What are we speaking about, nephew?"

"First," said Enriquillo. "We should areito to my uncle's deeds."

"I agree," said Guayo. "We should have Juqi, one of my lieutenants, start first. He has the best voice of this group." He called a tall man with grey peppered throughout his hair, to the fire. Three other warriors came, too.

"These four, more than the rest of us, have kept Jaceux's deeds since his birth." The areito went on for half the day, as the men sang and danced Jaceux's life. Enriquillo did not sing, but sat and cried at the loss of one so well loved. When they stopped, Enriquillo said: "I just wanted to understand all that I have lost, uncle Guayo."

"That we have all lost, nephew."

"That is why I came to seek your help. I want to strike at the troopers who took my uncle."

"Attack the white men?"

"Yes, uncle. For my father, my uncle and my friend. They don't respect our lives, and I intend to strike back."

Guayo's hair was not completely grey, but most of it was. Still, he was not seen as an old man. He had the body and strength of a young warrior, and his eyes were still bright. Only his manner was ponderous. He considered the boy's words.

"Did a spirit perhaps hitch a ride back from the underworld?" he finally asked. "These are bold words, nephew. Not for a boy."

"My great great uncle was bold and young. He fought the Castilians for years, and their king chose peace."

"Those were different times, nephew. This is not our way. And we don't have the men or the weapons for such a campaign."

"It need not be so grand, uncle. I only wish to send a message. To strike fear and make them not so eager to kill us."

"These white men don't fear us."

"That is why we must fight, uncle. They kill us like crows."

"Because they are skilled at killing, Enriquillo. Have you sought counsel with Agueybana on this? He could call upon *cohoba*'s wisdom."

"No," replied Enriquillo.

"So you have sought no word outside yourself?"

"I only ask for a few warriors, uncle. We will not engage the white men directly."

"Attacking is engaging."

"They won't see us, and so won't know who engaged them."

"That is not logical, nephew. How will they know to fear us, if you hide your actions? You must seek the *behike*, and he will ask *cohoba* for guidance."

"He will not agree."

"Then that is my answer, too. Now we must eat." He offered the platter of food and Enriquillo took a healthy helping. He was disappointed but held no animosity toward Guayo. He was only following tradition. Once the dancing and feasting concluded, Enriquillo headed back toward his village cave. As he picked his way through the last grove of fruit trees, someone called to him out of the bush. He saw that it was Bayamo, Guayo's youngest son.

"Taíno-ti cousin," the boy said. He was two years older than Enriquillo and was tall and wiry. He and a number of boys in his uncle's village admired Enriquillo's freedom and special abilities. "We will help you, cousin. Come this way." Enriquillo had to squeeze past thorn bushes, bramble and miniature pine trees to reach the small hidden camp. It contained ten other boys close to his own age.

"What will you help me do, cousin?" asked Enriquillo. All the boys stood when he entered. Most of them he recognized. One boy of sixteen, named Kaci, was the size of a full grown warrior.

"We will help you strike at the white men." As Enriquillo gazed around the camp, all the boys nodded their assent to Bayamo's statement.

"I had hoped for warriors," replied Enriquillo. "Who would know how to fight."

"We have—"

"I will teach them," said a man's voice from the bush. He stepped out and into the light from the campfire. Enriquillo recognized him from Guayo's camp. His name was Camaguey. When he came and stood beside Kaci, he realized they were brothers.

"I intend to strike the mounted police dwelling— to set it on fire," said Enriquillo. "We won't have but a few moments."

"I will teach them to shoot a bow on the run." Enriquillo looked at Bayamo.

"You would defy uncle?"

"I feel as you do. The white men think nothing of killing us. My father only barely escaped Jaceux's fate."

"They will continue to kill us. So we must strike at the right time."

"You can go invisible into the town," said Camaguey. "See when the dwelling is less guarded."

CHAPTER 36

THE ARCHDEACON COULDN'T get over the feeling that Camille was somehow responsible for the slave child's death. The boy was actually smiling as he bled to death, as if he was playing some gruesome game with her. That wasn't possible since she'd only arrived at the scene just before him. Also the other boy, Stephen, imploring her to help the child; he really seemed to believe she could. He wondered what Artemus might make of all this. The parish carriage stopped at the stables behind the cabildo. How had he gotten here so quickly? He didn't remember leaving the Dugard property. It was obvious that Peter, the old gelding, knew the way as well as he did. He stepped stiffly from the vehicle and waved at Porthos, the new groom. He was a lot younger than the previous one—he had actually been a man, while this boy looked no more than fourteen. The archdeacon limped across the yard to the building. He would not have the benefit of Artemus's conclusions in this matter. They had spoken little since the tribunal over a month ago. He had not found the words or the courage to approach his friend. Father Dominic imagined he would simply dismiss his suspicions of the girl. He would welcome that, would like to see the light in his friend's eyes as he proffered his own argument for her. He admired the man for his convictions. He believed Father Reyes was twice the cleric he was. Only his compassion and contrary stances hindered him politically. That was a shame. He had a brilliant mind and a saint's heart. He opened the door to the cabildo and saw a tall figure move from the ante-room into the secretary's office. He became excited.

"Artemus!" He hop-limped to catch up to the figure and reached him as he made it to Philomena's desk. He grasped the man's elbow and turned him around. "Oh Artemus, I—" It was not Father Reyes. It was a priest he'd never seen. "What—? Who are you?" The man rose to his full height. He was taller than Artemus.

"I am Father Nailand," he said, smiling. He had brown eyes too and appeared to be Latin as well.

"What are you doing in here? I am Phillipe Dominic, the archdeacon of this parish." Phillipe was both embarrassed and angry that he'd been ready to pour his heart out to this stranger.

"I just arrived, I—"

"Get out! How dare you invade this office!"

"I—I'm sorry. I was just looking for some tea. One of the other priests lent me his key and said the secretary had some in her desk."

"Tea is not permitted in this office, Father Nailand. Hand over the key. I shall have a word with this negligent cleric. What is his name?"

"I believe it was Reyes. A tall fellow. He was very nice. I don't believe he meant any harm, Archdeacon. I apologize for my presumption."

"Good night, sir," said the archdeacon, as he limped to

his office and slammed the door. He immediately regretted it. Now he would have to apologize to this priest, too. Phillipe felt almost too weak to walk to the dormitories across the square.

The next morning Artemus came to the cabildo with Father Nailand.

"I have come to introduce you to Father Nailand, Archdeacon. He is the auditor from the diocese. I would also like to request the return of my key." Phillipe was too embarrassed to speak for a moment. He did reach in his drawer and hand Artemus's key back.

"I must apologize for my behavior the previous evening, Father. Yesterday was a very difficult day."

"No apology needed, Archdeacon. I am well aware of the rigors of your duties."

"Are you an archdeacon as well?"

"No. I am primary assistant to his excellency, the bishop." It was worse than he'd imagined. "I would hope to secure a key of my own so that I might begin my task as soon as possible."

"Yes. I will see to it personally." He obviously had no expectation that the audit would be favorable.

CHAPTER 37

CHRISTIAN CONVINCED BRUNO that the kidnapping would only require five men from each of their camps. Then Christian showed up to the rendezvous alone.

"I decided to send my men to set the cane ablaze," he said.

"I see," replied Bruno, not sure what to make of it. Jungle bordered the road into town on both sides, so they took up positions on the left side of the path. Bruno had brought three other men and André.

"I guess this means we will be taking them back to our camp," said André.

"Yes. I guess that is what it means," replied Christian. "But don't kill them. It would make them less valuable." Christian chuckled at his own joke.

"We should probably be quiet if we intend to sneak up on anyone," replied Bruno. He was starting to feel less comfortable with this operation. Christian was acting very strange.

"Don't worry, Bruno," replied Christian. "It will all be over very soon."

"What are you talking about? What will be over?"

"I know it's not my child."

"What are you—"

"Quiet. I see the wagon," said André. As it got closer, he realized something was wrong. "That… is not Josephine. It's… master Bissett! Run, Bruno! It's a trap!" He burst from the bush and ran across the road in front of the wagon as Bissett brought it to a stop at the spot where they were hiding. The mounted police waiting on the other side surrounded and corralled André. They clubbed him when he put up a fight.

"Don't injure him," said Bissett, who did not step down from the wagon. "I want him completely intact." Bruno had never been this close to the man. He was thin and pale and looked tired. Unlike his younger brother, Henri, who had been big and loud.

"How much is he paying you for this?" Bruno asked Christian, as they clapped him in irons.

"Well, we were only after André. You are a nice bonus. Fifty livre for the murderer of his brother. Ten each for the rest of your camp. Five for mine."

"This proves it, you know," said Bruno.

"Proves what?"

"That she loves me."

"And once again, her love will not save you!"

"You don't understand love. I told her that. And you're a fool."

"I'm the rich fool who gets to watch you hang. I also get extra for your child."

"You'll never collect. You forgot someone." Christian looked troubled.

"The boy's not here."

"Is he?" asked Bruno. Christian ran to the mounted police captain.

"Send your troop quickly, before the Indian boy alerts his camp!"

"What Indian boy?"

"He's invisible! Hurry!"

"What? That's insane." Bruno started to laugh as they loaded him onto the wagon along with an unconscious André. "Don't worry. You'll get your bounty," said the captain. "They will be upon them before they know it."

Half a mile away, Enriquillo was running as fast as he could. There were a number of shortcuts through the jungle, and he took them all. He didn't need to make it to the camp. He just needed to get to the first signal point. A system that had, ironically, been instituted by André. He also taught him how to speak and understand the drums. The mounted police troop couldn't see him, but he ran across their path as they galloped up the pass toward Bruno's settlement. The rain started as he reached and began to beat the first drum. He had been too preoccupied to notice the flat black sky above. *Huracan* was even more dangerous than white men. The *behike* would have warned him of the coming storm during the dream walk, would have shown it to him. Now he would have to work his way up the mountain on his own instincts. He couldn't get to Nyira, but he had to find Juliette and get her to a cave. Get all of them to the caves, if he could. The Taíno knew to seek shelter at any sign of "The Big Wind." The runaways would probably try to move further up the mountain to get away from the white men. Enriquillo hoped he could find them before they were trapped by the storm.

CHAPTER 38

THE ARCHDEACON HAD been visiting a prominent, ailing parishioner on the Allard plantain. The wind and rain started as he headed back to town. Phillipe had only experienced one major storm, while he was on board ship bound for Saint Domingue. Luckily, they'd caught the tail end of it—but for half an hour, the rain had come down in blinding sheets, and gales pushed the vessel ten miles off course. It was a short duration, though he remembered the way the sky quickly changed with clouds that spat lightning like an angry deity. This was the same grey slate of sky. The clouds moved as if pushed by a vengeful hand. He slapped the reins on Peter, and the horse picked up his pace. He had been antsy when they got started as if he was trying to tell the Father they needed to hurry. The archdeacon wished he had listened. The rain caught them from the east as it blew in off the sea. Old Peter let out a scream and reared when lightning blew up a coconut tree near them. When he broke into a run, it was all the archdeacon could do to hold on. Although it seemed the faster Peter ran, the harder the rain came. It was a relief when he realized Peter had a refuge in mind: The Dugard property was right on their path. The archdeacon kept a tight hold on the reins and steered the gelding in the general direction of the manor house. That's when he saw a tree had caved in the roof. He had also not noticed the water pooled a foot deep in the yard. A strong gust caught the carriage and tipped it sideways, and Peter took off again, dragging the archdeacon through the floodwaters.

CHAPTER 39

WHEN THE FIRST winds started, Nyira was in the barn, milking one of the cows for butter to churn. Suddenly the front and rear doors slammed shut. This caused her to suspect tomfoolery on the part of the grooms.

"Stop it, Stephen," she said. "I have to get this milk to Nolwazie." Then something slammed into the east wall. When she went to inspect, she saw a corral post poking through the wood. She knew the boys weren't capable of something like that. Then the structure shuddered and shifted as if something was trying to lift and tip it over. She started toward the doors, but an object struck them before she got there. She wisely decided to climb the ladder to the hayloft and look out the door above. That loft door was gone, but she got a look at the storm coming, and the lightning firing from the black clouds, like doom come to life. She also saw the water from the rain and rising surf, streaming in through the crops in the eastern fields. She had to get out of the barn and make it to the manor house. It was about twelve feet off the ground, but she was more worried about the winds. Nyira climbed down the rope for the pulley, and the water in the yard was already at her ankles. Esmerelda met her in the kitchen.

"Nyira, are you all right?"

"I'm fine, Nolwazie. But I don't think we should stay in the house. The wind is too strong." Something smashed through a window in another room, and they heard Constance scream.

"Where else can we go?"

"Where is Father Reyes?"

"He's in the parlor with Constance and Madame."

"Ask him to take Constance and Madame and the rest of the servants to the sugar mill up on the hill."

"Oh, I'm so sorry this happened on your twelfth birthday, Nyira."

"It's all right, Nolwazie. We must get through this, and that will make it a good birthday." She headed back out the door.

"Where are you going? It's dangerous out there!"

"I must find Claude and the stable boys before it gets too bad." A huge object slammed into the house. When Nyira stepped out into the driving wind, she saw the massive old coconut tree that had stood near the veranda to the kitchen had fallen on the roof. She ducked just in time as an object flew past her head. The shovel that always leaned against the chicken coop lodged itself in the wall of the back veranda. All the chairs that had once sat there were gone, and the left support beam was cracked and off its base. This made the veranda lean to the left a bit. The rising water was already up over the first step to the veranda. Nyira was happy to see Claude moving slow but determinedly toward the manor house.

"Have you seen Esmerelda?" he asked.

"She's still in the house." Just then, the chicken coop, with chickens still squawking inside, sailed past them. It caromed off the veranda and took out the broken support beam. This caused the roof to shift.

"Claude, please go in and help Esmerelda and Father Reyes get everyone to the sugar mill. It's more solid."

"I know, Camille. But where are you going, girl?"

"I will try to find Diego and the other stable boys."

"I don't think that's wise, child. The water is rising too quickly."

"I will be careful, Claude. I have to try. Please go and help Madame." They heard Esmerelda call from the veranda.

"Claude! Let her go! She will be fine! Help us, please!" Esmerelda and Father Reyes were carrying Constance. Something had struck her on the head. Madame and the rest of the household servants followed. Claude raced up the steps. The sugar mill was a quarter mile up the hill, and the rising water was already at Nyira's knees. That's when she witnessed a sight as good as magic: Two Taíno canoes floated into the yard as if Enriquillo himself had provided them, which in fact he essentially had. They were obviously those the Taíno hid in the jungle near the beach. She pushed one toward the veranda where Claude could find it, and got in the other and paddled toward the stables. The boys were probably holed up there for safety. When she got to the structure, it too had been struck by a fallen tree. The tree had hit the rear of the building, and she could still hear animals trapped inside.

"Diego!" called Nyira. "Are you in there?" Diego and a

younger boy named Martime stuck their heads out a small window on the top level.

"Yes," said Diego. "Everyone but Stephen is here. But we can't get out. Something is blocking the door to the loft."

"I'll see if I can remove it." She paddled into the stables. The heat and stink of the animals' fear was as thick as smoke, and Nyira found it hard to breathe. She let out as many of them as she could; she felt they would have a better chance outside. She saw that a small beam had been broken when the tree hit the roof and wedged itself against the trapdoor to the loft. Moving it was a risk, but if she didn't the structure might collapse with the boys inside. She concentrated all her energy on the piece of wood, and it shifted. The boards around it were also unstable and threatened to cave in the whole framework.

"I have moved it, Diego! Please come out, before it all comes down!" They pushed open the door and the boys scrambled out. Diego was last, making sure all the younger children made it out first. The canoe could only hold five of the nine boys.

"I will get the small ones to the sugar mill," Nyira told Diego. "You will have to make your way there with the rest of them on foot." The wind was roaring, and they couldn't see that well through the towering wall of rain. Suddenly a horse came barreling toward them, and it was dragging a capsized carriage through the water behind it. Nyira put out her right hand, and the creature stopped cold.

"This is the archdeacon's carriage!" said Nyira. "Diego, quick! Check it!" Diego dipped under the water.

"Nyira! The archdeacon is trapped inside!" cried Diego, when he surfaced. "We must tip it up." All the boys that were tall enough grabbed the vehicle and pushed. The water held it fast.

"Move back," said Nyira. I'll bring it up. She put out her right hand, and the carriage rose out of the water and sat on its wheels. The archdeacon was unconscious. Nyira climbed in and touched his chest.

"He's still breathing. Let's get him to the mill." They left the archdeacon in the carriage. The other boys climbed in as well, as Diego sat at the reins. The boys in the canoe used boards that were floating in the water to paddle in the carriage's wake. As they made their way, they came upon a gruesome sight: Josephine Mallet, the household manager, floated face-up past them. Something had caved in the side of her skull. Nyira let out a cry and dropped her paddle as she tried to get to the woman. The boys in the canoe had to stop her.

"Please, Nyira!" they implored. "We can't help her. We must get to the mill." Still crying, Nyira picked up her paddle again. They passed four more bodies along their path. Apparently getting to the mill had been more difficult than Nyira expected. When they reached the high ground, Diego and the boys carried the archdeacon through the front door of the mill. There were more injured when they got inside. One of the most severe was Esmerelda.

CHAPTER 40

THE SEAWATER COVERED the road and was rising steadily.

"Monsieur Bissett," said the mounted police captain. "We will not make it back to your property. We need to find high ground."

"I don't know, captain," replied Bissett. "I'm afraid I will lose this slave before he can be properly punished."

"Never fear, monsieur. We have him in irons. There's no place he can go in a storm like this." An object flew by the captain's head, taking out the trooper to his left. "We must get out of this wind, quickly."

"I know a large tall tree not far from here," said Bruno.

"What kind of tree, slave?" asked Bissett.

"A giant elm, at the edge of your property. It's the best chance we've got at this point."

"You know this area, Christian?" asked the captain. "He wouldn't have a sentry set up there?"

"No, captain. The only men that came down the mountain with him are here now. I made sure of that."

"I guess we can try it then," said the captain. "We don't really have a choice. Lead the way, slave."

"You'll have to take the leg irons off," said Bruno. "So I can walk."

"All right," said the captain. "Take the irons off him. But if he makes any move to get away, shoot him."

"Don't worry, captain," said Bruno. "I have no desire to escape." They set off with troopers in front using machetes on the thick foliage. The wagon wasn't really suited for the jungle, but they made much better time away from the muddy seawater of the road. The deeper they got into the jungle, the thicker the foliage became. When they were about halfway through, the horses and the wagon got stuck in a swampy bog. The horses panicked and tried to turn, which flipped the wagon and tossed everyone into the muck. Bissett was furious.

"You did this on purpose!" he screamed as the mounted police pulled him and the others from the sinking mud. When he got to his feet, he snatched the whip on his hip. Bruno didn't try to shield himself and just stood looking at the old man. The whip was ineffective anyway, as it got caught in the dense branches and vines. Bissett only succeeded in looking more helpless as he wrestled with the worthless item. He finally gave up and leaned wet and exhausted against one of the cedar trees.

"I'd shoot you if I didn't intend to sell you," he said.

"I don't see how this is my fault," said Bruno. "I didn't make it rain. I'm trapped out here, too. We're all going to drown if we don't get to that tree."

"We're going to have to walk the rest of the way, monsieur," said the captain. "The wagon and horses won't make it through all the bogs in here."

The mounted troops dismounted and released their

horses. The rain and wind had picked up, but the jungle's thick canopy and dense foliage shielded them somewhat. The water was still rising, but they seemed to be traveling uphill, and it was only at their knees. A half an hour into their forced march, they lost their second mounted trooper. They had been trying to cross what once had been a quiet little stream, with a footpath of small boulders laid by the Taíno, to sit upon and fish. It was now a raging torrent, and one man fell into it when he lost his footing on the rocks.

"There is normally a small trail here," said Bruno, as they made it to the bank. "But I recognize these trees. It's not too much further." Bissett did not look well, and the strain of moving against the force of the water and driving wind was taking a toll on him. He'd already collapsed once, and would've been swept away were it not for one of the runaways getting his hands on him. The water was at their waists now. Two mounted troopers held him up.

"I would like to make a request, captain," said Bissett.

"What is it, monsieur?"

"I would like the use of a pistol so that I might execute my slave now. I don't believe I will make it to that tree." André was suddenly distressed.

"Wait! I didn't mean it!" he cried. "It was an accident!"

"Hold him!" said the captain. Three troopers took hold of André as the captain handed Bissett his pistol.

CHAPTER 41

ENRIQUILLO SAW THE bodies of four runaways with rifles when he made it to the camp. They had obviously been holding off the troopers so the others could escape. There were three dead troopers as well. Someone had attempted to burn the structures, but the wind and rain had snuffed it out. They had made their escape through the dense forest, which made it hard to pursue them on horseback. As Enriquillo searched the forest, he saw horses wandering loose. There were more dead runaways along the way, as they fought while retreating. He discovered about twenty horses tied as a group in a small copse of trees. The troopers were on foot. He heard weapons fire nearby. As he moved cautiously through the bush, he came upon another dead runaway. This one only carried a long bow with twelve arrows in a manati skin quiver. It had been a gift presented to Bruno along with the hammock and *duho* stool. The bow gave him an idea about how he might get through the attacking line of troopers. He wouldn't have much accuracy from distance with the winds, but he didn't need distance. The gunfire was close. As he came over a rise that led into a small gulley, three troopers guarded five runaways. Two others lay dead. One trooper was executing those lying wounded on the ground nearby.

"No use taking wounded," the trooper said.

Enriquillo set up behind a tree about five yards away. He hit the first guard in the center of his chest. "Near the heart," as Camaguey had instructed. The man let out a gasp and went down. When the executioner turned around, his heart was available, too. The third trooper, witnessing the invisible attack, must have assumed they were surrounded because he ran. One of the runaways picked up the first trooper's weapon and shot the fleeing trooper in the back and then shot the executioner again when he moved. Enriquillo walked over to the first man he'd shot and looked down at him. He didn't know how he was supposed to feel. This was the first white man he'd intentionally killed. But the man made a sound and turned over. He was bleeding badly, and the arrow had broken off when he'd fallen. The trooper looked at him. He had eyes the color of the water in the secret cove. The man reached out, and his face was anguished.

"Water," the trooper said. "Give me water." Enriquillo didn't like this. This man hadn't hurt him, and yet he'd caused him pain. "Water!" he cried again. He didn't know what else to do, so he rushed around the camp, searching for a gourd or a canteen. By the time he found one, he heard a shot. When he ran back to the trooper, he was already dead. Finished off by one of the runaways. A boy about Kaci's age and size, with angry eyes.

"Next time, kill them better," the boy snarled at him. Three of the surviving runaways gathered up the troopers' weapons and went in pursuit of their comrades. The others stayed to strip clothing and shoes from the bodies. Enriquillo didn't want to look at the other trooper he'd shot, for fear he might still be alive, too. He would have to answer for them before he could enter *Coaybay*. Something strange twisted in his stomach, and his head felt like it was coming off his neck. He bent over and everything he had eaten that day came out of his mouth. He didn't feel good. What was happening to him? Was this the sickness of those who've killed? He wanted to sit down, as his strength seemed to be seeping out of him. He had to get away from here. Then he heard a cry from the bush:

"Someone help us, please!" It was a woman's voice, and it sounded familiar. He searched through the forest until he discovered them hidden under some blown brush and broken branches. When he moved it aside, he found Juliette holding onto Yiella, who'd been shot in the shoulder.

"How did you get here so quickly?" he asked.

"I have a horse. When I heard the drums, I came to find her. I was almost too late. We hid when we heard the troopers coming, but she got hit anyway."

"We must get her to a cave before the storm catches us," said Enriquillo. He asked one of the remaining runaways to help them get Yiella on the horse. "You should get on too, Juliette. The cave is further down the mountain."

"We need to hurry," said Juliette. "She's bleeding a lot." Enriquillo took one of the trooper's horses and led them to a small cave hidden within a group of large boulders. It was along the route of a Taíno shortcut over the mountains. He'd only learned of it from Jaceaux in the last year. He helped Juliette down, and they both took Yiella from the horse. She was very weak, but Enriquillo had learned some wound cleaning and bandaging techniques from Nyira. There were pots and a supply of water in the cave. They made a fire to heat the water. Enriquillo went out and found herbs he had seen the girl use to heal the wounded on that first night in Bruno's camp.

"I have to go and help the rest of the Bruno's men get away," he told Juliette.

"Thank you, Enriquillo," said Juliette. "I can manage it from here. I've learned some things from Nyira, too." He rode hard to get back quickly. He found the last three runaways hiding in the jungle near the camp.

"You're the invisible Indian boy," said the boy with angry eyes. "You can sneak in closer than we can. Can you shoot one of these?" He handed Enriquillo one of the flint-lock pistols.

"No," said Enriquillo. "I prefer the bow."

"Okay then. We'll follow you. We can attack from the rear. If you kill a couple of the last guards, we can make an opening for our men to escape through."

"I have to kill more of them?" He looked ill at the suggestion.

"Yes. It's their only way out. Don't worry. It gets easier." It didn't get easier, and he was only able to keep going with constant urging from the angry-eyed boy. He shot one man guarding the rear, and the arrow went through his neck. He didn't die right away, but the runaways stabbed him to death before he could cry out.

"This actually works better," said Angry. "We can finish with a knife all who don't die quickly." Enriquillo preferred this method as well as any. As long as he didn't have to look the men in the eyes again. The next trooper he came upon was guarding a group of six runaways. He took position five yards away in the bush. When he shot the man, he let out a cry as he fell. The runaways moved up quickly to finish him, but a second trooper stepped out of the bush armed with two pistols and opened fire. Angry died first. The other two runaways shot the trooper, but his second gun went off as he went down and shot Enriquillo in the chest.

CHAPTER 42

WHEN NYIRA ENTERED the mill, she went to Constance first. The girl had been struck by debris when she stepped onto the veranda. Madame was sitting holding her daughter's hand, while Father Reyes was tending to the archdeacon.

"I can clean her wounds if we can get a fire going in the hearth."

"Do you know healing, child?" asked Madame.

"My father was a healer," said Nyira. "I was taught by him. Where is Esmerelda? She should help me."

"Claude carried her upstairs to the loft," said Daphne.

"Why did he have to carry her?" asked Nyira. Daphne hesitated.

"Esmerelda said you should tend to those down here. Claude wi—" Nyira rushed up the stairs. The second-floor loft was where the grinding wheel pushed by the slaves was located. Esmerelda was in the far corner by the window, lying on a pile of straw.

"Nolwazie," cried Nyira and went toward the cook. Claude blocked her.

"She asked that you not see her, Camille."

"But why? What has happened?" Claude choked up a bit.

"It's what she requested." Nyira tried to get by him again, and he grabbed her. "Don't, Camille. Let her go in peace." Nyira looked him in the eyes.

"I can help her, Claude. You want me to help her." Claude's huge hands slipped away.

"Yes," he said. "I want you to help her." Nyira rushed to the corner, and almost screamed when she moved the straw away. A stake protruded from Esmerelda's chest.

"Oh, Nolwazie," she said, fighting back tears. She rushed back downstairs. There were buckets of ash by the hearth. She dumped one of them and headed out the door.

"What are you doing?" asked Diego.

"Nolwazie is hurt, and I'm going to help her."

"If you fix her they will know, Nyira."

"Start a fire in the hearth please, Diego." She stepped outside with the bucket.

She used all her power to push back against the wind and hold up the bucket to catch water. She anchored herself against the wall of the mill. When the bucket was half-full, she ran back inside. Diego and Daphne helped push the door closed again. Diego had gotten a small blaze going with a few pieces of wood and straw. Nyira made it a full blaze by looking into it. She tore off pieces of her dress and poured half the water into the kettle hanging inside the hearth. When it didn't burn fast enough, she gave the heat a boost to get the water to boil. Father Reyes came over to watch her.

"What are you doing, Camille?"

"I must clean Esmerelda's wounds."

"That won't help her, child. Her wounds are…" Nyira looked him in the eyes.

"It's not that bad, Father. I can help her." Father Reyes looked confused for a moment.

"Yes. You're right, child," he said. "It's not that bad. You can help her." Nyira took the water up the stairs. Claude was sitting beside his wife. He could obviously do nothing but look upon her. He held her hand and let tears fall from his eyes.

"Claude you should go back downstairs," said Nyira. "I will tend to her now."

Claude wasn't sure why he agreed to such a thing, but he did and moved hesitantly down the steps. Nyira sat the bucket and rags next to Esmerelda.

"I hope you don't mind, Nolwazie. But I need a section of your dress, too. It's going to take a lot to wipe all this blood off." She rolled Esmerelda onto her side and tore the dress away where the stake had gone through her back. Esmerelda let out a groan that sounded like: "Please don't!"

"I'm sorry, Nolwazie. I just can't let you die. No matter what happens. Now hold still. I'll try to make this hurt less." Nyira put her ear to Esmerelda's chest, to listen for how close the stake was to her heart. She finally decided to pull the rod out of her back. The wood made a popping sound as it dislodged from Esmerelda's breastbone. Nyira had to stop from time to time when Esmerelda's body started to convulse. She put her ear to her chest again, to make sure her heart hadn't stopped. She would've liked to get it faster, but wanted to make sure the stake didn't splinter from the force she put on it. The entire process took almost forty-five minutes. The one mistake she made, she didn't leave a scar. She made

Esmerelda sleep as she wiped up all the blood, and wrapped and covered her chest. When she awoke, Esmerelda cried:

"What have you done, child?"

"She has saved your life," said Father Reyes, who stood about ten feet away. "And condemned her own." Nyira spun around and tried to make eye contact with the priest. Artemus quickly turned his head. "I've felt your power, Camille. You have influenced me once. I ask that you not do it again."

"I only seek to protect her, Father. I mean no harm."

"I believe you, child, and I still sense no evil in you. But that won't save you."

"Will you keep my secret, Father?"

"I am bound by my vows, Camille. And I am not the only one who knew her injury was mortal."

"When the storm passes, you must leave," said Esmerelda. "That is your only hope, Camille."

"What about you, Nolwazie?"

"I can't leave Claude. I don't know what he would do without me."

"You may have to consider it, Esmerelda. For I am bound by God to confess my sins."

"But she is not a sorceress," said Nyira.

"She has known, child. She has taken you into her home. The church is very specific in this."

"I had hoped to avoid this. You should have let me die, Nyira."

"I am not capable of that, Nolwazie. I promised to keep you from danger, and I failed. I'm sorry." Diego came up the stairs.

"Nyira, Madame has requested you come tend to

Constance. She has not awakened. Madame is afraid." Nyira looked at Father Reyes.

"If I help Constance, could she be condemned, too, Father?"

"No, Camille. Only those who were aware of your powers and concealed them."

"All right," she said. "Tell Madame I will be right down, Diego."

When Nyira got to Constance, the girl was very pale. More than usual and her breathing was very shallow.

"I will lay her head in my lap, Madame," said Nyira. "If you will allow it." The woman was obviously very fearful, but she moved aside and allowed her daughter's head to rest under Nyira's hands. She sat for a while cleaning the wound on Constance's head. Madame watched this very closely, her expression of perpetual surprise had devolved into stressed exhaustion. Her eyes were red from crying. Finally, Nyira put the cloth down and sat stroking the girl's face; her eyes soon opened.

"Mother?" was the first word she spoke.

"Oh, thank heavens!" cried Madame. Constance sat up slowly. That's when her mother took her in her arms. "My dear, dear child. You have frightened me."

"I had a strange dream," said Constance. "Camille was in it."

"Yes, child. It was Camille that nursed you back to me." Constance looked at Nyira.

"Thank you, Camille. That wasn't your name in my dream."

"That hardly matters, my child," replied Madame. "It was only a dream. Now you must rest again."

"Your name is Nyira," continued Constance. "I also saw your village and your people. How was that possible?"

"I don't know. I was hoping very hard for you to awaken. Me and your mother."

"That is not important," said Madame. "Rest now, and you will eat when you awaken."

"How was that possible, Camille?" This from a revived Archdeacon. "How were you able to share so much of yourself with Constance?" He was still very weak and was propped up by a pile of sacks near the window. "I ask this because I had a similar experience. Did you touch me as well, child?" Nyira didn't like where this was going.

"A number of us did, Father. When we righted the carriage, while you were trapped in the water."

"But I saw the face of your father, and I know his name. He was a healer."

"Yes he was, Father." Nyira sat quiet for a time after this exchange. She had no idea her touch had this kind of effect on people. It made her sad to think of her father again, at this time. She wondered if he would recognize her if he saw her now. The thought saddened her, and she couldn't help but cry to herself a little.

"I hope you realize that this is a form of sorcery, child," continued the archdeacon. "I shall have to convey this to the diocese." Nyira had no reply to this statement.

"That is not possible," said Madame. "She is not an evil creature, Archdeacon. She has saved my Constance, and you."

"It is a matter that the Church will decide, Madame."

"Will she be harmed by this inquiry, Father?" asked Madame.

"She was able to place a portion of her soul into another human being by touch, Madame. That is confirmed by myself and the girl. I have no choice but to send this information to the Bishop. I would be in violation of my vows not to." Madame looked stricken at this reply.

"But were it not for her touch, my Constance—"

"There is no need for further discussion, Madame," said the archdeacon. "Church doctrine is very clear." Father Reyes came down the stairs at that moment and sat down beside the archdeacon.

"You need to preserve your strength, Phillipe," he said. "Now lay back and rest." The archdeacon didn't argue with Father Reyes. He just sighed and complied with his direction.

The rain and wind had continued its onslaught, and the water had started to seep in under the door.

"We will not have the fire long," said Diego, as he stepped in a puddle on his way to add another item to the blaze.

"We had better move the injured upstairs to the loft," said Father Reyes.

"Oh, disappointment!" cried Madame. "I had hoped to have bread made from this fire."

"I'm sure you can leave a few slaves down here so they could make some," replied Father Reyes. When Madame beckoned the Father to come and sit beside her, she whispered:

"I am concerned about Camille. The archdeacon has decided to call an inquisition because she has touched him and healed Constance."

"Yes. I expected this," replied Artemus. "She has performed a miracle upon Esmerelda. I watched it myself. She removed the stake and saved her life."

"They will kill her," replied Madame, at this revelation. "My Constance would be dead if she had not touched her."

"Yes. And she is yet healing those in the room here," said the Father. "But there is no way to save her now that her secret is known."

"We must find a way, Father. I will free her before I see her destroyed. She is not an evil being. I do not agree with the Church."

"I am conflicted, of course. Because I am bound by the strictures of my order. And you will be in danger if you attempt to conceal her."

"I will not attempt to conceal her, only to help her get away."

"I must stop now. To even consider such a thing is blasphemous." They began the process of moving the injured to the top floor. Father Reyes wanted the storm to subside but knew another would be right on its heels after Phillipe's report to the Diocese.

CHAPTER 43

WHEN BISSETT PULLED the trigger, the gun didn't fire. He turned it around and gazed at the firing mechanism and powder. "It's wet," he said and tossed the weapon into the water.

"Don't worry, monsieur," said the captain. "We shall carry out your wishes when we reach the tree."

"That is not acceptable," said Bissett. "I want to see this slave dead. Why don't we just drown him?"

"That is not practical, monsieur. He might take some of my men with him."

"I don't care about your men!" screamed Bissett. "This slave murdered my brother! My brother!" They could all see that the planter had lost his reason.

"We must get going again, monsieur," replied the captain. "Someone help Monsieur Bissett to walk." When a couple of troopers took him by the arm, he became enraged.

"You will unhand me, sirs! I will not be moving until this creature is dead!" He tried to raise his leg so he could kick André, but lost his balance and pitched backward in the water. The troopers pulled him out.

"I do not want your help, sirs! Leave me!"

"What are you asking, monsieur?"

"Just what I said. Leave my slave with me."

"But monsieur," cried the captain. "If we left you, it would be certain death."

"As long as he dies, too. That will do, captain."

"Monsieur Bissett," said the captain. "Please reconsider. We are but a few clicks away from the edge of your property."

"Chain me to my slave, captain," demanded the planter. "I will deal with him in my own way."

"Sergeant," directed the Captain. "Chain Monsieur Bissett to his slave."

"But captain," replied the sergeant. "What if he is overpowered?"

"Monsieur understands the consequences."

"Yes I do, captain," said Bissett.

As three mounted troopers held on to André, the sergeant clapped both men in the same pair of cuffs.

"I shall leave you with a key, monsieur," the sergeant told the planter. "Should you succeed in your task."

"Thank you, sergeant. It will come in handy." Once the captain saw they had fulfilled Monsieur Bissett's request, they moved on through the flooded jungle. When André gazed at the planter, he was shocked at the hatred in the older man's eyes.

"I have the key to these cuffs, slave," said Bissett. "Perhaps you can get it from me before I kill you!" He snatched up a floating branch and clubbed André over the head with it.

"But if I die, I will pull you down with me, white man," replied André. Bissett swung the branch again, but André was quicker and caught it, snatching it away.

"Are you going to kill me with that?" asked Bissett. He purposely pitched over in the water and dragged André down with him. André managed to get to his feet, the water was chest level by this time. He realized that Bissett was insane and if he was going to get the key away from him, he had to be more aggressive. The planter surfaced, coughing up water and howling with laughter. André had heard that deranged men did not feel pain. He had to take a chance if he was going to survive.

"I have the perfect place to keep this key, slave," said Bissett. He placed the cuff key in his mouth. André jumped him and shoved him under. He got his left arm around Bissett's throat, to make sure he couldn't swallow the key. He shook his master as hard as he could as he held him down. He was drowning, too. He just hoped Bissett had taken in less air than he had. It wasn't going well. The old man fought hard, and he was scratching at André's arm and pummeling him in the face with his right fist. Still, he held on. He then dragged Bissett up and put his hand over his mouth. When he opened it to take a breath, André took the key out and took him down again. Bissett had no strength left this time. André was just strangling him then. Finally, his master went limp. When he came up for air this last time, the water was just below his chin, as he had a body weighing him down. He took another breath and went down to free himself from the cuffs. He came up and swam toward the nearest tree—a medium-sized palm. It was already tilting in the wind, so he didn't think his refuge would stand for long. All the larger trees were down. Then he saw something that gave him hope: one of the troopers horses swam past him. He knew it was a long shot, but he imagined that that horse knew where it was going. He jumped for it. The horse wasn't frightened. All he wanted was to swim alongside until it got used to him. He took hold of one of the stirrups to keep pace.

CHAPTER 44

THE ELM TREE was standing up well in the deluge. Only a few of the troopers made it there. They had had to swim once the water got so high. It was the only skill Bruno retained from childhood. The river had been a playground for the children in his tribe. The troopers had to remove all their weapons to stay afloat. Not all of them managed to accomplish this before the water overcame them. Five of them drowned this way. Four more drowned when they panicked as the water kept rising. Christian knew how to swim as well, also the captain. There was no more need for guards. They all knew where they had to go. Well, actually only Bruno knew, and they were following him. He was now glad he had only brought a few men. Neither of the last three survived the swim. As they came upon the tree, there were others already inhabiting it: three men and a woman. They had probably been hiding in the jungle after placing a potato there. Bruno recognized the woman. It was Babette, Juliette's sister. The runaways in the tree saw them and threw a vine down to Bruno first. He was a bit weary from the swim but was able to brace his legs on the trunk and repel himself up with the long vine.

"I expect that we will be mounting the tree too, soon," said the captain.

"You're Bruno," said one of the men waiting in the tree.

"Yes," replied Bruno.

"I'm Maurice. Me, Francois and Babette were coming to join your camp. And we were bringing these." He handed Bruno a machete.

"Thank you, Maurice," said Bruno, taking the weapon. "Well, as of this moment, this is my camp." Babette came over and embraced him.

"How is my sister?" she asked.

"I don't know," replied Bruno. "We should ask him." He referred to Christian as he made his way up the trunk. "Maurice and Francois, please tie Christian to a lower branch. If he resists, you can chop his head off."

"You do remember that you are still our prisoner, slave," said the captain.

"There are no more slaves here, captain," said Bruno. "And the only prisoners are you and your men. Welcome to my camp."

Maurice and Francois climbed down to a lower branch to intercept Christian. There were only three troopers left, including the captain. They had ample limbs to tie them to.

"I also have some good news for you and the others, Maurice," said Bruno. All the runaways rejoiced at news of the Master's imminent demise.

"So you say Master ordered the troopers to leave him chained to André?" asked Francois.

"Was he out of his senses?" asked Maurice.

"I can't say for sure. But he was willing to risk everything to kill André."

"André will not die easily," replied Francois.

"That's what I'm hoping—though his chances are slim." Babette climbed down to the branch Christian was tied to.

"How is my sister and her baby?" she asked.

"You mean Bruno's baby, don't you?" said Christian.

"I mean my sister and her baby."

"Get me one of those machetes, and I will tell you." Babette climbed back into the upper branches without her answer.

"You will pull me up, slave," said one of the troopers to Francois, as he tried rappelling up the tree by a vine; none of them held. "Pull me up, I say, and I will limit the number of lashes you receive for escaping." Francois thought about it for a moment and then tossed a vine to the trooper and hauled him into the tree. The trooper seemed very pleased with himself when he arrived. "Now that is a good sla—" Francois hit the trooper in the face with the butt of his machete. The man fell headfirst back into the floodwaters.

"There are no slaves here!" cried Francois. "I am a free and clear man!"

"You will pay for that," replied the captain. "If he doesn't come up, you will hang."

"You will hang if you don't shut up," said Maurice. "I lost a good friend to one of your patrols, captain. And I no longer have a master." When the captain made it up the trunk, they secured him to a branch away from his remaining man and Christian. The one Francois struck had not surfaced again.

"What have you to eat?" asked Bruno, as the wind gust picked up and slammed into the tree.

"We have fruit and some bread," replied Maurice. "It's

wrapped in oilcloth and tied to a branch further into the canopy, to protect it from the rain."

"It's about time for your baby to come, Bruno!" yelled Christian, over the wind. "Hopefully the wind doesn't blow it away." He chuckled at that idea. Bruno climbed down to the limb Christian was secured to.

"I want you to know that if we survive this storm," said Bruno. "I am leaving you in this tree and sending word to the slave quarters that you are here."

"So you are afraid to fight me then?" said Christian.

"That is an option, too. We shall see." A powerful gust pitched the tree left and right, and a surge of rain battered the inhabitants like a wet club. Christian discovered that vine did not make the best tying rope, especially when wet. He was soon able to loosen his restraints. When Babette climbed down with food, he asked: "Are you going to feed me?"

"Yes," she said and placed a bit of wet bread into his mouth.

"Will you help me get one of those machetes?" he asked Babette. "Because if they kill me, you will never learn the fate of your sister."

"Even if I do," replied Babette. "You will still be outnumbered."

"I only have to kill Bruno. Then you will all be a part of my camp."

"You won't hurt me, will you?"

"Why would I hurt you? You're my wife's sister."

The next morning when she came to bring him some fruit, Babette also smuggled a machete. When she turned to leave, Christian grabbed her and slit her throat. He then pushed her body out of the tree. When he climbed out of the lower branches, Christian discovered that Bruno and the other men were waiting for him.

"I warned her not to trust you," said Bruno. "But she was desperate to know the fate of her sister."

"It doesn't matter," replied Christian. "My wife hardly ever speaks of her. But I would have told her that her sister carries the child of a dead man." When Maurice and Francois made a move toward Christian, Bruno stopped them.

"This is my fight," he said. "Neither of you are allowed to help me. No matter what."

"But what if he—"

"Then so be it. Just make sure my wife and child get to safety."

"No more talk!" yelled Christian, as he slashed at Bruno's legs from below.

"No need to jump," said Bruno, as he used a vine to swing out of the arrow of rain that shot into the branches. He brought the blade down so hard against Christian's sparks flew. Christian wasn't ready for Bruno's burst of power and lost his footing.

"That's the only slip you get," replied Bruno. Christian lunged, holding a vine and barely missed Bruno's head. He'd ducked and got a nick on his forehead.

"Once again, I draw first blood!" cried Christian. Bruno dove at him again. When Christian tried to swing away, Bruno cut the vine. Christian dropped and hit the branch below him. There were more than enough vines to keep him from falling out of the tree. The fall definitely knocked the wind out of him.

"Now who is slow getting up?" said Bruno. He swung down and knocked Christian off the limb, with a knee to the chest. "That was for sweet Babette." Christian grabbed a small branch as he fell. It snapped under his weight. He dropped his machete as he plummeted through the branches, and hit a number of them on his way to the water.

CHAPTER 45

AGUEYBANA DID NOT trust the horse, but he couldn't fly and needed to get to the boy quickly. Guayo had shared his discussion with Enriquillo concerning his intent to attack the white men. The *behike* was already aware of the boy's intention. He hadn't needed a dream walk to know Enriquillo's heart. They had set out right after the storm hit. This was the time *cohoba* had shown it would happen. Agueybana just needed to find the exact spot in the mountains.

"The beast needs to slow down," he told Guayo. "I have to listen to the wind. It's too loud now, but *cohoba* has shown this trail."

"We shouldn't slow down too much, *behike*. Lest his soul be gone when we get there. Hold on tight. We must run." A number of the warriors were trailing them on their own horses. "Look! There are bodies," cried Guayo. "This must be the dark *cacique's* settlement. We're close." They dismounted and rushed into the jungle, passing dead troopers and runaways.

"It's not much farther," said Agueybana. "He has left a few bodies of his own. It's as I feared. We must hurry, Guayo. His soul will be hard to find if it escapes his body!"

The old man broke into a run, and it was as if he made no movement. Guayo and the warriors had never seen anything like it. Before they got to the woods, he ran back past them, carrying the boy.

"How did you—" said Guayo.

"Hurry!" said the *behike*. "I can't run as fast while I'm holding him. We must get to your horse, Guayo." It occurred to Guayo that the boy had been taller and larger than the *behike*. He wasn't now. He looked like a small child in the Agueybana's arms, and there was a lot of blood.

"You move so fast," said Guayo. "Why not use your speed to get him to your cave faster?"

"I have attached his soul to mine, and he is draining my energy. If I run, I won't be able to maintain it. If he dies, he takes me with him." The horse wouldn't cooperate.

CHAPTER 46

"THERE MUST BE some type of restraint," said the archdeacon to Madame Dugard.

"For what reason!" cried Madame.

"Just until this storm has passed and the mounted police can take her into custody."

"She is not a danger, Phillipe," replied Father Reyes. "Why should we restrain her?"

"So she cannot escape, Artemus. Had you not considered that? Some leg irons should be sufficient."

"We shall do no such thing," said Madame. "We don't put shackles on our slaves. We don't even have any."

"I only want to make sure the girl doesn't flee, Madame," said the archdeacon. "Have you at least some rope in this structure?"

"I have never been in this structure, Archdeacon. But I know we don't restrain our slaves."

"Then how do you keep them from running away?"

"We don't because they never do. It's unnecessary."

The archdeacon was aware of this fact but had never thought about it in any concrete way.

"So you have no means of securing your investment?"

cried the archdeacon. "That seems very irresponsible, Madame."

"On whose part, Archdeacon? Ours for not abusing them, or the slaves for not running away?"

"This discussion is pointless, Madame," replied the archdeacon. "I, as the church's representative, take custody of this girl. Father Reyes, please ensure that the child does not escape."

"I will do the best I can, Phillipe."

"We should probably search out some mechanism to keep her on the premises."

"I think we already have it."

"What would that be, Artemus?"

"The storm, Archdeacon." The archdeacon was quiet for a time, as he considered a reply.

"I would feel better if there was some rope involved, as well. I would do it myself, but I don't yet have the strength to stand."

"I will see what I can do." Artemus was starting to feel a bit of anxiety because the storm's strength seemed to be subsiding. He went and spoke to Nyira. "You must be ready when the storm ends, child. The archdeacon has taken custody of you."

"I am not concerned for myself, Father. I have not had to protect myself since I have been on this island. I fear for Nolwazie."

"That is true. He has not considered her; he is so focused on you."

"I would ask that you help protect her and Claude, for he is a true innocent. And Nolwazie will do anything to keep him safe. Would he be—"

"Yes, child. He is condemned as well." Nyira turned to look at Claude as he sat with Esmerelda's head in his lap and his hand stroking her face and rubbing her shoulders. "I have faced all manner of threat since my village was destroyed over four years ago, Father. This condemnation is something I never imagined. Even if I gave you my life, it would not save them?"

"No, Camille. It would not. They will seize all who attempt to coddle and conceal you."

"But I have listened to the stories of your God. His life was sacrificed to save others. Is that not something you hold dear?"

"It is not the same, Camille. It's more difficult to explain. And it will not save you. Simply stated: The powers you possess are meant only for the divine. I will leave it at that." As the Father finished speaking and sat quiet for a time, he heard a very unsettling sound. Silence. The storm's winds had abated, and someone was outside the mill, calling Madame's name. When he went to the window and looked out, there were boats arrayed around the mill, and standing in the bow of one of them was Major Dugard.

CHAPTER 47

THE RUNAWAYS SEARCHED the floodwaters for Christian.

"Maybe he's dead," said Maurice. "He hit a lot of limbs before he fell into the water."

"I will believe that when I find his body," said Bruno. "Now we both have a missed opportunity to kill the other. We must keep watch."

The water was not peaceful as the wind moaned and the rain growled and crashed into the tree. "I hope this storm passes soon, because we don't have enough food for a long stay in this tree," said Bruno.

"I have seen pigs swept by in the water," said Francois. "We could capture one and slaughter it."

"That will only be possible when the rain stops," said Maurice. "Because we would need to make a fire."

"We expected to be at your camp by now, Bruno," said Francois. "Or we would have brought more food."

"It does us no good now, though," replied Maurice. "We will have to think of something. Perhaps there is fish."

Just then, the body of the trooper that Francois struck floated near the tree. It looked like he might be caught on a vine. He didn't move with the churning water and seemed to be attached to the trunk of the tree.

"I don't know if I would eat fish from this water," said Francois.

"Why don't one of you go down and cut him loose," said Bruno. "So he can go with the tide." Francois took the task since it was he that killed him. He repelled down and got the task done quickly. The body was carried away by the churning floodwaters.

"We will wait a day and see how this progresses," said Bruno. "Then we may have to go back to the plantation to look for food."

"I had hoped not to see it again," replied Maurice.

"If we can locate some potatoes, or find the smokehouse, you will be happy."

"You're right. Hopefully, everything isn't under water."

"We can hope," said Bruno. "But we still have to swim a distance to find out."

"I still remember how, I think," said Francois. "I was the fastest swimmer in my village as a boy."

It took the storm a little more than a day to pass. In that time, the water rose five more feet up the trunk of the tree. When the winds and rain stopped, Bruno and Francoise got in the water and swam toward the center of the property, not aware of what they'd find or what refuge they might get to before fatigue set in.

CHAPTER 48

WHEN AGUEYBANA APPROACHED Guayo's horse, the animal backed away, pawed the ground and tried to rear. Guayo tried to hold it, but the stallion wouldn't allow them to place Enriquillo onto its back.

"There must be something else around the boy's spirit that's scaring this beast," said Agueybana. "I will have to frighten it away if we want to get him to the cave in time." He placed Enriquillo on the ground and lay beside him. The *behike* appeared asleep but had actually pushed his spirit out of his own body and into Enrquillo's. He recognized the thing immediately.

"It is a knef," said the *behike*, getting up and going to Guayo's horse

"What kind of creature is that?" asked the commander. Agueybana untied a pouch from Guayo's horse's long thick mane.

"It's a creature that feeds on fresh vulnerable souls. I'm glad I got here when I did, because if that thing damaged the boy's soul and he dies, he will be left wandering with no possible rest. They're attracted to war and death." He took a hand full of something from the pouch and laid back beside Enriquillo. Once he was back inside the boy's spirit, he took the cemi from around his spirit's neck and placed it around Enriquillo's. *I would fight you myself*, he told the flimsy one-eyed being. *But I must get this boy to his home, so I can save his life.* He also flung the handful of burned gold dust at the thing to disorient it for a while. It blinked when the dust landed in its eye and floated off. Agueybana then went back to his own body. "Quick! Let's get him on the horse! The dust won't hold it for long, and the Cemi won't matter if he dies." They put Enriquillo on the horse, and Guayo rode away.

"They will have everything ready when you get to the cave," said the *behike*. The commander saw a blur of him shoot up a trail leading over the mountains. When Guayo reached the mother cave, a number of ni-taíno tribe members were already waiting. They wrapped Enriquillo in a cotton garment and quickly took him into the cave. Higuamota was in the dark chamber with the *behike*.

"Give me your hand, Higuamota," said Agueybana. The *cacica* presented her hand, and the *behike* sliced it in the palm. He then placed it on the wound in the boy's chest. "He has lost a lot of blood. So we must be very diligent in replenishing it throughout the night."

Meanwhile, Enriquillo was in a fight. The knef had returned and was pursuing him. He was running and shooting arrows at it and ducking when it swooped down at him. He tried hiding in the forest, but wherever he went, it was there waiting, as if it knew what he was thinking and what he might do before Enriquillo did.

Agueybana was worried because the boy wasn't getting stronger, and he was sweating like he was working in the sun, when the cave was cool.

"I think I know what's happening," said the *behike*.

"The monsters are chasing him?"

"Not the ones from his dream. The thing that would feed on his weakened soul must've come back. You will have to go and help him, Higuamota. Let him know he has nothing to be ashamed of, that he is safe here with us." Higuamota lay down beside her son while keeping her hand upon his chest.

"Don't fear, my son. I'm coming to give you courage." The *behike* placed his hand on the *cacica*'s stomach, which was the center of the soul.

CHAPTER 49

WHEN THEY HAD swum for about twenty minutes, Bruno recognized the tree that stood out behind his old shack.

"We could climb it and take a break for a moment," said Francois.

"No. Let's not," replied Bruno. "We have a bit further to go. There are more trees along our path. So we should try to make it to the middle of the property if we can." They swam on. The first body they found was the boy, Octavius.

"He must have been heading to put a potato in the jungle, too," said Bruno.

"No. I doubt it," replied Francois. "This boy and his father were known informers for the overseers. He was probably a spy."

"I will never understand how some slaves can do such a thing. Especially when it gains them nothing."

"Maybe some extra food or no lashes for a month," said Francois. "Bissett wasn't going to free him." They came upon a few floating structures which Bruno realized were shacks taken apart by the winds. Some of the debris was buoyant enough to climb upon and rest awhile. They took turns, so as not to sink it. They were trying to make it to the slave quarters, but Bruno had forgotten about the ancient coconut tree that stood midway into the property, right after you got out of the eastern fields. It was leaning badly. Not quite to the water, though it might not be long before it plunged in. There was a woman and her child in it. They had found a way to tie themselves to it. He couldn't imagine how they had survived this long in the awful power of the winds and rain.

"Hello!" Bruno called to the mother.

"I recognize her," said Francois. "That's Simone, and her son's name is… was Nicholas." The woman didn't respond. She looked glassy-eyed. Bruno wondered when was the last time she'd eaten. The body of her child was tied to her back. It lay as if it were sleeping, with its head leaning on her shoulder. She barely seemed to notice them—if she did at all. She must have been trying to get to the jungle as well. They took a moment to rest against the leaning tree.

"If we can find some food, we will come back to you," Bruno called to her. The next stretch took them into the slave quarters. There weren't any buildings, but some industrious individual had built a rather sturdy looking raft. There was a man and his two children on it.

"That's Charles, the carpenter," said Francois. "His wife died last year, and he's been trying to keep his children from being sold away from him."

"He won't have to worry about that now," replied Bruno.

"Hello!" cried Charles. The children, a girl and a boy clung to their father. "Francois! Is that you?"

"Yes! It's me, Charles, and this… can we come aboard your raft?"

"Yes," said Charles. "Who is that with you?"

"This is Bruno. Remember—"

"Arnaud's young friend! Yes. You look different now, Bruno."

"That's probably because I am tired, Charles. Can we board?"

"Oh, yes. I'm sorry. Just make sure you come from opposite sides. So we don't tip from your weight." This made sense to Bruno, so they did as the slim short man suggested. Bruno came up on the side of the little girl. The child looked a little scared, but what she didn't look like was hungry. Francois came up on the other side, near the boy. The children didn't look more than four or five. But when they boarded, Charles had a surprise: a pistol pointed at them.

"Now I know you, Francois, but I am going to protect my family. So don't do anything stupid." Bruno liked this man and decided he would invite him to be in his camp. If he didn't shoot him.

"That probably won't shoot," said Bruno. "What with all the rain. The powder is surely wet."

"I'm not a fool, man. I made sure to wrap it in some oil-cloth. Now if you two want something to eat, I've got some food and some water."

"You did this before the storm, didn't you, Charles?"

"Yes. I was going to get some of the other slaves to help me get it to the shore behind the property."

"I don't know how far you would've gotten, but I like your idea," said Bruno. Charles had some meat wrapped in oilcloth, too.

"I know where he got this!" said Francois. "Charles built the smokehouse."

"Where did you hide this thing?" asked Bruno.

"In the grass under the trees behind the *calenda* field. I've been working on it for a year. Since after Miriam, my wife, died. I have to get my children away before master sells them."

"You don't need it anymore," said Francois. "Bissett is surely dead. He won't be selling anyone."

"I don't think that will last," said Bruno. "This storm is over, so there will be other masters soon. I have another idea you might consider." The raft was very well constructed, and even had a makeshift sail to take advantage of the ocean winds. Bruno knew it was a plan doomed to fail, though. He was lucky to have met Charles because if they survived and made it back to the mountains, they would need someone to help rebuild the settlement. They took off from the raft after Charles gave them some idea of what shape the manor house was in. The mistress and most of the children had perished as well when the floodwaters overwhelmed them. Charles had also told them that there were still a number of overseers hiding around the property. He had shot one as they made their way toward the raft behind the *calenda* field.

"Just be careful," said Charles. "I left a stash of smoked meat in the barn—if it's still standing. I had to leave it. There was only so much I could carry with the children, even on a horse."

CHAPTER 50

NYIRA WAS TOO busy tending to the sick to realize the significance of the major's arrival, but Esmerelda wasn't.

"You must hide, Nyira! Please, go now!" The girl put down the bloody rag she was using to wipe the face of an injured house slave.

"Where am I to go, Nolwazie?"

"I—I don't know, child, but—"

"Where will you go? You are in danger, too."

"Don't worry about me! Please run!"

The major was calling into the building:

"Madame Dugard, are you well?" he asked. Madame left Constance's side and rushed to the window, but she couldn't manage to get it up.

"Someone, please help me to open this," she cried. "I must speak to my husband."

One of the slaves obliged her. "Yes, Ferdinand, my love!"

"Is Constance—"

"Yes, she is well, too! Please get us out of this structure!" She broke down in tears again.

"Never fear, my love. I shall toss up a Jacob's ladder to the window. Have one of the slaves catch it." This was done. Christophe, the butler, caught the thing. He called to Gilbert the blacksmith and a large field hand named Felix to hold and secure the ends of it.

"Gilbert, will you hold Constance so that she might get down the rope first?" There was no need. The major had climbed up himself. He was an older, slim man, but he took his daughter in his arms like she was still a small child. "Hold on tight, Connie. We go back down to the boat." He deftly descended the ladder as those in the mill watched. A trooper situated in the boat took Constance from his arms. And then Madame made a suggestion that had to do with Nyira's safety.

"Now you must go, Archdeacon," she said.

"Yes, I will help you to the ladder, Phillipe," said Father Reyes. The archdeacon was halfway to the window before he realized what was happening.

"I will wait until last," he said. "To stay with the child. You should wait as well, Father Reyes."

"It's not necessary," said Madame, a bit distraught. "I will stay with my slave, Archdeacon." Phillipe was on to this attempt at subterfuge.

"I am sorry, Madame, but she is no longer your slave. I have taken possession of this witch in the name of the church."

"She is not a witch!" cried Madame, and looked like she might cry, but realized it wouldn't deter the archdeacon. "I will stay anyway. To see she is treated well."

"As you wish, Madame. Christophe, please ask Major Dugard to dispatch mounted police to arrest this... sorceress?" He looked at Nyira. "Is that the proper term, child?"

"Yes, Father," replied Nyira. "It is the proper term." Esmerelda broke down in tears.

When a mounted policeman came through the window, the archdeacon asked him a question:

"Have you a pair of shackles in your possession, sergeant?" This brought an anguished cry from Madame Dugard, and Father Reyes went and consoled her.

"She has saved our lives, Father! Does that mean nothing?"

"No Madame. No, it does not."

As the trooper approached Nyira to place the shackles upon her, Esmerelda brained him with the water bucket.

"Run, Nyira!" she cried. "Get away, girl!"

"Nolwazie, what are you doing?"

A second trooper climbed through the window, pulled his club and rushed Esmerelda. Nyira stepped in his path and pointed at the club; it burst into flames, and the trooper's sleeve caught fire. Soon he was almost engulfed in flame. The man staggered to the window and jumped into the water.

"Someone stop this witch!" cried the archdeacon. "She will burn us all!" It was Artemus who found the solution. He picked up the hem of his smock, came up behind her and covered Nyira's head.

"Now be still, child," he whispered to her. "Don't give them a reason to harm you."

"I'm sorry, Father. I only meant to protect Nolwazie."

"Someone cut the cloth and tie this covering around her head," said the archdeacon. "Thank you, Artemus. You have saved us." Father Reyes didn't reply, instead whispered to Nyira:

"You have not helped your case, Camille. Now they fear you."

They used a separate boat to transport Nyira—in a pair of shackles, no less. They took her to the only undamaged vessel anchored in Port-a-Piment's harbor and locked her in the hold. Nyira was consumed by melancholy as she descended the ladder. Where was her beloved Benzia when she needed her?

Chapter 51

When Enriquillo saw his mother, he knew she would be in danger.

"I am here my son," she cried. "You must—" The knef went for her at once.

"Mother, run!" He threw himself in the path of the thing. And something about his gesture made it back away.

"What is that, Enriquillo?"

"It wanted something from me when I was afraid. But now that you are here, it seems to want it from you. We must get away."

"No, Enriquillo. We will not run. It feeds on weakness and fear. I saw how it backed away when you bravely came to my defense. We must fight it together. I will not be afraid and neither should you." Enriquillo realized she was right. But there was must still be something clinging to him because the thing still waited.

"You are a good son, Enriquillo," said Higuamota. "The ancestors will welcome you when it's your time."

"Mother, I have done terrible things. I have killed," he said and sat down and sobbed. "I was sick from it. I am a killer!" The knef moved toward him.

"You have only injured, my son. *Cohoba* showed the *behike* the battle. You have only wounded. Others completed the kill."

"But the white man on the mountain," said Enriquillo.

"That we cannot take away. You will answer him with his own crimes, that prompted your fury."

"That's true," said Enriquillo. "I was blind with anger over Abiodun's death." He got up and looked the knef in its one eye. "I am not afraid of you. We have nothing you want." He picked up a hand full of dirt and flung it at the thing. It began to fade as Enriquillo and Higuamota advanced upon it. "It's fading, mother. Now I know its weakness. If your spirit is strong, it can't hurt you."

"I believe you are correct, my son. Now you must awaken." She disappeared, and he was alone.

CHAPTER 52

THE BARN WAS partially submerged, but a good part of it was yet above the floodwaters. As they swam into the yard, they saw a number of individuals on the roof of the structure. At first, Bruno was afraid they might be overseers. As they drew nearer, he saw they were not. Although there was one white person among the group, a boy of about eight, it appeared.

"Who is that?" Bruno asked Francois.

"That is Gustave, the master's son."

"Maybe all the overseers are dead?"

"It's possible but unlikely," said Francois. "There are many more structures on the property." Before Francois could finish his statement, a boat came around the side of the structure, carrying a group of white men.

"I should have known someone would have access to boats," said Bruno. "We need to stay out of sight before they—" Another boat came up behind them.

"We have them, Mister Miles!" said a white man in the boat.

Francois submerged quickly, followed by Bruno. They had to put some distance between them and the boats.

Bruno went the opposite way to Francois, feeling they'd have a better chance if they separated. Bruno's lungs felt like they were going to burst as he pushed himself, desperately trying to find a structure to surface next to. He finally noticed what looked like a series of boards, about twenty yards away from their original spot. He came up slowly and saw it was debris, and not far from it were a group of floating bodies. One of them was a white woman. The others were a black man and a woman. He thought he recognized them. These must be the remains of Mistress Bissett and Josephine and Pierre Paul. There was no way to be sure since they were badly bloated. He turned around and saw the manor in the distance. It had shifted sideways like an unbalanced ship. He submerged again and moved west toward the house. He didn't know if he would find food there, but perhaps a refuge from the overseers in the boats. He stopped at the old tree that had stood near it. It had fallen over, and he worked his way around the trunk. He waited a moment to be sure no overseers had concealed themselves around the corner. When he was about to move, something grabbed his foot. Francois came up grinning near him.

"I was wondering why it was taking you so long."

"You nearly scared me to death," said Bruno, and might have hit him, if he hadn't wanted to conserve his energy.

"I have been in the manor house," said Francois.

"What did you find?"

"I haven't looked yet. I was waiting for you."

"Lead me to it," said Bruno.

"We have to go through a rear window. There are items blocking the front door. They must have been trying to keep some of the panicked slaves out."

"And they waited too long to get out themselves. I found Mistress Bissett and her maid and butler not far from here." They swam around behind the sloping manor house and climbed in through the back veranda. Bruno had never been in the house, obviously, but he was struck by the grandeur. His father had told him about the palace of the King of Kongo and described the walls coated with gold and the bright, colorful interior, and the people in all their finery. There were no people here, of course. But from the crystal chandelier that hung from the ceiling in the large central room, to the golden drapes upon the windows and the elegant paintings along the walls with silver flecked wallpaper, it was still the grandest place he'd ever been in—but no masters. He knew that was temporary. When the water receded, this would be a slave owner's manor house again. The thought infuriated him. If it were possible, he would burn this building, burn this whole place.

"Look," said Francois, "let's go up the stairs and see what's up there." Bruno wasn't sure that was wise, though it was above the water. They swam toward the marble stairs rising out of the floodwaters and leading to the second floor. When they reached them and pulled themselves out of the water to rest, Bruno realized how fatigued he was and regretted this rest, because it was deceptive. They would die if they stayed here too long—either that or be recaptured. Francois didn't appear to need a rest. He sprang from the water like an excited boy and ran up the steps.

"Come on. I want to see what's in here," he said. Bruno got up slowly.

"Wait, Francois," he said. "We should get out of here."

"What? But why? I have always wondered what they—"

"I don't like the way it feels in here."

"It's quiet, that's all."

"It's—" They heard something fall and shatter in one of the near rooms.

"Someone's still here!" Francois ran up the stairs and turned the corner.

"Francois, wait! What the hell are you doing?" Bruno ran up after him.

CHAPTER 53

THE GUARDS IN the prison were afraid of Nyira. Especially after they heard how she set their comrade on fire. She had to wear a hood, but they made a point to be very kind to her. They were told not to feed her very often so that she might grow weaker. None of them wanted to risk her being unhappy, so they fed her the best water and food—from their own personal rations. There was an opening in the hood so she could eat.

When she had been in the hold for a few days, Father Reyes came to visit her.

"Good morning Camille," said the Father. "It's Father Reyes."

"Hello, Father. Is it morning? I can't tell."

"I would have them remove the hood while we speak. You won't set me on fire, will you, child?"

"I could never do such a thing to you, Father."

"Good. Then I would like to talk with you a while." He looked at the guard "You may remove the hood, sergeant." The man was hesitant for a moment, but finally stepped up and removed the lock and little chain that secured the hood in place. "Is there possibly a seat or a stool I could sit upon, too?" The soldier left and returned quickly with a sturdy tall stool for the priest.

"I'm glad you've come, Father," said Nyira. "I was starting to get a little lonely."

"I don't see how that's possible, Camille. You and I both know you could leave whenever you chose. Isn't that right?"

"Yes," replied Nyira, sitting down on the bunk in her cell to look upon the priest."

"So you really are a sorceress, Camille?"

"Yes, Father. I have been since the day I was born."

"And are you in league with Satan, then?"

"How could you ask me such a thing, Father?"

"It is not I who will be asking, Camille. I'm only trying to prepare you. I do have something that's been troubling me."

"What is that, Father?"

"The powers you used to set the trooper's club ablaze, where do they come from?"

"I don't know, Father. I had never done such before. I was only trying to protect Nolwazie."

"So you had no knowledge of this ability until it happened?"

"No. I never know until the moment I or someone I love is attacked." He leaned forward, sighed and placed his head in his hand.

"This is what I feared." He stayed quiet for time as he considered the implications. "You do understand, that this is the reason you are all to be condemned. You, Esmerelda, Claude and the boys."

"Have they taken them? They're not sorcerers, Father."

"It is written in our texts and our doctrines, Camille. That your kind and any that would shield or coddle you shall be condemned to fire." Nyira turned her face to the wall and cried a little. "But the question that is most crucial, Camille: is would you harm others to protect them?" Nyira sat for a moment sniffling and looking down at her hands, as a bit of sunlight came through the portal and cast small shadows off them onto the floor by her feet. She finally looked up at him.

"I don't care what happens to me, Father. But I have no choice but to protect those I love."

"I see. They would burn someone with even the hint of your powers, child. And you could very well destroy this town and everyone…Lord give me strength."

"I have only ever sought to protect those I love, Father. Where are Nolwazie and the boys? Are they safe?"

"I don't know. They have been arrested, though. I believe the archdeacon is keeping them hidden, to control you."

"Where? Everything was destroyed by the storm."

"They've been busy constructing new barracks for the troopers and new jails. But they are not anywhere I can find."

"Are you not in danger as well, Father? Just by speaking with me?"

"I am committing blasphemy. Like you, I am more concerned for others than myself. And I fear what you might do."

"I don't choose to do anything. I have only sought to live with those I love, and who love me."

"What if you I can locate your family, child? At least Claude and Esmerelda?"

"Why would you do that?"

"I am only being practical, Camille. You and the others will have a trial. The diocese will send a vicar general to organize and preside over it. Unless they designate the archdeacon, a prosecutor will be appointed. These are all formalities. They don't need evidence. Their ultimate end is to execute you and your family. When that occurs, you will be forced to protect them, causing the troopers to attack you, and be slaughtered. I seek to prevent that. Now, if I can find them, could you get to them by some means?"

"I, or someone that I send, Father."

"Someone that you...there are others like you? Where child?"

"It doesn't matter. They, like me, are only concerned with the safety of those they care about."

"But you must promise not to harm others, Camille."

"I promise to do the best I can, Father. I have no control over what other people might do." Father Reyes got up and left the cell after Nyira's reply. He was well aware of what "other people" would do and felt it best he get to the girl's family as quickly as possible.

CHAPTER 54

"WE MUST NOT interfere, Enriquillo," Agueybana said. This after Enriquillo learned that Nyira had been captured and likely faced execution for witchcraft.

"How long was I sick?"

"It took us two weeks to heal your wound and secure your soul," replied Higumota.

"I should have seen it in my dreams. Why didn't she come to me?"

"She is being condemned for healing those injured during the storm," replied Agueybana. "The white men have always had a strange type of justice. It is based on cruelty. She was condemned by the very one she healed."

Enriquillo was still weak and had not fully regained his stamina. As he lay in his father's hammock, he remembered something from his first dream with Nyira, that he only had to want something and he would see it. He had an idea—and very much wanted to be a small insect to carry it out. His first couple of tries at wanting, nothing happened; and afterward he was exhausted. The next morning, when he opened his eyes, there was a fly alighting on his nose. This insect sat for a moment, rubbing its legs together and looking in his eyes:

You are going about this all wrong, it seemed to say. He realized it was right. So he took a small dipping gourd out into the jungle. When he got to the remains of the fish they'd cleaned the evening before, he trapped one of the flies swarming over the smelly pile and took it back to the hammock. He didn't tell anyone what he was doing, and while he was healing, Agueybana didn't do a dream walk with him.

He ducked under the covers on the hammock and released the fly, and spent that day and the next two studying its every detail. On the fourth day, he let it go and then sat down on the floor of the *bohio* and wanted again. After two hours of this, one wing sprouted from his back.

This is much easier in dreams, he thought.

Then a scary thought occurred to him: *What would happen if I became a fly, but one that was the size of a human?* It would frighten Higuamota and probably the whole village. So he wrapped a blanket around his shoulders and went out to the secret cove to practice wanting. It took two more days for the second wing, and he was actually able to take off and fly up into the trees. But he had to use a vine to get down because he didn't know how to fly down. He had to remind himself to keep trying to get small as well. By the end of the week, he could transform completely into a fly. When he flew over to the cove to have a look at himself in the waters, it frightened him. A fly had so many eyes that he was horrified, and wouldn't do that again. Once he'd mastered the shape, he had to shrink himself down. It was only after he had attained fly smallness that he realized how many spider webs there were in the cove. He was caught by one as he rose into the air to fly out of the pine and elm trees. When the spider tried to attack him, he grew out to the size of a pine-apple to escape.

When he arrived at the ship where Nyira was being held, he couldn't find her. He'd never been on a ship. It occurred to him that he didn't need to know where she was, he just had to follow the white men; they would lead him to her. When they entered the hold, he still didn't see her but heard her voice.

"Here is your meal, Camille," said the guard. "We have placed some fresh bread here, too. Please let us know if you want more." He placed the plate on the floor not far inside the door.

"Thank you, Paul," said Nyira. Enriquillo realized that she had a hood upon her head.

"What are you doing, my love?" asked Enriquillo, as he crawled up her arm to her shoulder. "Why are you allowing yourself to be held in this way?"

There was a mounted police just outside her cell, so she could only speak to him in his mind.

Enriquillo. I am so happy to see you. They are holding my mother and Claude and the boys in some secret place. Father Reyes told me as much. The archdeacon believes I will not try to escape if they are hidden from me until the trial. He's right, of course. I'm bound here until I learn of their whereabouts.

"But what if they've already been killed?"

I would know if Nolwazie was dead. The archdeacon knows I will do nothing as long as they're safe.

"But they mean to kill you; you know this. Why don't we escape and search for them while you're free?"

They won't live long if I don't stay here. I have to,

Enriquillo. I'm the reason their life is in jeopardy. I have to do all I can to save them.

"Even if you die? Even if I lose you? What about me, and our life together?"

You are strong Enriquillo. You will still be strong without me. I don't have a choice. My heart would die if I left without them. I wouldn't be much good to you then. So please be patient. I sense they are well, but they must have them a distance from me. I can no longer hear Nolwazie's thoughts.

Enriquillo left the cell dejected. He couldn't argue with her. He would do the same if his mother or Agueybana were held captive somewhere. He made it back to the cave before his mother knew he was gone. There had to be something he could do. He would not accept the loss of his dark princess. Not without a fight. He lay down in the hammock and rested a while. The transformation had sapped his strength. He knew now that he had to save it for emergencies only. He had an idea but would wait a few days before he acted on it.

CHAPTER 55

HER NAME WAS Cassandra. Both Bruno and Francois had heard of her, but only glimpsed her once. In a carriage, beside Master Bissett. She was a slave, but there was no way to tell by looking at her. She was about sixteen, tall with auburn hair and brown eyes. She was the most beautiful person on the property. The mistress hated and resented her, of course. Bissett paraded her around the town like a prized colt, and he refused to sell her. She was his daughter, so it wasn't even considered. She was hiding behind the armoire in the first bedroom when they rushed in.

"What are you slaves doing in here!" she said. "Get out. Or I'll call the overseers!" Francois was not fazed in the least. He just stood there grinning like a fool who'd just captured an angel or a unicorn.

"I never thought I'd get this close to her," whispered Francois, as if the girl wasn't standing right there in front of him. "What are we going to do with her, Bruno?"

"We need to get out of here, Francois," said Bruno. "We're not going to do anything with her."

"But we can't just leave her. I want to touch her." He moved forward, and the girl backed all the way to the window.

"Get away from me! I'll scream."

"You better do as she says. We can't take her with us, you fool. Let's go look for the food and get out of here." But Francois was transfixed. "Let's go, Francois. We—" Someone outside yelled into the building.

"Hey! Anybody in there!" Francois rushed the girl and put his hand over her mouth.

"Okay, girl," he said. "We don't mean you any harm. We're just looking for some food. Nothing else. Tell us where you've got some and we'll leave you in peace." She nodded her head, and he took his hand away.

"I'll tell you on one condition," she said.

"What condition, girl?" asked Bruno. He didn't like the sound of this.

"You have to take me with you when you go."

"Yes! Absolutely!" said Francois. He almost started to dance at the idea.

"No! No! No!" said Bruno. "Are you insane? They might be waiting out there for us when we come out."

"I'm not insane. I'm in love," said Francois.

"You can't leave me here, Mistress Bissett wanted me to die. That's why she wouldn't take me with her. She had Josephine tie me to the bedpost." She still had the rope tied around her wrist. "But Josephine doesn't tie too well. I'm glad it wasn't Pierre Paul."

"They saved your life," said Francois. "The master and the mistress are both dead." Cassandra thought about the implications of this for a moment.

"What about Gustave?"

"He's up on the barn with some of the slaves," said

Bruno. "We can't take you, girl. We swam in here. We have to swim out soon, too."

"I can swim," said Cassandra. "I was taught with Gustave. I can read and write, too."

"None of which we can eat. You'll just slow us down."

"Then I want to put a potato in the woods. Can you help me do that?"

"It's underwater. He wouldn't find it."

"If you try to leave me, I will scream, and they will come back." Bruno pulled out his machete.

"We need to cut her throat and get out of here, Francois."

"No wait, Bruno!" said Francois. "Let me talk to her first."

"Well, I'm going to go look for some food or whatever they have we can take with us." Bruno left the bedroom and walked cautiously up the hallway like the place was still inhabited by the Bissett family. He didn't know what this girl was up to. For all he knew there were others hiding up there. When he searched the rooms down the hall, he found a stash of smoked meat in a cabinet next to the bed in the largest bedroom. This was probably the bedroom of the master and mistress Bissett. There was a large armoire with expensive looking clothes. He also found a pistol and ammunition. He didn't think he'd need the weapon but tucked it in his waist anyway. He cut a sheet to wrap the meat in and tied it around his waist. He then went back down the hall to the first bedroom to get Francois so they could leave.

"I can't leave," said Francois.

"What's the matter?" asked Bruno. "Are you injured? I'll swim close to you. You'll be fine once we get in the water."

"I can't leave her, Bruno. She wants to escape. We have

to take her." Bruno considered using the pistol in his waist, but it wouldn't take care of both of them. It would also make a lot of noise.

"You are a fool, Francois. I don't know why I didn't see that when we started. How is she going to swim with what she's got on? Not to mention she's a white woman. She'll stand out."

"I'm not a white woman. I just look like one. And if I stay here, I won't be safe without master to protect me."

"I'll give you a few more minutes to make up your mind, Francois. Then I'm leaving." Bruno hoped the man wouldn't be difficult, because he didn't want to have to kill him, or the girl. He went back and searched the bedrooms again. Francois had to know his was a foolish idea.

CHAPTER 56

NYIRA WAS CORRECT in her blind assessment: Almost everything in the town had been destroyed. What still stood included the forty-foot bell tower and the cabildo, which had been badly damaged but was yet intact. Most of the structures built with granite or limestone had held up, too. That meant the church still stood and a few brick buildings as well. Unfortunately, the stores were all gone. The public market was just an empty flat space as if it had never existed. The auction house was also badly damaged. The section that had existed before the large brick auction area was added had collapsed. Artemus had witnessed the devastation after a war: the final campaigns during the war of Spanish Succession. This, along with the scent and sight of death, was not new to him. The dormitory had washed away, along with most of his cowls and his papers. The priests, as a rule, did not maintain many possessions. He did miss the journals he took notes in and a pendant given to him by his mother when he left for seminary. They were now housed inside the chapel, which had a number of offices now used for quarters. These were only for senior clerics. The deacons resided in tents on the land where the dormitories once stood, and thus assisted in their re-building. The cabildo was cleaned and the damaged furniture removed as the carpenters replaced the paneling and the baseboards along the walls.

A week later, Artemus was having a casual conversation with one of the troopers guarding the cabildo, when he asked where they were keeping prisoners, with no jail available. At the end of a week of subtle inquiries, he received a message from a captain of the mounted police, a man by the name of Patrick Dumaine. Captain Dumaine had not consented to meet the Father at the church as he'd requested. Instead, Father Reyes was directed to meet him at the rear of the newly constructed livery just off the downtown square of Port-a-Piment. Artemus found this strange but decided that perhaps the man was operating so far outside channels, that he didn't want to be discovered. He could definitely appreciate that.

It was a late afternoon meeting, and being it was in town, he didn't need a buggy, so he walked.

The livery was closed at that point in the day. Or perhaps the proprietor had boarded all the horses and buggies his establishment could hold. Artemus entered through the stables. He suddenly realized how strong and unpleasant the smell of horses and their dung was. Why this should occur to him then, he didn't know. The parish had also rebuilt the stables behind the cabildo, but the odor of it had never seemed this strong.

Perhaps they're not cleaning it properly.

He moved quickly past the stalls and headed toward the office. The door was open, and a lamp was lit.

"Hello?" called the Father. "Is anyone about? I have an

appoint—" A short, bald, fat man stuck his head out of the rear of the office.

"Yes? How may I help you?"

"I'm Father Artemus Reyes. I have an appointment with Captain Dumaine."

But someone else came out of the office behind the little man. It was the archdeacon. Father Reyes was flabbergasted.

"I… what are you doing here, Phillipe?" The archdeacon just stood and gazed at his fellow priest for a long moment.

"I am here as Captain Dumaine," he finally said.

"What? What are you saying?"

"What are you doing, Artemus? That is the quest—" The archdeacon's knees buckled, and Artemus rushed to his side.

"I'm all right. Just let me sit for a moment." The stable owner rushed over with a chair for the priest.

After the archdeacon had recovered, the stable owner brought him a cup of liquid.

"Here you are, Archdeacon. This should help revive you." Phillipe accepted the cup without question and to Artemus's surprise, took a sip.

"Oh, that is quite delicious! What is this wonderful concoction?"

"It is only tea, Father."

"Oh… well, it's delightful. Thank you, Monsieur Devoe." Artemus stood watching this scene, still not sure what it meant.

"When did you decide to become Captain Dumaine, Phillipe?"

"I didn't decide to do anything, Artemus. I was forced to. To save you from yourself."

"I don't—"

"At the very least you have committed blasphemy, just by speaking with the child. And with the plans you made, you fell into coddling. If I had allowed you to reach her parents, that would be concealment. For you to stoop to these acts, she has obviously bewitched you in some way."

"She is not evil, Phillipe..."

"You—" The archdeacon tried to stand too quickly, but his legs wouldn't cooperate. "You are a... let me calm down a moment. My heart feels like it might come out of my chest." He took another sip from his cup and found it empty. "Monsieur Devoe, might I have another cup of this?"

"Yes, Archdeacon." The little man retrieved the cup and returned with it a few moments later. Phillipe took a sip to resume his argument.

"You are a most gifted cleric, Artemus. But your heart makes you a fool. You are lucky that I stopped your demonic errand when I did. For you were headed towards the gallows, and I am implicated as well now. But by heavens, I couldn't see my only... I am not loved, as you are. I have only you to spar with sometimes, and we... are we friends? I have never had one before, so I'm not sure."

"Yes, Phillipe. We are friends."

"Then you must forgive me for what I must do, my friend. For your own safety. Guards, please come." Two mounted policemen came from the rear of the stables behind Father Reyes.

"Phillipe, what are you doing? This is not necessary."

"Yes, it is, Artemus. Until the vicar general comes and I can be sure you are no longer under the sorceress's influence."

"So I am to be placed in jail, then?"

"No. Nothing that harsh. You will be confined within the renovated auction house."

"But this is insane."

"No more than what you were planning, my friend. I am just thankful that the guard who reported you held you in some regard. Otherwise—oh, I don't even want to think about it. Guards, please take him away—and please be gentle with him. He's only a danger to himself."

The two mounted policemen escorted Father Reyes to a wagon waiting in front of the stable. They did not place him in irons (Artemus was grateful for that), but one sat beside him in the front, while the other rode behind on his own horse.

CHAPTER 57

WHEN BRUNO WENT back to the bedroom, he saw a strange but not unexpected sight. Francois was holding Cassandra on his lap.

"We have to go, Francois. We can't wait any longer. The sun's going down, so we should be able to get away before they see us." Francois didn't seem to have heard him.

"I can't go, Bruno. I can't just leave her," replied Francois. He looked strange to Bruno. His eyes were glassy and his movements lethargic, like a man who'd been drinking too much of the palm wine the slaves produced. "She can't swim out with us, so I have to stay and protect her, Bruno."

"You have lost your mind, you know. This is a trap, and you've fallen into it. How are you going to protect her?" Francois furrowed his brow as he thought about this and then looked frightened for a moment. But Cassandra wrapped her arms around his neck and looked Bruno in the eyes.

"He'll keep me safe," she said and placed a kiss on Francois's cheek. Bruno saw the way the man's eyes lit up, that it was like a type of poison subduing him, muddling his thoughts.

"I can't leave her, Bruno." Bruno could see he was lost.

"Okay. If that's how you want it." He backed out of the room and went down the stairs. He tied the meat around his neck, feeling since it was smoked it should be fine. The pistol would be useless once it got wet, and it was just something to add more weight. He climbed through the window on the back veranda, and waited almost half an hour, near the fallen tree. He wanted it to be dark, in case anyone was waiting in ambush. When the night descended, he swam underwater, only surfacing periodically to take in air. He did this until he was a good distance from the manor. All the markers they'd followed were there. The moon was out of the clouds and very bright when he got to the raft with Charles and his children.

"You'd best come with me, Charles," he told the carpenter. "You can't just sit here. The water level is going to drop in few days. I have a good place to hide while we wait." He handed him the meat he was carrying. "You can put that with the rest of the food." They paddled the raft half the night until they made it back to the big elm tree.

"Hey," said Maurice. Then he looked puzzled. "Charles. What are you doing here? Where's Francois?"

"I need to rest for a while," said Bruno. "Then I'll tell you the whole story."

"They are going to kill him," said Maurice, when Bruno finally told him. "That's why I didn't want to go back there."

"He's knows that, too," said Bruno. "But it's like he's stuck inside some dream and can't free himself."

"Some of the slaves told me stories they heard from the ships when they worked on the docks," said Charles. "The sailors talked of sea sirens who lured men away from the ship.

They were always very beautiful, and when the men rowed out to them, they would drag them down to the depths."

"It sounds like what's happening to Francois. I couldn't save him. If I'd stayed much longer, I would've been trapped, too."

CHAPTER 58

THE EYE OF the storm must have passed over because André noticed that the wind had shifted, and wasn't pushing against them as much, but the rain still beat at them. Fatigue had begun to slow him down, so he gave a few desperate kicks and got a hand on the saddle horn. From this position, he was able to mount the horse. He realized his body might weigh the animal down, but it was better than sinking on his own. The horse's survival instincts were what he was relying on. It didn't seem to mind him on its back, or it was too focused on its destination to care. Either one of those ideas worked in André's favor. He didn't want to relax too much though because he needed to be prepared should the horse lose buoyancy and start to sink. This had been a crazy idea, but he didn't want doubts to enter into it. He would either die with this creature or get lucky with it. There was something comforting about just trying to survive, versus a helpless submission. They made their way through the jungle without much difficulty and then came to the edge of the town. He could have jumped off at any time and taken refuge atop one of the structures still above water. That would eventually place him at the mercy of the slavers when the waters receded. He spotted a number of whites clinging to the roof-tops. They would not welcome a slave into their midst. He had no misconception about that. Some even called to him. What they said he couldn't really make out over the roar of the wind. Perhaps they were praising his ingenuity or his courage. He doubted that. More likely they wondered whose horse he had stolen, and what had he done with its owner.

The church bell tower was a good marker for where they were in the town. He kept clear of it though. He could see troopers situated at the top, along with priests from the chapel and anyone else who were able to make it to the structure. As always, there was no safe haven for a slave. He would live or die with this animal, rather than surrender his life to eventual retribution and death. Lucky thing he had not drawn closer to the tower, because one of the troopers, possibly recognizing the horse, took a shot at him. Thankfully the wind was too strong for it to get anywhere near him and it didn't spook the horse, and they kept moving. He started to worry when the horse's breathing started to change. Was this the end? Had his luck run out? Before there was an answer, the horse stopped and began to walk. They'd made it. He was on some part of the trail toward the mountains. The trees looked familiar. He slid from the horse's back and sunk. His legs had lost their strength. He struggled until he realized he only had to stand up. He gained his footing and moved up into a copse of trees at the edge of the water. He lay down and rested for few moments. They provided a small bit of shelter from the rain, but he was still worried with the way the wind could change and make his refuge a death trap. He looked back and thought to thank the horse for his life, then realized that he'd better secure the beast because he still needed it to make it back to the high camp. He was half way up the mountain when he saw Juliette's horse, Josephine, tied to a tree next to some boulders along the trail.

CHAPTER 59

FATHER REYES SPENT the next week in the auction house. There were a number of shackles along the walls in the facility, but none was used on him. He was treated very well by the guards, who enjoyed his ritual of the morning blessing. They even came and had their meals with him so they could hear his humorous and unorthodox opinions. Everything that could be done to make him comfortable was accomplished, without releasing him.

The vicar general, Henri Dumont, arrived a week later. Unfortunately, he brought with him Father Guillaume Montaine. Dumont would be the judge for Nyira's trial, and to the archdeacon's dismay, Father Montaine was assigned as prosecutor. Phillipe was so distressed by this development he went to the auction house where Father Reyes was being held so that he might take counsel with his only friend.

"There is no to need to be distressed, Phillipe," said Father Reyes, as he reclined on a cot near a barred window. "Perhaps vicar general Dumont is not aware of your diligent efforts in this matter." The archdeacon stood up then—he had sat down on the cot as he spoke with Artemus.

"Yes. You're right, Artemus. I will go and speak with

Bishop Dumont. He surely is not aware of my excellent work on this case." He hurried away, confident that some oversight had occurred that had assigned Father Montaine versus someone like him, who had intimate knowledge of this matter.

Earlier that afternoon, the vicar general had taken up all the offices in the cabildo and half of the chapel. He and Father Montaine were housing a large entourage to take care of the administrative duties involved in the coming proceedings. Phillipe entered the chapel and found that he no longer had his quarters. Father Montaine was installed in them. He had to knock on his own door to address the man.

"Yes," said Father Montaine when he opened the door. He was a tall man with a rather regal air about him. He couldn't help but look down upon the hunched, shriveled form of the archdeacon.

"I'm Archdeacon Phillipe Dominic," said Phillipe, as if he needed to convince himself as well. "These are my quarters. I will need to retrieve my belongings—my clothes, my papers, and my books."

"Oh. Yes," replied Father Montaine. "They've been bundled up and sat in the office of the cabildo." He turned and closed the door, leaving Phillipe to stand incredulous.

Phillipe's belongings had actually been stored within the stables, as the newly restored cabildo had only room enough for the administrative staff of the vicar general. They had been placed inside an unused stall that had not been cleaned very well. A number of bundles from various other priests were piled one on top of the other, with horse dung sandwiched in between. Phillipe sorted out his items and Porthos, the groom, carried them back to the tented residence of the lowly deacons for him. More tents had been erected that housed two priests each. After he had established his living quarters, Phillipe walked back to the cabildo to seek an audience with the bishop.

He only got as far as his secretary, a tall, wiry-looking man.

"How may I help you?" said the secretary. He didn't actually look at Phillipe when he limped in. He seemed to be at some very important task—that required most of his attention. Phillipe was angry all of a sudden, as if this whole affair had been contrived to bring him misery.

"I'm Archdeacon Phillipe Dominic!" cried the archdeacon. "I must speak to his excellency at once!"

The secretary didn't appear the least impressed with Phillipe's tone of urgency.

"For what purpose?" he demanded, his voice very monotonal and dismissive. "The bishop is preparing for the witch trial."

"I am the reason there is a trial!" cried Phillipe. "It was I who apprehended the creature!"

"Why should that matter to his excellency?"

"Because I... the prosecutor—"

"Father Montaine is the prosecutor, sir. He is in another office. This is the vicar general's office."

"But I thought..."

For some reason—at that moment—the archdeacon couldn't say exactly what he thought.

"I'm very busy, sir," said the secretary. "Please take your business to the prosecutor's office at the other end of the building."

The archdeacon turned and trudged out of the office.

He was no longer feeling panicked, just confused. How was he going to let the bishop know that this was really his case, his chance?

By some administrative oversight, Father Reyes was released earlier that day, following the vicar general's arrival. Phillipe had gone to the auction house to find that Artemus was no longer there. What had they done with Artemus?

There was a duty sergeant stationed in the office— the auction house had all the accessories of a jail, if not as many cells.

"When was Father Reyes released?" the archdeacon asked the burly, agitated soldier seated at the desk.

The sergeant thumbed through the paperwork piled in front of him. He let out a sigh as if he had already been put upon by a number of demanding priests that day.

"There is no record of such a person," said the soldier.

"But there has to be!" cried the archdeacon, reaching for the pile of documents. The mounted police sergeant snatched them back.

"What crime has he committed, Father? Perhaps he has been moved to the regular stockade."

"Ugh… blasphemy?"

The soldier frowned at the priest.

"Blasphemy is not an enforceable crime, Father. If it were, we would need a stockade covering the whole of Saint Domingue."

"Yes. I see." The archdeacon walked out of the building, not sure where he was supposed to go. What was he supposed to do now? What if Artemus had decided to hide from him? What had he been thinking to place his friend in such a precarious state?

Oh, Artemus! What have I brought us to? It has come to nothing! And where have you gone, my friend? Who will care enough to even offer me ridicule?

He went to the chapel to begin evening confession and found Artemus there.

"Artemus!" cried the archdeacon, and ran to embrace his friend. "You're free. What—how—"

"They released me, Phillipe."

"I was so afraid I wouldn't see you again, that you had hidden yourself from me."

"Why would I do such a thing?"

"Because I—"

"You didn't do anything, Phillipe. Nothing happened."

The archdeacon looked at his friend, confused, and then realized that Artemus was correct. Nothing had occurred. No blasphemy, no coddling, and no imprisonment. It was as if the girl's trial had been created out of some anomaly that he was not attached to.

"I'm sorry, Artemus."

"So am I, Phillipe."

CHAPTER 60

ONCE THE WATERS receded, and the ground was solid enough to walk on, Bruno's new camp set out for the trail leading into the mountains. He considered releasing the troopers but decided he would take advantage of the head start. Maurice helped carry one of the children. The little girl, Amelina, had attached herself to Bruno. She had noticed his mutilated hand and had taken to rubbing it and holding it.

"Does it hurt, Bruno?" she asked.

"Not anymore."

"I think if I hold it and wish, they could come back."

"I would like that very much. How long do you think it will take?" She crinkled her little nose in thought.

"A week?"

"You are truly a miracle worker!" he said and scooped her up for a hug. It suddenly occurred to him that he could very well have a daughter of his own somewhere. He decided not to say it out loud to anyone. Even to precious Amelina. It would be too much if something had truly happened to his beloved Juliette and the child. They passed a number of the drowned troopers on the way, and Amelina asked if the men were sleeping.

"Yes," said Bruno. "They are tired after the storm." He looked at Charles, to check his response to his answer.

"It's as good as any," Charles replied.

They moved quickly through the bush but slowed when they got closer to town.

"You might want to get your pistol ready, Charles," suggested Bruno. The town looked deserted. Bruno knew that was because most of those who survived the storm had either taken to high ground on their property or climbed one of the remaining taller structures. All these people would be hostile to slaves traveling through the town. "I've followed this trail for a couple years now, Charles, and I never feel safe until I get to the end of it and away from where the mounted police might be."

"I wish you had kept that other pistol you found," replied Charles.

"Me too. But we have machetes. That will have to do for now." Bruno put little Amelina down.

"We have to play a game, Amelina," Bruno told her.

"What kind of game?" the little girl asked, with excitement in her eyes at the prospects.

"A quiet game," said Bruno. "We want to see who can be the quietest."

"I'm much quieter than Michel," she said.

"Shhh," whispered Bruno. "It starts now. You can't say another word until we get to the mountains." Thankfully her little brother had fallen asleep in his father's arms, or this game might not work. He hoped they would not have to fight their way through this section, not with the children. They sent Maurice ahead with a machete, to scout for possible ambushes. Just as he feared, a mounted police unit rode past them in the bush. One of the last troopers in the procession stopped and started to move through the jungle toward their position. Charles held the pistol at the ready. Bruno had forgotten to ask the man if the powder was still dry. A captain called to the trooper:

"Clement! Are you looking for drowned bodies?" He turned his mount to keep up with the rest of his unit.

"We need to pick up the pace," said Bruno. "There may be more of them passing through like that."

"I win!" said Amelina.

"You what…?" said Bruno. "Oh. Yes, you do win. We have a little further to go, yet. The game is not over." It was late evening by the time they made it to the lower camp. They rested for half an hour, and it was another two hours before they reached the main settlement.

All the structures had been destroyed by the winds, but the lumber was still dry and the ground solid. Bruno noticed someone had done some digging. André came out of the woods.

"I had to do some burying when I got up here."

"André!" cried Bruno and rushed to embrace his old friend.

"I didn't realize I was missed so much. I should go away more."

"I have come to appreciate your reckless sense of survival, my friend."

"My what?"asked André.

"It doesn't matter."

"And someone else is waiting for you a little further into the mountains," said André. "Take that trail through the forest, and you'll come out near some boulders."

"What are you talking about, André? Who's waiting for me?" André just shook his head and walked away.

The moon and stars were both in attendance on this night, and Bruno could see the path clearly. So he pushed past the overhanging pine branches and fern bushes to begin following it. But why was he going? Love had ended up just as badly as he'd expected. First, he was a coward when he didn't want it, and when he accepted it and tried to defend it, he almost died—should have died. He couldn't imagine it would be any different now. It would be better if he let her go. Someone else would be better for her, could protect her better. These thoughts and arguments were ready on his tongue when he reached the edge of the path leading to the cave. He could see from the shadows at the entrance that she'd gotten a fire going. The aroma of her stew cooking reached him, and his hunger almost buckled his knees. But no... he had to be clear, firm. She would be better... she stepped into the mouth of the cave and just stood watching him. She had on one of her colorful *pagnes*. He was suddenly afraid... if he could just turn back now—

"Bruno..." she said. It was a whisper, but it hit him like a hot arrow to his heart. "Bruno...I—"

"Wait! Just wait... I need to... think."

"Please come, Bruno. I need you. We need you." He started to cry and dropped to his knees.

"You know that's not a good idea. I've warned you before. Why don't you listen! I'm just... I'm not..."

"You're the only person I've ever loved," she said. He looked up, and she was standing over him. "And you're..." He saw that the moon seemed to be doing something to her eyes, and her smile. "... You're never getting away from me again." Did she lift him? Because he was suddenly on his feet, moving toward the cave, toward the fire, toward the stew and… he heard a baby's cry. He stopped again and made to pull away, but Juliette's grip was like Arnaud's; he was pulled by her incredible strength. "No turning back now. It's time she met her father."

"She?" he said.

"Yes, she."

"A daughter?" She led him into the chamber, and it was as if his cabin had somehow been transported here. There was the wooden table with the chairs and wildflowers for a centerpiece. In the far corner, two wooden beds stood side by side. Only now, there was a smaller strange looking contraption at the foot of them, and a cry issued from within it.

"What… what is that?"

"It's a bassinette. I remembered it from when the master's first child was born, and the wet nurse brought him out on the veranda, where it was cooler.

"But how did it get here? Everything in the manor was under water."

"I described it to one of the Taíno carpenters, and he recreated it exactly." The baby made a sound, as if not wanting to be ignored. "Oh, and it's occupant wants to meet you." She reached in and picked up the infant and placed her in Bruno's hands. "Babette, say hello to papa." The baby began to cry at the same time that Bruno did. "I guess we know where she gets her emotions from."

Chapter 61

"We should attack the vessel now," said Camaguey. "It only holds a few guards."

"That's what I would like to do," replied Enriquillo. "But she is worried about the fate of her family."

"Yet we know they are only concealing them as they plan her death. Why not attack now? Even if we don't take her. So they know we are watching."

"No. I don't want to risk my cousins lives just yet, and we wouldn't have the advantage of surprise. We should be practicing, though."

"We have also acquired some of the fire sticks."

"That's good to know. We may need them. The arrows are good, but they respect the sound of the fire stick."

"We have also been given more warriors from Guayo's camp. We have twelve now."

"Guayo is worried about Bayamo. Cousin still wants to fight. Something else is happening, too. The runaways say the white men have sent for a special *cacique* to pass judgment upon her. The people are allowed to watch. I will watch, too."

"Count the number of guards they have left since the storm," said Camaguey.

"That's a good idea."

"I would also like to say: the scar becomes you, young *cacique*," said Camaguey. "You have been in battle and survived."

"It was not what I thought it would be," said Enriquillo. "I didn't manage to kill anyone. I may not be so lucky this time, or someone will end my life. If I have to… it doesn't matter. I will do what I must for my dark princess."

"We will be with you, Enriquillo."

They were crouched in one of the cedar trees in the upper mountains. The Taíno were helping Bruno rebuild his settlement at a new site. All the runaways that had survived the battle with the troopers had acquired a horse from those left wandering in the forest. They had also captured more guns. Enriquillo led them to a fallback location. In case the camp is overrun again: A large cave nearby. It wasn't as large as the mother cave, but it provided more shelter from the chill at that altitude. Bruno preferred that his wife and child reside there with the women. Juliette had already managed to fill her chambers with every manner of accessories: flowers, weaving and carvings from Higuamota and the artisans of the tribe. There was even a pictograph showing how Bruno had been captured, escaped, and survived the storm to return to his love. It was created by the warriors of the tribe, and Enriquillo himself. He enjoyed coming to the cave and playing with the small children. He even shared a dream walk—he convinced Agueybana to assist with this—to show them their homeland.

"Who was the girl, Enriquillo?" asked Amelina.

"That is my dark princess."

"She is very pretty. My mother was pretty. Is she asleep, too?"

"Asleep?"

"Bruno said the troopers we saw on the ground when the storm was over are sleeping. Is your dark princess sleeping, too?"

"No. She's awake. I will try to bring her back from where she is, so she can meet you."

"I would like that."

One of the most important features of the cave was an underground water source. It would make the runaways impossible to find. This dwelling did not have as many dark chambers as his mother cave. Those had developed over thousands of years, as spirits came to inhabit them. The runaways might not stay in the caves as long as the Taíno. This land wasn't their home. They often spoke of returning. Though no one had any idea how that could be accomplished, without one of the large vessels that brought them.

It didn't take long to for tragedy to strike the camp. A group of the women went out into the lower valley to pick flowers and gather pretty stones to adorn their chamber. Amelina had begged her father to let her go with them. She was like any other child: she insisted on going further away from the women, in search of any flower that she had never seen. When she ventured down a little gully to the left of the women, she saw a man lying near the stream. She immediately had an idea.

"You can wake up now," she said, poking the large man with a stick. "The storm is over. You can wake up." The man did open his eyes and looked at the child.

"And who are you?" he asked. He sat up and smiled at the little girl.

"My name is Amelina. I'm picking flowers for our home. We will also give some to Juliette." The man became very interested at the mention of Juliette.

"Oh, I know Juliette," he said, grinning like an old friend excited to learn of a past acquaintance.

"You do? She is very pretty, and her baby is, too."

"Is it now? Well, that's wonderful. I happen to know where there are some pretty flowers you can take to the baby. Is it a girl or a boy?"

"It's a baby girl," said Amelina.

"I know where there are some special baby girl flowers."

"Oh good! I'll go tell the others. They will want to pick some, too." Christian thought about this for a moment.

"That's a good idea and very nice of you. Let's go tell them together." He stood up and grabbed his machete as he followed the child. As they were climbing out of the gulley, one of the women met them on the rise.

"Look, Yiella. I woke him up. He's going to help me look for some special baby girl flowers for Juliette's baby." Yiella froze for a moment, and Christian smiled.

"Good morning, Yiella." The woman came to life suddenly and scrambled backward so quickly she fell. Christian advanced on her. She could see he had cuts on his face and a wound on his head where he must have struck a limb as he plunged through the tree. Christian reached down and pulled Yiella to her feet.

"Don't kill me, Christian. I've never done any harm to you."

"You are right about that, Yiella. I'm sorry for all the

things I've done to you. I don't plan on killing you. I want you to take a message to Bruno. My friend and I are going to be picking some flowers in this valley for the rest of the day. If he shows up tomorrow, alone, she will get to bring them to his baby. If not… well, tell him not to take too long. I'm not good with children."

CHAPTER 62

THE TRIAL STARTED about two weeks after the vicar general arrived. The proceedings were to take place in the chapel. That was the largest structure and also very close to the Cabildo. It wasn't until the townspeople began to gather outside the church that the archdeacon got a sense of the spectacle he had contributed to. Although he wasn't entirely shut out of the process; he was named as a witness.

"This is insulting," he complained to Father Reyes.

"Yes, it is, Phillipe. You still must attend. Lest you be charged with concealment. The child healed you, as well."

"Oh. I hadn't thought about that."

The church pews had to be pushed back in order to allow for the pedestal upon which the vicar general was to be seated. There were chairs arrayed to the left of the judge's podium, which were designated for the witnesses.

Phillipe noted that the group of people lined up before the front door of the building, were only there to view the entrance of the child who was to be judged. Nyira was transported chained to the rear of a wagon, and accompanied by a guard on each side of her. When she arrived, she smiled at the people as if she were a princess in a parade, and tried to wave, but her hands were secured to the side of the vehicle. The crowd appeared confused at the sight of her. She didn't have the air of someone soon to be condemned. No one thought to yell derisive comments or fling objects, as were common during such gatherings. It wasn't until she stepped from the wagon and they saw the chains, did they realize that this sweet child was the one to be tried and burned.

The archdeacon decided to avoid the gauntlet out front; he came in from the rear of the chapel as most of the priests. When he entered, he saw Father Montaine standing before the podium of the vicar general, and it was all he could do not to rush him and tear out his throat.

CHAPTER 63

ONCE THE DEFENDANT and the spectators were seated, the prosecutor brought out the first witnesses. Eight of the stableboys were marched to the witness section. Diego had been badly injured and had to be carried to the witness stand to give his testimony. He glanced over and saw Nyira sitting in the box before the vicar general. He couldn't make eye contact.

Don't worry, Diego, she communicated to him in his mind

I'm sorry, replied the boy. *They have nearly murdered me and threatened to hurt the others, to make me speak against you.*

The evidence was clearly against Nyira, as each boy described a wound he'd sustained, and how Nyira had fixed it. After this, Constance Dugard came and added her testimony.

Nyira decided that the best course for her was to be completely honest.

Nyira's examination:

"Are you in league with Satan, child?"

"No, I'm not."

"And yet you have been observed performing Satanic acts. Who do you serve then?"

"I serve no one. I am as I've always been."

"But do you deny that you are a sorceress?"

"No. I don't deny it."

A gasp went through the spectators. They were then wooed by her sweet smile. Montaine stood quiet for a moment as if to allow that answer to sink in.

"So you confess to turning chickens to stone?"

"Yes."

"You seem very pleased with yourself. Are you not afraid of the consequences of your actions?"

"My actions were not meant to harm anyone."

"But you agree that you are evil?"

"No. I don't agree. I am who I was born to be. I was born a sorceress. I don't regret it. How could I? It would be as if you could regret your white skin."

"I'm not to be compared to you, child. I am a holy man of God."

"What does that mean?"

Montaine looked confused.

"It means that I follow the tenets of our Lord. Are you familiar with our commandments?"

"Yes. I have read them, and I feel I understand them well enough."

"What is it that you understand, girl? Can you tell them me, so that I might understand what you mean?"

"That you should respect your neighbors as you would yourself. That you should do to others only what you would do to yourself. And you should not kill. Is that so?"

"Well, yes," replied Father Montaine. "It's a rather general definition. But not untrue."

"That is why I find this proceeding so puzzling, Father."

"Why is that, girl?"

"Well as you know, I and my kind were brought here against our will. Most of our families were murdered. Yet I hold no ill feelings toward you or your people. And I am condemned only because I saved some of your lives."

The archdeacon could hold his tongue no longer.

"How dare you twist the holy words, devil!"

The vicar general looked very calmly upon the archdeacon's outburst and dismissed him with just his look.

"I—I'm sorry, your grace," said the archdeacon, looking up at Vicar General Dumont. "I couldn't sit and allow this creature to spout such blasphemy."

"I hope the court considers," replied Father Montaine, "that it is just such blasphemy that will seal the fate of this child."

The archdeacon saw the comment as a direct attack on him—but didn't dare stand to answer it.

Nyira displayed a very calm outward demeanor, but she was distressed by the fact that Claude and Esmerelda were not brought out to testify. She at first imagined that this was a contrivance of the archdeacon's, but he didn't appear to be in charge at the moment. She decided to reach out with her mind and try to communicate with Esmerelda.

Nolwazie, she asked. Are you well? Are you close?

Oh my goodness, child! replied Esmerelda. It is so good to hear you! Are you well?

Yes. Do you know where you are being held, Nolwazie?

We have had our heads covered when the mounted police came to retrieve us.

They mean to keep us apart.

It is very confusing that I can't see you. Oh, this is such a cruel affair!

"Are you listening, child?" asked Father Montaine.

Nyira was pulled back to the courtroom.

"Yes."

"Good. The court would ask that you give a demonstration of your evil powers. Heal the slave, Diego."

Nyira didn't initially respond to this request. She seemed to be considering the consequences of such an act. She then decided that she had the perfect example that she would like to give.

"Please place him with the others," said Nyira. "So that I may heal him from a distance." The guards were directed to place the boy among the other stable boys.

Nyira stood up, faced the stable boys and closed her eyes. When she opened them, all the boys vanished.

At first, there was clapping from the spectators. Father Montaine stood stunned. When Nyira turned and looked at him, her eyes had their hot green glow. The priest threw up his arms.

"No! Don't look at me!" he cried.

"In the name of our Lord!" cried the vicar general. "Guards, seize her!"

"Cover her head!" cried the archdeacon from the witness section. "If she can't see you, she can do no harm! Put the hood upon her!"

The mounted police rushed to her, but Nyira only stood looking calmly at Father Montaine.

A hood was hastily drawn down upon her head.

I'm glad Nolwazie is not here, Nyira thought to herself. *She would be very disappointed.*

"Is that what you wanted to see, Father?" asked Nyira through the hood.

"Yes… yes, that will do fine, child," said the vicar general. "Can you tell us where you sent them? Are they alive?"

"No, I will not. But they are alive and safe."

Nyira had never been to Bruno's main settlement. She did know of the lower camp. When the boys appeared there, they startled André, who'd just returned from a fishing trip to the secret cove.

"Where have you all come from?" he asked.

"We were at Nyira's trial," said Diego, who could walk now. "After she healed me, she sent us away. So we'd be safe."

"Why didn't she come, too?"

"She is probably trying to find Claude and Esmerelda."

"Enriquillo said he would be there, too," said André. "I hope he can get her out before they burn her."

"We do, too," said Diego. André led them the rest of the way into the mountains, to the new site of the settlement.

The mounted police guided Nyira back to the defendant's box.

The prosecutor seemed apprehensive about how to begin.

"I… I think that I will rest my case now," replied Father Montaine. "I believe the court has enough evidence to make a decision."

"Yes," replied the vicar general. "I believe we do. The evidence is very clear, Father Montaine. Guards, please remove the girl to her cell."

The mounted police escorted Nyira back to the jail.

CHAPTER 64

JULIETTE DID NOT want Bruno to go meet Christian.

"I don't want to go either," said Bruno. "You know I can't leave the child in his hands." Juliette could only cry then because she knew that was true.

"What if he has—"

"I don't want to think about that. I have to go."

"Maybe I can go and speak to him," replied Juliette.

"You will never speak to him again! I don't care if he kills me! You will never speak to him while I live." Bruno took one of the horses and sent a scout to survey the location, in case Christian had planned an ambush. Bruno had no doubt he was capable of it. The scout came back to say Christian was waiting just at the beginning of the drop off into the gulley. He and Amelina were sitting on the ground. Bruno was relieved. At least he hadn't killed the child. It was bad enough she was still with him. He took off on the horse at a quick trot; he wanted a show of strength that the horse could provide. He had told his men to stay back, and that if he fell, they were to make sure Christian didn't leave the valley alive. To make sure he was no longer a threat to Juliette and his child.

When Christian saw him coming, he stood up, holding the little girl's hand, like a kindly friend. She had a bunch of flowers. Christian released her hand as Bruno rode up. The little girl ran to him.

"Look Bruno. I have a lot of flowers for the baby!" she said. Bruno dismounted.

"Thank you, Amelina. Give them to Yiella. She's waiting there just over the hill."

It was early, so the sun had not reached its peak, and the mist from the forest was still floating along the valley floor.

"She is a sweet child. She knows her flowers," said Christian.

"Is that what this is about, Christian?" asked Bruno. "You came here to pick flowers?"

"No, Bruno. I'm here to kill you. We each have a missed opportunity. It ends here, though." Bruno drew his machete and smacked the horse on the rump, to send it away.

"I agree. I'm tired of thinking about this all the time."

Christian looked past him to the hill where a crowd had gathered. Most of Bruno's men were armed. Some of them had been his men. That changed when they learned of his intended betrayal.

"I gather I don't get out of here, even if I kill you."

"You gather correctly. This ends here and forever."

So Christian charged and brought his blade down with everything he had. Bruno wasn't fazed; he met the strike quickly and held the weight, not letting Christian pull back and slice again. He pushed back, but wouldn't let Christian move back to gain momentum with his size.

"You've been training," said Christian. "It won't help. I have anger on my side."

"Me too," snarled Bruno, who slid his blade down and sliced Christian's thumb. Christian was surprised by the precision of it. "But I have more anger and practice." Christian looked at his own blood for the first time and went crazy slashing and chopping, using his weight to take Bruno off his balance. While Bruno did have more practice, Christian's bulk moved him around. Their blades clanged across each other and Christian was still pushing. Bruno didn't know why Christian suddenly looked very confident. He smiled a bit, and just then Bruno's blade caught him across the nose.

"Bruno, look out!" called a voice from the hill. It was Juliette.

"It sounds like my wife is worried about you," said Christian. "She should be!" He charged, and Bruno took a chunk out of his shoulder. But Christian kept coming and took another slash across the chest. Suddenly Bruno was falling. He had forgotten where he was and Christian had maneuvered him to the edge of the gulley. He fell hard and then rolled down to the bank. He turned over just in time as Christian was coming down at full stream with his blade. He hacked off Bruno's left hand with it and raised it again. Bruno knew this was—

"Christian! Don't!" came a voice from the top of the gulley. It was Juliette. And she was standing holding her child. "Don't kill him, Christian. You have no reason to. I love him, and you can't do anything about it." Christian thought about it for a moment.

"All right. On one condition."

"What condition?"

"Give me the baby as a hostage. So I can get out alive."

"Juliette, no!" cried Bruno. "Let him kill me. But don't give him my child!" Christian raised his blade.

"It's his choice."

"No, wait!" said Juliette. "I'll do it. But you must promise not to harm her."

"I promise," said Christian, as he moved to go up the gulley.

"Juliette!" cried Bruno and tried to rise, but Christian slashed him across the back of his left leg. "Juliette, please! Run!" Christian charged up the slope.

"Don't worry, Juliette. You know you can trust me," said Christian. "It's probably my child anyway. I would never harm my own child." He made it to lip of the rise and moved toward her. "On second thought. I think I have another option!" He raised his blade and rushed her.

"Juliette! Run!" But Juliette didn't move.

"That's what you did to my sister," she said. She dropped her bundle and had a flintlock pointed at him. She fired and blew him off the ridge. "Babette trusted you, but I never did."

CHAPTER 65

"WE MUST KEEP the child away from her mother and father so that we might be better able to carry out her sentence." This from the archdeacon.

His obvious knowledge about the girl had finally gained him an audience with Father Montaine.

"Yes. You have a point, Phillipe," replied Father Montaine. The archdeacon was delighted to hear someone of significance say his name out loud—and to heed his recommendations.

"I suggest the hood be kept upon the girl. That way she can't focus on anyone to work her evil magic."

CHAPTER 66

THE TRIAL OF Claude and Esmerelda was much quicker than Nyira's. It was an already established fact that they had coddled and concealed her. The proceedings were merely a formality. Their sentence was decided and pronounced to them while they were still in the room: death by hanging, to be carried out immediately. That's when Claude lost himself and dropped like a stone falling from a cliff. He had never really grasped the nature of his crime, nor the consequences. When Esmerelda kneeled down and cradled his precious head, he asked:

"What have we done? How has this come upon us?"

Esmerelda didn't have a real answer. None that would make it easier for him to accept.

CHAPTER 67

THE COURT WAS more cautious when giving Nyira her sentence.

"What has become of my mother and Claude?" she asked the officials through her hood, as they stood before her cell to deliver the vicar general's ruling.

"They have been treated well, child." This was Father Reyes's voice she heard. The vicar general and Father Montaine felt it might be safer to have someone she was familiar with issue the ruling. "We must take you to the plaza now."

"Am I to be killed now, Father?"

"You will be with your family, child. Is that not what you have wished?"

"Yes."

They walked her to the wagon sitting in the yard behind the jail.

Nyira was a bit nervous as the wagon progressed silently around the rear of the Cabildo and then made its way through town—as if to put her on display. She heard various words of malice from those they passed. That was the only way she was aware that they were going through the city.

CHAPTER 68

ENRIQUILLO AND CAMAGUEY had been preparing for this inevitability. He felt it a lucky thing that the priests were still in the tent city. He needed something they possessed. Bruno had even lent a few of his horses and five of his men. Enriquillo was sitting on Nyira's shoulder when they delivered her sentence.

"Don't be afraid, my princess. We will be ready."

Please don't do anything, Enriquillo. I must see my family safe.

"But they are taking you—"

Please, Enriquillo. You must trust and be patient.

"I suppose you are right, Nyira. But how long should we wait?"

You will know when the moment presents itself. My papa used to say that.

"But what does that mean?"

It means be patient.

That was not the answer he had hoped for. Though he was aware of Nyira's incredible powers, he was afraid she was overlooking her limitations. Like suppose they kept the hood on when they set the blaze? He couldn't argue really. It was her life. And the white men were counting on her subdued state until the last moment.

CHAPTER 69

WHEN THEY PULLED into the plaza, the wagon stopped. As Nyira was taken from the vehicle, the hood was removed. That's when she saw that the square in front of the cabildo was filled with people. The day was clear and bright, and not a cloud came anywhere near the sun. The crowd was so large it clogged the streets all the way to the market. She'd loved that market and all the merchants who had been so kind to her. Like the baker that gave her a sweet bun when she and Esmerelda came to his stand. Even now, the boy Archie hawked them through the crowd. The children whose parents could afford to buy one for them, skipped through the throng laughing. Nyira found herself smiling too, as she watched them. She had not seen this many people in the square since the juggler and the circus laid anchor in the harbor. This seemed to be an almost festive occasion. But then she gazed toward the center of the square and saw the pyre.

A number of slaves milled around the area, as well. Most of them were household slaves coming from the market with the food they had purchased. Nyira noted the small children with the servants, some of them little girls.

She made eye contact with one small dark child holding a basket as she had on her first day in the market, though this child's master was not as rich and generous as Major Dugard. She could tell by the fact that neither the child nor the older slave wore shoes and their clothes were torn and filthy. She obviously would have rather not be a slave, but it made life bearable when the owner chose to treat them well. Nyira smiled at the child, and she smiled back and then hid her face in the dirty skirts of the woman she accompanied. That was when the archdeacon crossed into her vision.

"You will not be smiling for very long, witch."

He turned to see if he could discover who or what she was smiling at.

"I see no smiling in the pyre." He appeared furious that viewing her fate had not caused her to tremble and plead for her life, as others had.

"You shall not have the satisfaction of my fear, Father," said Nyira. She focused on the end of the rope that cinched his cowl around his waist. The end of it suddenly began to smoke. The priest recoiled and quickly put the rope out.

"Cover her head again!"

They walked her across the plaza. When they removed the hood again, Nyira saw Claude and Esmerelda standing at the base of the bell tower. When Esmerelda saw her, she broke down in tears. The sight hurt Nyira's heart, for she had never seen Nolwazie so afraid. They quickly replaced the hood again.

"I just wanted you to know the fate of your family," said the archdeacon.

"Why harm them, Father? Isn't it enough that you are to kill me?"

"They are just as guilty as you are. Coddling and concealing is punishable by death as well."

Nyira was more afraid of Esmerelda's pain than any that might be inflicted by the pyre.

She reached out to her:

Please, Nolwazie. Don't cry. I promise to think of something.

I'm not crying for myself, replied Esmerelda. *I cry for Claude. He doesn't understand what's happening. I would rather die alone than to watch him die not knowing why. He is concerned about you.*

I will try to speak to him? Will he be frightened if he hears my voice in his head?

He might. But I believe it will allow him to be at peace if he can have counsel with you.

So Nyira reached out.

Claude? Can you hear me, Claude?

Claude jumped and looked around like he'd been struck.

What? What sorcery is this?

It is mine, Claude. Camille. I just wanted to put your mind at rest. You have done nothing wrong. You were a good father to me.

This didn't stop Claude's sobs, and it only added to Esmerelda's.

"These good people shouldn't have to die for my actions, priest," replied Nyira, and began to sob as well. The archdeacon smiled and made sure to stand behind her.

"Now we're getting somewhere. Show the proper remorse, witch. But this is not the best part. Your family will watch from the tower as you burn. That will be the last sight they see, as they hang. And their bodies will remain in view for a week."

Nyira thought that he was wise to have her head covered. She was so furious that she would have broken her promise to Father Reyes. But Artemus was watching as well. He was standing just behind the archdeacon.

"There is no need to taunt her, Phillipe," he said. "They will die just the same. What benefit is it to display such cruelty to the people?"

"So they might see that evil will have no quarter in my—"

"Your...?"

"I meant to say... his majesty's colony."

At that moment Nyira felt a buzz at her ear. It was a small, oddly colored fly.

"Now can we attack, my princess? Your family is here," buzzed Enriquillo.

I have a plan of my own, replied Nyira. *So do nothing.*

"What? I—I... but they—"

You must trust me, my love.

The mounted police escorted Esmerelda and Claude up the steps to the bell tower, while a second troop along with the priests marched Nyira to the pyre.

A larger crowd of townspeople had gathered in the area. The wood was stacked so high that at first there was no way for Nyira to be tied to the stake protruding out of the pile. Once she was secured, the hood was removed again.

Even though Nyira knew she was condemned, she held no bitterness toward the people in the square, as they called for her death and flung fruit or other objects. Some of which struck the priests, particularly the archdeacon. One little girl, having made eye contact with Nyira—she gave her brightest of smiles—flung a tomato that caught the archdeacon on his narrow evil nose.

The brightness of the sun and sky continued to defy the solemnity of the occasion. As if they both knew something she didn't. But Nyira was still wondering what she might do to prevent Claude and Nolwazie's impending death. For once, she was at a loss. She didn't want Enriquillo to know this, lest he start a war with the few warriors that were left of his people, and get himself killed, too. It was also much harder to think once she saw Claude and Nolwazie up in the bell tower, with nooses displayed ominously before them. She could see the terror on Claude's face, but Nolwazie's had become serene. When a flicker of sunlight glinted off the shiny brass buckle of a mounted policeman in the tower, Nyira knew that the fire would take her.

Father Dominic took advantage of his opportunity to be in the middle of this event and spoke some words to the crowd: a bitter, vitriolic sermon on the merits of good and the wages of sin. Nyira barely heard it. She was focused on Claude. If she had time, she would have gone into his soul, just to reassure the entity waiting there. To ask it not to desert too soon, for Claude would need it to be strong.

She was impatient for them to get it over with, and she hoped that they wouldn't kill Claude and Nolwazie before they set her aflame. She had no desire to watch them die. She would go first. That was what the archdeacon had promised. The last words the priest uttered were: "Burn, witch!" And the pyre was lit…

CHAPTER 70

ENRIQUILLO WATCHED AS they set his dark princess ablaze. He felt his heart and his hope begin to burn with her. He had seen others in the square when they were burned on the pyre. First, they screamed from fear of the fire, and then they screamed as it actually overwhelmed their flesh. It made them look like the demon they were accused of being. None of these things happened to the dark princess. He realized something different was occurring when he didn't feel her pain. He had linked his soul to hers, which essentially meant when she died, so would he. He felt no pain. He did feel some heat, but not a burning heat, just a glowing, pulsing ember of light. Like a small torch ignited in the darkness that kept getting brighter and brighter until it engulfed the dimness of the cave. And since she was not burning, she didn't cry out.

The people in the square noticed this right away.

Some had started a chant of: "Burn, witch! Burn, witch! Burn…"

They couldn't get through the last pronouncement because the witch was not burning. This gave Claude and

Nolwazie a momentary reprieve. The mounted police were as confused as the people in the square.

"She is not a witch!" cried a child in the crowd to its mother. "If she doesn't burn, how can she be a witch?" The mother shushed the child and pulled her away, as the archdeacon scanned the throng with murder in his eyes, seeking the one who had uttered such a thing. The mother moved herself back further from the fray, out of the priest's line of sight. The Father soon realized that this was not going as planned, for even the girl's clothes were not burning. But he had a thought and another option. He looked up at the bell tower and saw that it was there that the girl appeared to be getting her power, her inspiration.

"Hang the conspirators!" he called to the tower. "Hang them now!" This order roused the mounted police. They pushed Claude and Esmerelda to the edge of the tower, looped the nooses around their necks and shoved them over.

CHAPTER 71

IT WENT VERY fast to the naked eye, but to Nyira it was like a dream, a nightmare in slow motion. She was not sure how she did what she did. She just found herself in flight, like a cannonball, or a blazing comet. As Claude and Nolwazie dropped, she met them in mid-air. What was even more astounding, she was still ablaze. When she caught them, she had morphed into some type of enormous firebird. She caught Claude by the arm with one giant talon, and the other Nolwazie had the presence of mind to reach out and grasp on to. The ropes burned away like paper, as Nyira took flight over the square. The people in the square were dumbstruck…

The archdeacon, on the other hand, was furious. He screamed at the brigade stationed near the pyre.

"What are you doing? Don't let it get away! Shoot! Shoot it down!"

The firebird flew in close range of the soldier's rifles. The captain commanded: "Ready!" The troopers raised their rifles.

This was what Enriquillo had been waiting for. The warriors were stationed among the priests, lined up right behind the brigade. But Enriquillo had to act quicker. So he buzzed quickly toward the brigade, and in mid-air transformed into a massive African elephant. Just like in the dream. He dropped out of the sky and crushed the middle contingent of the guard. Then he rose up and let out a trumpeting roar, and leveled the remainder with a sweep of his huge trunk. Soldiers and weapons went everywhere. Then the fourteen warriors dressed in priests' cowls rushed in armed with macana war clubs and made it difficult for the unit to regroup. The war clubs were easier to conceal beneath the disguise than a bow or a rifle. It was pandemonium. The soldiers didn't know who they were fighting, or who to shoot. This gave the firebird enough time to fly out of range. Before the troopers were able to regroup, the warriors made for the horses tied up near the stables behind the cabildo. As they mounted and raced off, one lone rifleman took aim at the last warrior and fired. Bayamo was hit. Camaguey grabbed him and held him up as they raced toward the jungle.

Nyira flew Claude and Nolwazie into a valley just east of the mother cave. She put them down in the orchard of Jaceux's lower camp. Claude was a bit confused when his feet touched the ground, but Nolwazie had a lot of questions.

"Where are we to go, Nyira?" Nolwazie asked.

Nyira had transformed from the firebird and walked toward a copse of fruit trees.

"I will need to rest for a while. The bird has made me very weak."

She looked very much like a small child as she laid herself in the grass under the trees.

"Enriquillo will come to get us soon. We should be safe here for a while."

"Where are we to live, child? How are we to survive?" asked Claude, who had finally come out of his daze.

"You will live where and how I live. But you must remain hidden. The mounted police will not give up their search for you. Neither will the archdeacon."

Once they were settled and felt safe, Nolwazie started to look at the orchard Nyira had brought them to. The trees around them were full of the various fruit she had been buying from the market for years, like star fruit, chironja (half orange and half grapefruit), coco plum and guava. Just to name a few. There were even some banana and orange trees along the ridge of the valley.

"We will at least not be hungry," Nolwazie said as she began to wade through the grass and flowers in the area. She did not have a basket, so she collected fruit and piled it in her skirt. "Claude, come and help me gather us something to eat while we wait for the boy."

"Who is Enriquillo, Esmerelda? And how did our Camille become... oh, this is too much. I want to go home. What are we going to do now?" Esmerelda felt it was finally time to explain it all to Claude.

"So the child we have had in our home all this time was a sorceress?" He sat down in the grass and said nothing for about ten minutes. "But she is not evil?" he finally said.

"No Claude. She is the sweet girl that we know and love. She was just born the way she is."

"And she has saved us?"

"She has, yes." He looked over at Nyira as she slept in the grass.

"And now we must live... we are free?"

"We are. There are other parts of the island that we will be led to, that will allow us to live our lives in peace. Is that not a good thing?" He considered this thought for a long moment.

"It is a good thing, yes. It will take some getting used to, but I don't mind being free."

"Neither do I. We are together. That's the most important part."

"That is," said Claude. "Now when is it that I will meet this boy who has caused all this?"

"Soon," said Esmerelda, as she walked toward the trees and began to gather fruit again. She turned and looked at Claude. "Are you going to help me?"

Claude rose and stood frowning for a moment; he was not accustomed to engaging in women's work.

"If you don't help, it will be just that much longer before we are able to eat."

Claude's stomach grumbled at that moment as if to confirm the urgency of Nolwazie's mission. He walked up to a tree and just stood there as if possibly the fruit might tell him what to do. Nolwazie chuckled as she came over to help motivate her truculent husband.

"You will have to reach for it, my sweet man." She took one of his large hands and guided it to a star fruit. He grasped the thing and then examined it.

"I have seen this," he said, looking as though he was just discovering his own hand.

"Yes, you have," replied Nolwazie. "You carry them with you into the fields."

"They are good." He took a bite. "I like them." He reached for another.

"Please, Claude, we must pick them first. Do not eat all of the fruit before we can gather enough."

"But I am hungry."

"We are all hungry—Nyira will be, too. When she awakens. So we need to pick enough for all of us to eat."

"Yes… I see." Once he had grasped the idea of harvesting for more than just himself, Claude worked quickly and diligently. The same attributes that made him a good field hand that had never felt the whip.

Once they had collected a decent amount of fruit and piled it at the base of one of the trees in the grove, Enriquillo rode down the trail leading into the valley, but he was not alone. There were at least fifty people following along behind the tall, handsome Taíno teenager. Each of them carried a basket filled with various types of meat, fish, and fruit. Nolwazie had obviously seen him before, but he seemed… different somehow. Taller perhaps. But it had only been a few months. He stopped at the grove of trees, and Nolwazie went and wrapped her arms around him

"We are so happy to see you, Enriquillo! My Nyira is very lucky!" Enriquillo was caught off guard by Nolwazie's enthusiasm. But he welcomed her touch.

"It is I who is lucky, Nolwazie. You have protected my dark princess. And it almost cost you your life. She could have no better mother. My people will need your wisdom and strength if we are to survive." Nolwazie was suddenly struck by the magnitude of what the boy had revealed to her. These people were now her people.

"I—I will do my best, my *cacique*. That is what you are called. Am I correct?"

"Not quite yet. My mother yet lives. She awaits you in our cave."

CHAPTER 72

FATHER DOMINIC WAS still on the platform.

"What are you doing!" he screamed at the mounted police. "Get up all of you! Get after them! She's going to get away!" Artemus approached the platform.

"Phillipe," he said. "Phillipe, please come down from there. They have no chance of catching a bird in flight."

"But I have done…"

"You have done everything you could," said Father Reyes. "Please come down." The archdeacon looks at the steps and does not recall how he managed them.

"How did I get up here, Artemus?"

"Come on," said Father Reyes going up the steps and offering his friend his hand. The archdeacon looked at him with almost tears in his eyes.

"We have failed, Artemus."

"That is not true, Phillipe," said Father Reyes. "I have not failed. I wasn't attempting to do anything."

"Oh, if you are going to be difficult about it. Then I have failed. Is that better?"

"No, it's not. But please come down from the platform before you fall, Phillipe." The archdeacon sighed and accepted his friend's hand to get himself to the bottom of the platform.

"What are we going to do now, Artemus?"

"There is only one thing we can do right now, Phillipe."

"What is that?"

"We must go and find something to eat, and possibly a good cup of tea to go with it." He then turned and walked across the plaza toward the food vender's booth.

"Oh, all right!," said the archdeacon, trailing after his friend. "Don't walk so fast. Wait for me."

CHAPTER 73

HIGUAMOTA HAD PUT on her best Nagua, designed with the image of her favorite creature: the turtle. Her hair was adorned with hawk and parakeet feathers. Around her neck she wore a necklace of coral and carved gold nuggets. The necklace had been a gift from Enriquillo's father upon their marriage. She and Agueybana were standing in the mouth of the mother cave.

"How do I look?" she asked Agueybana.

"The same as you did yesterday," replied the behike.

"I don't look even a little bit better than yesterday? Do you think she will like my necklace?"

"Are you going to present it to her as a gift?"

"Well, no. Why would I do that?"

"Then it does not matter whether she likes it."

"I am trying to look special! And you are not helping!"

"You are already special. You are Cacica." Higuamota sighed heavily and leaned against the side of the cave wall.

"I can't stand this waiting. What is taking them so long?"

"She may be a little tired," said Agueybana. "She flew over an army as a fire bird carrying her mother and father in her talons."

"Her mother and father are coming, too? I need to sit down. She went and dragged a duho stool to the entrance. "I don't know what I am supposed to say to them. Please, Agueybana! Tell me what I should say!"

"All right," said the behike. "If I give you powerful words you can say, will you stop pacing like an anxious crow?"

"Yes, yes! Please tell me!"

"Okay. Close your eyes and breathe deeply. Relax. And listen." Higuamota leaned back against the cave wall."

"You must be completely calm or the words will not work," said Agueybana."

Higuamota had reclined her head against the rock of the cave wall; it looked like she was asleep. She was putting her whole self into receiving the words of power from the behike."

"I am ready, my behike," she said. "Please give me the words."

"Not yet," said Agueybana. "You must remain relaxed. Your eyes must remain closed. The words are too powerful. And you can only use them once."

"They are that powerful?"

"Yes. I will wait until the time is right, and then whisper them to you."

CHAPTER 74

JULIETTE WAS FROZEN as she watched Christian fall and roll limp and lifeless back down into the ravine. He landed awkwardly about twenty yards from where Bruno lay bleeding. That's what jolted her back to reality. She flung the pistol aside.

"Someone, help me!" she screamed as she raced headlong down into the ravine toward her husband. Bruno attempted to get up when he saw her. But was having no luck at it.

"Juliette," he said, and fell again. "I'm…"

"Don't try to get up, Bruno! You're still bleeding." She took the blanket that was supposed to be swaddling clothing and wrapped it around the bloody stump that was his left hand. "Please, my husband. Lie still for a moment until they get here." She wrapped her other arm around his shoulders.

"I'm sorry," said Bruno and looked very forlorn.

"Why are you sorry, my love?" asked Juliette, as she placed a gentle kiss on his tired and sweaty left cheek.

"Because once again, you have had to save me." Horses were heard coming along the ridge above them.

"They're down here!" cried Andre.

"He can't walk Andre!" called Juliette. "He's bleeding

too much from his left hand, and his left leg has been cut! You will need something to carry him on!"

"And now, I must be carried, like a cripple," groaned Bruno.

"No," replied Juliette. "Like a chief." Bruno smiled after she said that.

"And I suppose you will be a bossy, chief's wife." The men were making their way down into the ravine.

"If that is what is required, yes," replied Juliette. "And our child will be a chief's daughter. Who will probably be spoiled by her father." She kissed him again—this time on the lips.

"If that is what is required, yes," said Bruno, and kissed her back on the lips. They then engaged in a passionate kiss.

"Hey!" cried Andre, as he and the other men approached with what looked like a giant basket with poles running through it for handles. "You are bleeding too much to be doing that!" Both Bruno and Juliette looked at him and began to laugh. Four of Bruno's men helped him into the basket, and with Juliette walking alongside to hold the bandage over his bleeding left hand, they carried him up out of the ravine.

Chapter 75

"ALL RIGHT," SAID Agueybana. "It's almost time. Stand up and get ready." Higumota stood up and moved next to him in the mouth of the cave. "When I tell you to, open your eyes and I will whisper the words of power. Now...open your eyes." Higuamota opened her eyes and saw a beautiful, tall, dark child with amazing green eyes standing before her.

"Oh!" said Higuamota. "I—I," Agueybana leaned over and whispered in her ear.

"Say: Hello and welcome."

"Hello and welcome!" cried Higuamota. "You are so beautiful." Nyira smiled and wrapped Higuamota in a hug.

"So are you," said the girl.

"I would like a hug, too, mother," said Enriquillo. "If you have any left." Higuamota was crying now.

"Of course I have more," she said. "I have enough for all of them." Nyira waved Claude and Esmerelda forward.

"Come on, Nolwazie. Bring Claude." Claude looked a little awkward, but he was big enough to wrap his arms around practically the whole group.

"I smell food," said the big man. "Can we eat after this?" Everyone began to laugh.

"Oh, Claude," said Esmerelda. "Your appetite is bottomless."

"I just had a little fruit," complained Claude.

"It's all right," said Higuamota, wiping the tears from her eyes. "We have prepared a feast. So I guess it's time to eat," said the Cacica. Everyone followed her into the cave, as the drums signaling the beginning of the feast began to play.

Acknowledgements

A FEW PEOPLE were key in the production of this bit of literature. Okay. A little too formal. I wrote this thing in front of my friends at the Fairhope Writers Forum, in Alabama. And by "writing in front of", I mean I literally wrote the first ten pages and came in that next Saturday and read it to them. I can only imagine they found me a bit odd. Hopefully, you'll all be famous now. And John, thanks for the question that opened the door to this.

Now a note about the research: There are a number of articles and books on Taíno culture and Haiti in general. But sadly, a lot of Taíno data was lacking. Different references seem to repeat the same information. But Jose Barreiro's wonderful novel: "Taíno" opened a nice window for me to peek through. I'm still peeking. And the Dominican Republic was helpful as well. They still have a thriving nature reserve on that side of the island. I got a sense of the beauty and immensity of a Caribbean jungle.

And thanks also goes to everyone who helped me clean this up:

Scott Pack (my first editor!) no-nonsense kind of guy. Really liked that.

@meandmybigmouth
Helen Burroughs—my wonderful beta reader
@HKelleyB
Sukhy Samani–my generous beta reader
@sukhysamani
Courtney M. McMeekin—my insightful beta reader

References

Maroon Societies (Rebel Slave Communities in the Americas)

Richard Price

The Slave Ship (A Human History) Marcus Rediker

The River Congo

Sir Harry Hamilton Johnston

The Taino: The Rise and Decline of the People Who Greeted Columbus

Irving Rouse

A Short Account of the Destruction of the Indies

Bartolome de La Casas

Cautio Criminalis

Friedrich Spee von Langenfeld

Caciques and Cemi Idols: The Web Spun by Taino Rulers Between Hispanola and Puerto Rico

Jose R. Oliver

And a thousand other various papers, library documents, dissertations and internet searches…

GLOSSARY

Taíno (Tah-ee-no) The aboriginal inhabitants of Cuba, Hispaniola, Puerto Rico, Jamaica and other lessor Islands; self-descriptive, meaning "noble" or "good" people.

Higuamota (ee-wa-mo-tah) (Cacique—chief of Enriquillo's tribe. Also his mother)

Agueybana (ah-way-bah-nah) behike—medicine man/ Shaman of Enriquillo's tribe)

guaxeri wa-zeh-ree (citizens of the Taíno nation)

Hutia (who-tee-ah) Rodent of the West Indies. Eaten by early Taíno and present guaxeri.

Coaybay—(ko as in Colorado)-(a as in Alabama) (ko-ah-ee-bah-ee) Taíno place of the dead

behike (be (like the e in elevator)(be-hee-kay) Medicine man or healer

bejuco (be (like the e in elevator)-who-(ko—as in colorado) (be-who-ko) various types of vines used as purgatives and as cord rope for construction

Carib—(cah-rib) Caribbean indian people from the lessor Antilles. A term chosen by the Spanish for people reuputedly canabalistic

Batey—(bah-tey) A plaza or ceremonial field where areitos and ball games were celebrated.

Areito—(Ah-ree-toe) traditional dances and recitations among the Taíno behike and cacique.

Cacique—(Cah-see-kay) chief

Enriquillo—(n-ree-key-oh)

Duho—(dew-hoe) a ceremonial seat or stool, low to the ground and fashioned from wood or stone.

Manati (manna-like manna from heaven) ti-tea (mana-tea)

BELOW ARE TERMS AND THEORIES I MADE UP FOR THE NOVEL

Knef—(like nephew) an almost transparent one-eyes entity. About the size of a 9x12 sheet of paper. It hovers and descends when the newly separated soul is weak enough for it to feast. Hunts at the edges of wars and natural disasters.

Dream walk—an act performed by an experienced behike or shaman. Used to eradicate evil spirits. It is also a bridge between the human world and other realms. Only the behike/shamans know this. It is also where Nyira takes Enriquillo to play and meet some old departed friends.

Kopai—(ko as in coke) (pai as in pie) guards the realm leading into Coaybay. They take various forms, from blue giants, to Raven-headed griffins and anything in between. Depending on their mood. Once you enter their realm, you have a short time to converse with your recently departed, If you linger too long, they will keep you. Which means you are dead, too.

About The Author

K.M. Harrell travelled all over the world as a member of the USAF. He is also a history buff and an avid reader of literary, fantasy, science fiction and, of course, nonfiction. He is originally from Louisiana, and is the eldest and only boy in a family of five siblings. He has written all his life, and has had a few short stories published in small literary journals. This is his first novel. He can be reached at:

www.kmharrell.com
@kmharrell2
https://www.facebook.com/ken.harrell.71653